Exteriors
and
Interiors

Exteriors and Interiors

C. McGee

Winchester, UK
Washington, USA

First published by Roundfire Books, 2016
Roundfire Books is an imprint of John Hunt Publishing Ltd., Laurel House, Station Approach,
Alresford, Hants, SO24 9JH, UK
office1@jhpbooks.net
www.johnhuntpublishing.com
www.roundfire-books.com

For distributor details and how to order please visit the 'Ordering' section on our website.

Text copyright: C. McGee 2015

ISBN: 978 1 78535 516 5
978 1 78535 517 2 (ebook)
Library of Congress Control Number: 2016941204

A CIP catalogue record for this book is available from the British Library.

Design: Stuart Davies

Printed in the USA by Edwards Brothers Malloy

We operate a distinctive and ethical publishing philosophy in all
areas of our business, from our global network of authors to
production and worldwide distribution.

For Bethy K and Daddy Doug.
Both of you are going to hate this book.
Nevertheless, I could not have done it without you.

Part I

Chapter 1

A Shitty Disguise

I'm not a fan of babies. I was a fan of Jonathan Swift, but then I figured out that he was being satirical. The proposal seemed modest enough to me. Adults are slightly better, as most of them can take care of their own basic needs. Babies can't; they shit themselves and require feeding from a nipple. Pathetic. Sometimes I wonder what would happen if we allowed infants to be raised by machines. Rumor has it that the Russians tried this during World War II. It was not by choice, all their adults died so they were left with a disproportionate amount of babies. They should have let those little bastards fend for themselves. What a suck on the war effort. Think about all the resources that were devoted to keeping those kids alive that could have been devoted to taking down the Nazis. If the Allies had lost, I would have blamed those children.

I didn't used to hate them—babies, that is. Indeed, I used to feel nothing more than a mild dislike for them. But that was before, back when they were a peripheral element of my life. Now they are a conspicuous part of my day-to-day, an obnoxious byproduct of my crap job. I did not set out to be the healthcare equivalent of a peon. I set out to be an architect. Unfortunately, the universe had other plans; fuck-you plans. My college graduation coincided with the demise of Lehman Brothers, Bear Stearns, and the entire U.S. economy. Obviously, this was not the best time to be designing outlandish homes. So, now I am not so much of an architect as I am an orderly. Beggars can't be choosers.

The hospital where I work is fine. The food is fine. The pay is fine. The physicians are fine. Lauren is fine. The only thing that is not fine are the fucking babies. But Lauren, Lauren is really fine. Not in the way that the food is fine, more in the way that a large-breasted, small-waisted woman is fine. That's actually what she is, a large-breasted, small-waisted woman. At work, when infants aren't wailing and geriatrics aren't whining, I dream up ways to ask her out. I also devise ways to "accidentally" touch her breasts. But mainly I think up ways to ask her out. Most of these plans are not feasible, some because I am not a knight, others because I am an orderly.

When I saw Lauren today, I was covered in shit. Literal shit. Although far from ideal, the situation could have been worse. Lauren could have responded to my disgusting appearance with the repulsion that it warranted. Instead, she maintained a professional decorum throughout our entire interaction. Obviously, I would have preferred that she had given me the commiserating look that everyone else did, but given the circumstances I can't complain.

My appearance was repugnant. The fecal matter was everywhere, it covered my scrubs front to back and top to bottom. In some places it was splattered, as though a Pollock-inspired artist had decided to use diarrhea as a breakthrough medium; in others, it was smeared like war paint; and in a few spots, it was blotched and raised, as if someone had ladled a mixture of beef gravy and cottage cheese directly onto my clothing. The smell was more consistent than the visual but infinitely harder to describe. When poop is unfiltered, freed from the tempering effects of water or soil, the odor that it produces transcends description. It does not, however, transcend taste. The gustative quality of the stench was both tangible and terrible. It hit the palate like a hammer and clung like plastic wrap. By comparison, the auditory aspect of my appearance was rather fleeting and subtle. That's not to say that the aural was less vile than the oral, just less noticeable. The squishy sound made by stool-saturated socks was hard to hear.

To put it simply, all of Lauren's senses were attacked by my presence. Correction—all of Lauren's senses save touch.

Fortunately, she did not have to touch me. Part of me still wanted her to, perhaps a brush of her breast against my poop arm. A disgusting appearance does nothing to squelch my sexual appetite.

People were nice to me despite my condition because they thought that I was covered in shit due to the hazards of the job. In a way they were right, and in a way they were wrong. My occupation was the cause of my condition, but not in the way one might expect. I was not covered in feces because I was cleaning up after some lady who pushed from her anus while giving birth, or because I had to go to the psych ward where crazies sling their shit like chimps. It was in fact because I eat my feelings. Like a flag girl on the high school marching band, I counteract my shame with snacks; chips usually, cream cheese when things seem really bleak. My lactose intolerance should prevent me from using dairy as a source of solace, but it doesn't; and as a result, I occasionally get myself into trouble. That's what happened today, that's how things went wrong, that's how I ended up with excrement all over my body. Perhaps I should explain further.

Today was a cream cheese day. A message from my college roommate made it so. Although his e-mail contained only good things, it made me feel bad things. It forced me to compare my life to the life of someone that was doing something, and in the process left me severely dejected.

The recent achievements of my former roommate easily trumped my own. My successful disposal of six trash bags filled with amniotic waste just couldn't compete. As a result, I went to the cafeteria and got a container of cream cheese and then one more. Garden veggie balanced out with strawberry. I ate them with two bagels and then with a spoon. While scraping the sides of the second container, I received a call, not on a smartphone like a dignified human being but over the crackly loudspeaker like my fast-food order was up. According to the person on the intercom it was "urgent." It wasn't, but I didn't know that so I ignored the lurching sounds coming from my stomach and hurried off.

When I arrived on the scene, it took me a few moments to figure out what my eyes were seeing. It was a woman but didn't look like one, more like an enormous ball of dough that had been left to rise on the linoleum floor. Her blubbery body was everywhere, and her clothing was nowhere, or so it seemed. Further inspection revealed that she was wearing an oversized hospital gown; it was hard to tell because the gown was so outmatched by her mass.

Understanding that I had been summoned to help this woman, I turned to leave. The hoisting of an overexposed blob monster was a daunting endeavor that I wanted nothing to do with. Regrettably, as I went to step away, one of the nurses called my name and pulled me back in.

After strategically maneuvering into an optimal lifting location with the nurse and another orderly, we leaned over and began to raise the dough ball. It was then that I realized things were about to go badly. The woman was too big and the stool that was waiting to come out of my asshole was too watery. As I strained to lift her, my brown starfish loosened. It did not do so for long, but it does not take long to shit your pants and that's exactly what happened. As I strained to lift the woman, my asshole opened up a bit, and some liquid gurgled out. Acting on impulse, I dropped my portion of the blob monster and headed toward the bathroom. On the way, more lactose-fueled stool made its way out of my anus and began its descent of my leg. When the runny shit came into contact with my calf, I picked up the pace from a walk to a jog. I would have run but that always makes shitting your pants worse.

Fortunately, the full-fledged anal release didn't come until after the restroom door closed. Unfortunately, it did come before the stall door opened. My asshole relaxed, and my stomach lurched, and my bowels emptied. My underwear filled, and my pants stained. I felt better and worse all at the same time.

As the realities of the situation settled in, my calculations began. I was far from the closet that had the extra scrubs, too far to make it there unnoticed. It was not an option. Neither was removing the stains in the bathroom sink, as they were too entrenched for the likes of hand soap. As for taking off my bottoms and running to the scrubs closet bare-assed, well that might have resulted in jail time; also there was telltale shit dried to my legs and butt crack hairs. Also, when I run fast my penis goes into athletic mode—that is, it gets real small and hides away, like a bald man nose-deep in a beige turtleneck. Humiliating. Needless to say, none of these initial ideas seemed like viable options, and for a moment, it appeared that I was stuck. Then genius struck. I was in a predicament because my backside was covered in shit, but I could get out of the predicament if the rest of me was covered in shit.

I had crapped my pants. That was the problem. The fecal matter that riddled my clothes was obviously my own, and that was embarrassing. However, it would be less embarrassing if it looked like the excrement was produced elsewhere and then imported onto me by force. If an orderly has crap on the seat of his pants, he draws attention and ridicule. If an orderly has crap everywhere, he draws attention and pity. I proceeded accordingly.

After checking the stalls to ensure their vacancy, I locked the main door, took a deep breath, and relaxed. As expected, the diarrhea that was left seized the opportunity to erupt out of my asshole. With empty bowels, I looked up at the mirror, gave myself a reassuring nod, and then began the process of disguising my accident. Reaching back, I grabbed a handful of the liquid stool residing in the seat of my pants and brought it forward. En route the aroma caught my nostrils resulting in a minor dry heave. I thought about stopping, but I didn't; I went all out, I threw the handful of shit at my chest. It didn't work very well. It's hard to throw things at your own chest; you can't wind up and you look stupid, like a territorial ape slapping its pecs. Attempting to do better the second time around, I threw the next handful in the air. I let it rain down on me, chin up, eyes closed, arms spread, like it was washing away my sins. This method proved more effective. When I reached back the third time it became apparent that there was not enough to grab so I smeared it around instead, mashing it into the fabric around my hips and toward the front of my thighs.

Having rubbed the crap in thoroughly, I looked up in the mirror to examine my progress. My initial thought was that it looked good. Then the ridiculousness of the situation struck me and I laughed. I laughed hard, the way a grown man that is standing in front of a bathroom room mirror analyzing how well he is covered in his own shit should laugh.

After a minute or two, I composed myself and returned to the mirror. With a determinedly straight face, I attempted an honest assessment of my appearance. It looked good, authentic, save for the fact that there was no splatter. There needed to be splatter. Unsure of how I was going to achieve this aim, I scanned the room for an answer. It came in the form of a toilet brush stored under the sink.

I removed it from its box and ran it under hot water. It was new, but I wanted to make sure that it was hygienic. The absurdity of this action was not lost on me. Having sanitized the brush, I reached around and began to scrub my crack, back and forth with a slow and deliberate motion. Twenty or thirty strokes later, satisfied with the thoroughness of my scrubbing, I brought the brush around. Holding it firmly in one hand, I pulled the bristles back with the thumb of my other and then released them slowly, a couple at a time. As each bristle released it flicked a little speck of brown onto my clothing. Gradually, my scrubs began to accumulate the authentic-looking spray that I sought. The effect was perfectly random. Pleased with the finished product, I walked out of the bathroom a bit proud. I doubted anyone had ever worn shit so well.

Within a couple of seconds of departing the lavatory, everyone's eyes were on me. Their faces conveyed messages of deep sympathy, each one attempting to outdo the empathetic look of the person before them. I responded with the appropriate face, that of a distressed and tired blue-collar worker. An expression that said, "I'm upset, but I'm not going to complain. I'm just a hardworking guy trying to fulfill his meager lot in life." No one questioned it. As the bulk of the staff at the hospital were upper-middle-class armchair liberals, they dared not laugh at the plight of the workingman. While fighting back a smile, I inwardly reveled. Each and every one of those people was being duped, and I felt superior because of it. I had known I had the capacity to fool, but not with such flair. Arriving at the locker room, I was tempted to turn and take a bow. Mastering the impulse, I pushed open the door and allowed a grin to spread across my face. It was a clean exit, a glorious exit ... for a moment anyway.

As the locker room door swung shut, my name came over the PA system. Evidently, it was another "urgent" matter. My glorious exit was spoiled. Begrudgingly, I jogged off toward the room number given, cursing each squishy step of the way.

When I arrived, I found Lauren leaning over some geriatric shining a light in his eyes. I wondered if the old man could see down her shirt, and if he could, whether or not he could tell if her bra was the type with extra padding that pushes the breasts up and together. Those bras are the best. Rather than passively envying the old man's visual, I attempted to move myself into a location that afforded a similar line of sight. Sadly, it is difficult to be sneaky when you are covered in shit, and as such, it quickly became clear that Lauren's cleavage would remain hidden from my view.

Surrendering to the limitations of the moment, I shifted my

gaze from Lauren's tits to her face. I was bewildered, but not surprised, to find her sporting an expression of earnest concern. This patient, this ancient fuck, was about to die, and it genuinely bothered her. She spoke to him softly, as if direct speech would hurt and wiped spittle from the side of his mouth with a tissue. It was a futile effort to give the old man a dignified look as he inched nearer to the grave. She did it anyway. She even held his limp hand in hers for mere words could not convey her emotions. As always, this amazed me.

Lauren had dealt with numerous dying patients. I had personally seen her care for at least a dozen, which means that she had cared for dozens more. But the casual observer would never have been able to guess this fact. They would have thought that this patient was her very own grandpa that lay dying in her arms. That she was embracing the last new memory of the man that taught her to fish for muskie or drive a golf cart or cut a grapefruit or some other thing that grandfathers teach grand-daughters. But it was not her grandpa. It was some anonymous old man; some ass that was probably on the business end of a fire hose in early 1960s Birmingham. How could she feel that much for a stranger? Why would she want to?

I was unaware when Lauren first looked up at me. Lost in thought, I was caught without my face on. I did not wear the expression of a blue-collar worker bearing his difficulties with quiet dignity. I am not sure how I looked. Probably like a grown man covered in shit. As a result, Lauren returned an expression that was different from everyone else's. She didn't look angry or disgusted, just less empathetic, more professional. She told me to clean up the old man's vomit, take out his bedpan, and then take a shower. I did as instructed, she thanked me, and I left.

I put my face back on for the walk to the locker room. People gave me the same sympathetic eyes that they had before, but the feeling of satisfaction was gone. I washed the shit off in the staff shower and left for the day.

Chapter 2

Unjustified Ennui

"Welcome home, you sexy fuck."

This is how my roommate greets me on a daily basis. It's not an exception. It's a rule. Sometimes he mixes it up and says things like, "Goddamn you're a handsome son of a bitch," or "Hey beautiful, those pants make your crotch look good." He is not homosexual so the lines are not genuine, and he is not homophobic so the lines are not mean-spirited. The lines are what they are, although I suppose they reveal something about him. Perhaps they reveal that as an upper-middle-class white male from suburbia, he is comfortable. He is comfortable with his life, he is comfortable with his friends, he is comfortable with his sexuality, he is comfortable with society, and, most of all, they reveal that he is comfortable with having a good time. His name is Brad and he is fun to drink with.

I'm like Brad in many ways and unlike him in a few. I too am an upper-middle-class white male. I also went to a good college and used to be a reasonably talented athlete. Like him, I have slept around a bit but still have standards. We are both decently good looking and we both get along fairly well with our families. Both of us are also somewhat dependent upon our parents for financial help. Not in a pathetic way, more in a slightly spoiled way. Mine pay my cell phone bill and send me gift cards for gas; Brad's pay his car insurance and allow him to charge seventy-five bucks a month on their credit card.

The main difference between us is that Brad is legitimately happy. He graduated from college and got a fairly well paying job as a consultant. He doesn't find the job challenging or stimulating, but he is pleased with it. His pay is above average and he gets to travel. When he is on the road, he gets per diem and he gets to hang out with other young professionals with whom he goes out and gets appropriately drunk. Not frat-party-Jägermeister-in-the-beer-bong drunk, but rather scotch-with-a-microbrew-back drunk. He enjoys most of the people around him and most of the activities that he does during his free time. I envy his contentment.

Unlike Brad, I suffer from an unjustified sense of ennui. Indeed, the very fact that I use the word *ennui* demonstrates the reality of this claim. I learned the term in a Philosophy in Film class; a class that I was able to take because it fulfilled a requirement for my minor, a minor that I was able to choose because I didn't have to worry about making myself employable. Indeed, neither my architecture major nor my philosophy minor ensured any sort of financial stability, but they didn't have to. Employability didn't need to factor into my decision-making process because there were no struggling family members in need of my help or any student loans in need of my attention. My debt-free status is due in large part to my parents and in small part to baseball. The former paid for most of my tuition, while the latter paid for the rest. Although I suppose that my parents could be credited for the baseball scholarship as well. Their money allowed me to attend elite sports camps in the summer and their genetics made me left-handed—southpaws are always needed on the mound.

I assert that my ennui is unjustified because I believe that listlessness, dissatisfaction, and all of the more seriously negative emotions should be exclusively reserved for individuals that have actually had to deal with hardship. I have not. The toughest thing that I have ever had to endure is a tie between blowing a save in the super-regional my senior year of college and burying our family's greyhound, Olive Oil, when I was twelve. I was not a child soldier and my parents were never addicted to meth. Hell, my parents are happily married. They share one bottle of wine every night after work while holding hands and discussing their days. Adorable. I have no reason to be unhappy, and since I know that I have no reason to be unhappy, I feel guilty for feeling unhappy. Goddamn, when I say shit like that I realize what a whimpering bitch I am.

I could try and substantiate my unhappiness by dwelling on my crappy job, but that would be a bullshit move. Sure, I did not begin a career in my chosen field immediately after college, but when the economy improves, I will. Sure, I am an orderly, but if I really wanted I could get a white-collar job. If I'm honest with myself, I took the orderly job to fish for sympathy. My friends and family took the bait. They provide frequent reminders that my lack of initial success is due to the state of the economy and not to my lack of ability or effort.

"You want to go out tonight, handsome? There's dollar drafts at the brewery. Plus, Sandra that hot Indian girl will be there. You know, the girl I was telling you about; Gandhi Indian not Sacagawea Indian." Brad asked this as he stood up from the couch in excitement. A pinch hitter had just driven in two on the television.

"Sounds good, fatty. We better get ready." I headed to the kitchen, took two mugs out of the cabinet, filled them halfway with coffee and the rest of the way with whiskey. Before putting the liquor away, I turned and asked if Robert was home.

"No, he said he would meet us there," Brad replied. "You know he wouldn't want one anyway. He only drinks shit that eases his menstrual cramps."

Brad's right, Robert drinks like a bitch. Everything he likes tastes of pomegranate. Robert is our third roommate, a tall, skinny black guy with really white teeth. His parents are first-generation Kenyan immigrants who worked their asses off to ensure that he was afforded the right opportunities. Robert works at the same place as Brad. They have similar jobs, but Robert works a little harder. It's not that Brad is lazy, he just does what is needed. It's not that Robert is a workaholic, he just does a little more.

I walked over to Brad and handed him the coffee mug.

"You smell like ass," he said.

"That's because I got shit on today," I replied. "Literally shit on."

"Did you? Well, happens to the best of us. Man I tell you, if I had a nickel … Wait, is this poop on my cup?"

I shrugged and gave a frowny-face head bob. Brad did the same and took another drink. Laughing, I walked toward the bathroom.

In the bathroom, I went to the sink and washed my hands. While working the soap through my fingers, I noticed some shit around my cuticles, which meant that it really was poop on Brad's cup. "Fuck it," I thought. "He didn't seem to mind." My hands washed, I grabbed my Irish coffee and hopped in the shower. I considered rubbing one out but decided against it since we only had the exfoliating body wash left. That stuff is trouble; it's like masturbating with deceptively smooth sandpaper. The last time I used it, I got a raw spot on my dick. There was no chance I was going to run that risk again, not with vestiges of shit still on my hand; who knows what sort of nightmarish affliction might result from such careless self-pleasuring. In lieu of masturbation, I drank the whiskey and coffee. It was a decision that immediately proved to be a poor one. The coffee was hot, the shower was hot, and I was already hot from the walk home. It was too much. Attempting to counteract the uncomfortable warmth, I got out of the shower, set the coffee on the sink, and ran to the fridge to grab a beer. I didn't bother to throw on clothes. Brad yelled at me as I entered the kitchen.

"Goddamn man, shave your pubes, this isn't the eighties."

"I know, I know," I replied, while grabbing a can of some mid-range beer. "It's just that the last time I shaved my pubes it didn't work out well. I hooked up with that Natalie chick and we went at it, and I got a weird bruise right above my dick. I think that pubes might play some sort of vital cushioning role."

"Oh no, you got a bruise from fucking a cute girl who liked your shaved balls," Brad replied. "Quit bitching and man up. If a girl sees your junk looking like that, she'll run the other way. Your sack looks like Albert Einstein's head. That's not a turn-on. Girls don't go, 'Wow your balls look like the smartest patent clerk that ever lived, let me put them in my mouth.' I am telling you man, tame those brambles."

Following Brad's advice, I returned to the bathroom, took out the clippers, snapped on the shortest guard, and shaved away. I didn't use the razor. God knows what disasters would ensue if I cut myself with poop hands. After finishing with my pubes, I hopped back in the shower, drank my beer, and got ready for the night.

Chapter 3

A Little Lie and Some Good Stuff

I checked out Sandra's breasts as we sat at the high-top table. They were nice, and she knew it. She also knew how to display them. Although her shirt was revealing, it wasn't trashy. It covered her bra completely and remained securely in place at all times (none of those whorish nip slips). She must have been wearing that two-sided tape that keeps material in place, thus ensuring that just the right amount of skin shows. I have no problem with beauty accoutrement like that. If tools exist that allow people to look better, why not use them? They make the people using them feel better because they look better, and they make the people around them feel better because they get to look at a better-looking person. Women with low self-esteem are the only ones who don't think this way. They prefer to assuage their own insecurities by suppressing the potential attractiveness of everyone around them. Fuck those women, they should work out more and learn to utilize accoutrements.

Sandra's tits shook a little as she laughed at something Brad said. I piggybacked on Brad's comment and got more laughter. It was a good time. Everyone there was intelligent but no one took themselves too seriously, the conversations were erudite but not pretentious, the humor was clever. Robert was the most reserved person present, but he still laughed at all of the jokes and contributed to the conversation in a meaningful way. The drinks came steadily. The guys drank a heavy porter and as our bellies filled moved on to scotch. The girls and Robert drank some fruity concoction.

Over the course of the night, I made a few witty remarks that resulted in a fair amount of amusement. Somewhere in between the fourth or fifth comment and the third or fourth drink, Sandra started to focus her attention on me. Occasionally, when I was talking to someone else at the table, I caught glimpses of her looking at me with a fond and intrigued smile. It was cute.

I was glad that Sandra was showing an interest in me. In addition to having quality breasts, she seemed to be a worthwhile person; someone that I would want to spend time with, not just someone that I would want to fuck. More important, it appeared that she might be thinking the same thing about me. The entire situation was quite promising ... until it wasn't.

Roughly halfway through the evening, Sandra inquired about my career. The fact that it took a couple of hours for her to ask this question speaks to the quality of the discussion we were having. There had been no need to employ conversation starters because the dialogue was so organic. But now the time had come. I would tell her that I was an orderly, and she would slowly disengage from our conversation. She wouldn't be mean, in fact she would be pleasantly surprised and continue to talk with me for a while. She would find it fascinating that a manual laborer could be so bright and insightful. It would give her a little faith in the populace, providing her with the comforting knowledge that some members of the working class are able to hold substantive conversations and enjoy intellectual pursuits. But eventually it would come to an end. I could be an interesting friend to go out drinking with, but there was no way that I could be a potential partner.

I couldn't blame Sandra for this. I would never date a girl who worked a manual labor job. A partner should be someone who complements and challenges you. As an orderly, I couldn't do either of those things for her. I can just imagine, we would come home from work and she would tell me about a case she was trying or a hostile takeover her business was plotting or a family's beloved pet that had died on her operating table, and I would tell her about the way I mopped up the vomit of some scab-riddled hooker that wandered into the ER.

I had experienced the rejection that was about to come many times before. I opened my mouth to tell her that I was an orderly.

Brad interjected, "The buildings this guy designs, un-fucking believable." He wrapped his arm around me and said something in a drunk-but-not-wasted whisper.

"Oh yeah?" Sandra replied. "You're an architect." She clearly liked this. It was a unique career; kind of creative but not too offbeat, an imaginative job but one with real-world application. Architects are artsy but they don't starve.

I smiled and nodded without hesitation. Acting modest, I allowed Brad to go on. His expression indicated that he was impressed with how quickly I got on board.

"An architect!" he exclaimed. "This man is more than an architect, he's a visionary. He's like ... oh, who is that one famous guy whose family got set on fire and chopped to bits by the psychotic butler?"

"Frank Lloyd Wright," I said.

"Frank Lloyd Wright!" Brad echoed with gusto. "This guy is the next Frank Lloyd Wright. Better even. His buildings, I'm telling you, they're ingenious but they're not over the top. That cabin, that little no-carbon-footprint bastard, it's brilliant— affordable but classy, small but spacious. It's great, and it will allow way more people to have second homes without slumming down the vacation neighborhoods. Of course, all the good you do for Mother Earth by making the cabins self-sufficient will be counteracted by the fact that way more people will have second homes. But fuck it. You'll be rich. If all the extra homes that get built because of you destroy the environment, you can just buy yourself some sort of protective dome. You better let me stay in that dome, man. You owe me for all those times I got you laid in college."

"Please," I said. "I got you laid. I always let your roommate crash on my futon so that you could hook up with those girls, and that chubby bastard snored, too. It used to rattle my loft."

"True, but a lot of the girls I hooked up with were chubby, and a lot of them snored, and very few of them made my loft rattle, so I'm not sure you did me any favors." Brad slapped me on the back and winked. He went back to the discussion on the other side of the table and let us talk.

As Sandra and I continued, our conversation only got better. We talked about architecture for a while. She wasn't an expert, but she knew more than most. She said that she saw the Guggenheim in Bilbao while studying abroad, and that she was not sure what all the fuss was about. I told her not to worry because the Basques would blow it up some day. She laughed and said that she didn't hate it that much.

"I want to see it defaced, not blown up," she declared.

"Well, I'm glad that your penchant for terrorism is within reason," I said.

We both laughed.

The Basques led to talk of separatist movements, which led to talk of genocide. Genocide is not typically viewed as a romantic discussion topic, but in this case it was. The fact that Sandra had knowledge of human-rights violations impressed me. Whether or not a woman can talk about history and politics and philosophy and international affairs is hugely important. If I grow old with a woman, I want her to be able to have substantive conversations. Discussions of reality television and other people's relationships can only go so far. When the bartender announced last call, we were talking about our college experiences.

"What's odd," Sandra said, as the bartender yelled, "is that you always hear about how fantastic college is. Parents tell you, friends tell you, even movies and books tell you. They all say that it's the time of your life. The hype is unparalleled. Then you get there and you think, 'Well this is fun, but it's not fantastic,'" so you are a little disappointed. The years go by, and it's nice. You meet some interesting people, and you meet some assholes, and you meet some people that know how to have a good time. You study enough, and you go out more than enough, and eventually you realize that college is fantastic. You have this subliming moment when it dawns on you that all you do is learn about interesting things, drink, and hang out with friends, and even better, you realize that more often than not all three of those things happen at once. Then immediately after you have this epiphany you think, 'I need to make sure the bookstore received the order form for my cap and gown.'"

I laughed but with an exaggerated frown to convey the insightful and funny, yet sad, nature of what she had just said. "Then at your graduation you go and tell your younger sibling what a great time college is," I added.

"Yeah," she said, through a smirk. "It's a vicious cycle."

We both laughed.

"But you know what," she went on, pausing to finish off her drink. "It's not so sad, because the bottom line is that I had a good time. I was there to enjoy all of it. I experienced the happiness of those years even if I wasn't fully aware of it at the time."

I leaned back in my chair and smiled a little from each corner of my mouth, a little more from the right. I tried to let my expression convey my thoughts. This was a difficult task, as I didn't know what I felt. I can tell you that it was something good. Sandra smiled back. It was an unapologetic smile, broad and bright. When she gave it, there was no hesitation nor was there any sign of manufacturing. It was a genuine moment, and I was afraid to end it. I was worried that my smile would fade awkwardly, or I would say something unworthy of the moment. Just as these thoughts came to my mind, Sandra exited the pause beautifully.

"Then again," she said. "Maybe I'm upbeat about the whole college experience because I talked my Dad into paying for a fifth year. It was a pretty fantastic victory lap."

It was perfect. Her comment was clever and on point. It ended the moment with a spot of levity, yet it did not cheapen it. We transitioned into a conversation with the whole group, discussing plans for the rest of the night. Everyone decided to go to their respective homes except for the girl on Brad's arm and Brad. She said that they were going back to her apartment to watch a movie.

"You guys should come," she told Sandra and me. The invitation was not hollow. If anything, it was an order rather than a request. She wanted to bring Brad home, but she didn't want to appear slutty. She also wanted a contingency plan in case she decided against sleeping with him. You know, the classic "Oh I want to, but I have to drive Sandra home" bit. Brad knew that he was going nowhere without us, so he encouraged us to come. He even gave me the big-eyes-mouth-together-head-jerk-toward-the-door face when the girls weren't looking. I owed Brad for covering up my occupational shortcomings so I agreed to go. I would have gone anyway. Brad was a good guy and he was always enthusiastically appreciative when you acted as a solid wingman. Also, I wanted to talk more with Sandra.

It surprised me that I thought about talking with her and not about seeing her tits. Then I wondered if her girls were big enough to have that little line underneath where the breast folds over. Not too much as that makes them look saggy, just a bit. For breasts, bigger is not always better. Far too often large breasts are floppy and undefined like an amoeba. They are also prone to nasty areolas, huge circles that look like an invasive species slowly taking over the nice, smooth skin working their way out from the center nipple. Sandra's looked like they avoided the amoeba and the invasive species problems. I took her hand and squeezed it affectionately as we exited the bar.

* * *

The four of us walked back to watch a movie. The girl that was hanging on Brad's arm at the bar continued to hang on to his arm the entire way back to her apartment. I was glad I was not Brad. I dislike when women get drunk and slovenly lean on me. If you're going to hold on to me do it with some goddamn dignity. Stand up straight and casually lock your arm with mine, don't yank it down and stumble to and fro. Girls that do the latter remind me of a small dog on a chain. They go speeding away from the object that they are tethered to and then when the chain, or in this case arm, reaches full extension, they get jerked back toward the object holding them.

Sandra and I walked a little behind. Talking to her I found out that the terrier-like woman pulling on Brad's arm was her friend Hayden. She explained that Hayden and Brad work together, and that she knows Brad because she occasionally stops by their office for lunch. She continued on, telling me that Hayden is attracted to Brad but has yet to make a move. Typically, when girls discuss matters such as this I get bored, or frustrated, or both. When Sandra told me, I did not. Her tone was different. She didn't talk in an immature gossipy squeal, and she didn't have an attitude of disapproval. She simply explained the situation to me. She made it clear that she liked the potential match and wanted to facilitate it but that she did not want to meddle. She noted that if they were going to get together they would. It was up to them.

After Sandra revealed the dynamic playing out in front of us, I explained to her my feelings on arm yanking as well as the act's visual resemblance to small canine behavior. This was a simple comment, but it was also a test, a test that, if I'm honest, was rigged. If Sandra laughed with me and ridiculed her friend, it meant that she was not loyal. It meant that she did not really like Hayden, and I dislike people who are "friends" with those that they don't really like. If, on the other hand, Sandra took offense and was overly protective of her friend, it meant that she couldn't take a joke. I asked the loaded question on purpose; I liked Sandra, but I wanted my positive feelings toward her to diminish.

Sandra laughed a little and then said, "Hayden does look a bit like a bichon frise, the light curly hair and all." She paused briefly, and then went on, "But you can't blame her for acting like that. That's what a lot of men want."

"Oh yeah," I said smugly. "Guys want women to be lapdogs." As I said this, I pictured scratching Betty Friedan behind the ears while reading *Playboy*, a dusty and unopened copy of her *Feminine Mystique* in the corner. I thought wryly, Betty's book is wrong, it isn't the "problem with no name," it has a name, it's called the "lapdog problem."

"No," Sandra said, as she smirked indulgingly. "Men do not want a lapdog. This isn't Betty Friedan–era suburbia."

Shit, I thought.

"She has to act like that precisely because men, at least reasonably intelligent men, don't want a lapdog."

I was confused. I said, "I'm confused."

"Okay, so Brad is a good guy. At times he acts like a fraternity pledge, but overall he is a good guy. In fact, his occasional fratastic behavior is part of his charm. He is kind of loud, extremely sociable, occasionally crass, and really fun, just like a frat cliché. But unlike the frat cliché, he does not torment the fragile, he can have substantive conversations, and he genuinely cares about those close to him. While guys like that are not horribly uncommon, they are extremely difficult to bag because lots of women want them. Women want them because they want a guy's guy, but they don't want an asshole. They like men who love sports and beer and shooting the shit with their friends. They like that these men fulfill many of the archetypical male roles, but not all of them, especially not the antiquated sexist ones or the emotions-are-best-bottled-up ones. So even though there are a decent amount of these guys, they are hard to land because there is a lot of competition for them. They are also hard to land because they are hard to read. Although they deviate from the archetype, they don't deviate too far. Consequently, women have to slow-play their hand to gauge the extent to which each particular guy will stray from the paradigm. If they try to get them to diverge too far too soon they will lose them. Not because the man doesn't like them but because the man feels like he is betraying his gender."

"But how does that explain the bichon frise before us?" I asked, trying, and failing, to act unimpressed.

Sandra's indulgent smile grew. She knew I was legitimately interested. She continued, "So, Brad clearly wants to sleep with Hayden tonight. Hayden also wants to sleep with Brad, but you see it isn't that easy. This is the first time they have gone out, and, as of yet, they haven't gone on any actual dates. If she sleeps with him this soon, Brad will think she is slutty and thus not girlfriend material. He will dip his pen in the well and then dismiss her. Therefore, Hayden has to balance her desire to sleep with Brad against her desire to date Brad."

"Oh yeah," I said through a laugh.

"Oh yeah," Sandra's smile grew more. "Hayden simply has to act fairly drunk. Even girls that you bring home to Mom get loose when they drink. But, she can't act too drunk because that will prevent him from sleeping with her. Not because he's above sleeping with a girl who is wasted, but because he has probably had a bad experience in the past. Some girl that took him to bed when she was smashed either passed out while they were doing it, or felt ashamed afterward and hid from him, or perhaps even vomited on him. So, in order to reveal that she is just the right amount of drunk she does the arm yank thing, or as you so kindly put it, acts like a small dog on a chain. She demonstrates that she is totally capable of walking on her own, but by occasionally swaying or walking toward something that captures her attention she also reveals that she has drunk a fair amount. As a result, when he wakes up the next morning he will feel satisfied but still interested and, assuming he lasts at least a few minutes, so will she. He will try to sleep with her again in the morning when they are sober. He will do this partly because he has an erection and partly because he wants to determine what type of girl she is. Hayden will kindly turn him down. She will then reveal that she enjoyed herself but that she doesn't normally do stuff like that. They will both have had a fun night, gotten laid, and possibly found a new significant other, and it is all due to the arm yank. So you see, Hayden is not acting like a bichon frise, she is acting like a spider. She is luring Brad into her web so that she can sample him."

"That's good," I said. I thought a great deal more than I said. I thought that the question that I had tried to trap her with now seemed to be the effort of an amateur, like I was a Little Leaguer trying to strike out Ty Cobb. She was Ty Cobb. Well, not really, she wasn't a racist white male with a temper and a great batting average. She was an articulate Indian woman with perky tits and a solid grasp of world affairs. Nevertheless, she made me feel immature and outmatched. I had tried to trip up a girl who didn't deserve to be tripped up, a girl that had something.

It's not that what Sandra said was groundbreaking in its insightfulness; it wasn't. Many have commented on the ridiculous games played during the courting process. Nor was it that she delivered this information without a hint of condescension. Many great intellectuals have conveyed their brilliance without talking down to their audience. It wasn't even that she maintained a cute innocence as she talked about erections. It was that she did all of these things while standing beside me. She was a genuinely beautiful, intelligent, and fun woman and she was amenable to holding my hand and probably playing with my cock. It struck me that this had never happened before. I had engaged in intellectual conversations with women before, but they typically looked like they were in need of a diet and a bath. I had attracted sexy, well-dressed women before, but they had always been vapid or crazy. I had flirted with cute, innocent, and kind women before, but they were always too cute, too innocent, and too kind. I had read about girls like Sandra. That was it.

Awareness of Sandra's exceptionality made me nervous. It shouldn't have, she was interested in me, and I had been myself … or, I had mostly been myself.

When we got to Hayden's apartment, she put in a movie. We didn't really watch the film, it was just background noise for drinking. All four of us switched away from our previous beverages and instead had shots of cinnamon schnapps. It tasted foul but freshened our breath, which is probably why Hayden selected it. Brad would have normally objected to such an emasculating alcohol, but he knew what the drink selection meant so he swallowed it with a smile. I thought briefly about how pliable men become in promising sexual situations. It's an accurate and justified stereotype.

After a while, Brad and Hayden stood up and told us that they were going outside to talk. If I had been more inebriated I would have kissed Sandra the second they departed, but I wasn't so I didn't. Instead, we turned our attention to the movie, or at least we faced the television that had the movie on it. I wasn't actually paying attention to the events unfolding on the screen. My mind was too preoccupied with the moment at hand, anxiously debating whether or not to make a move. It felt like high school all over again but in a good way—that sense of disbelief at the good fortune of being alone with a pretty girl that might want to fool around.

As the minutes wore on, I stole a few glimpses of Sandra out of the corner of my eye. I didn't want her to feel like I was gaping, and although I wasn't, I felt like I was. Sandra didn't take her eyes off the screen, and she didn't move closer to me, yet she still managed to convey a longing for closeness. It was a subtle and warm invitation that for some reason, took me roughly ten minutes to act on. Eventually, I remembered that I was a grown man, mustered up some balls, and moved my hand to her thigh. Her leg welcomed the touch, relaxing at the arrival of my fingers. Emboldened with confidence by the positive feedback, I leaned over to my right to kiss her. Since it was a move that I normally make to my left, it was not smooth. Consequently, before our lips touched, I had to adjust my body. The pause that ensued allowed us to catch a glimpse of one another up close. Sandra was not expecting it so I know that her endearing reaction was sincere. Her eyes widened, both sides of her mouth curled up, and her tongue stuck out a bit extending just beyond her two front teeth. Enchanted, I remained still until she leaned forward and closed the gap between us. Her lips were soft but not greasy. I worried that mine were too dry. She lay back on the couch and pulled me on top. Her body was warm and it felt pleased, perhaps even relieved, that I was there. I got extremely hard. She felt this happen, paused for a second, and looked at me affectionately. She then leaned up a bit and kissed me lightly while simultaneously using her thigh to press against my cock.

We ended up making out for a long time. Sandra's hands never moved toward my crotch, and while mine occasionally cupped her ass and pressed her hips toward me, they never made a legitimate effort to touch her between the legs. After we stopped but before we got up off the couch, Sandra gave me a quick and affectionate kiss on the lips as if we had been dating for ages.

Once our make-out session concluded, Sandra went over to the sliding glass door, opened it, and informed our friends that we were leaving. When we got to the front entrance of Hayden's apartment complex, she took both of my hands in hers, stood up on her tiptoes, kissed me on the cheek, and said, "I think I like you." Then she turned and walked off toward her house.

The night didn't end in an orgasm, but it was still fulfilling.

Chapter 4

Ryne Fucking Sandberg

When I say I hate work, I mean I hate work; it is an assertion totally devoid of exaggeration. My hatred for my job is sincere and raw, and sometimes consuming. It becomes clear that the hatred has consumed me when I begin stalling for seconds. Many people stall for minutes, but only those who truly loathe their jobs stall for seconds. I do it on a regular basis.

Typically, my stalling routine begins with my heading to the vending machines in the basement, a strategic choice from the outset, as it usually takes longer to get to them than it does to get to the ones on the first floor. Upon my arrival, I pull out a bag of nickels and begin to insert them into the appropriate coin slot. Nickels are my coin of choice as they are the smallest denomination accepted by the machine; if it were possible to pay in pennies, I would. Twenty nickels later, I select my soda. After it falls, I tap the top of the can a couple of times with my finger and then lift the tab. The can now open, I proceed to slowly wiggle the tab back and forth until it snaps off. Once the tab is removed, I make my way over to the oncology unit where I place the scrap of aluminum into the fundraising bin for the leukemia kids. Although it's unlikely that a single soda tab will make a difference in the fight against shitty white blood cells, it still seems like a worthwhile thing to do (especially when one factors in how long it takes to get to the oncology unit). On the way back, I stop by the restroom, whether or not I actually have to go is of little consequence. If my bladder is empty, I just stand in front of the urinal and fake it. Following the pee (or faux pee), I walk over to the sink, turn on the water, wait for it to get warm, and then place my hands underneath. In order to guarantee a thorough washing, I make sure to keep my hands under the water until I'm done singing *Twinkle Twinkle Little Star* at the appropriate 4/4 tempo. Outside of the restroom I kneel down, untie, and then retie my shoes. Finally, I slowly walk the last few yards back to my point of departure. Each of these activities gives me at least twelve seconds, some of them as much as ninety-five. It is a routine of unrivaled beauty.

Of course, a magnificent stalling routine would be fairly useless if it didn't get me out of the worst parts of the job. As such, I'm always careful to deploy it at just the right moment, to time it so that the routine coincides with the nastiest of the orderlies' assignments. It's not hard to do since most of the disgusting tasks at the hospital tend to happen at specific times. The exacting nature of my approach typically pays off. I clean roughly half as many colostomy bags as the average orderly and sponge bathe about seventy-five percent fewer bariatric patients. The other orderlies are borderline retarded so they don't pick up on this fact.

Having accorded a great deal of praise to my routine, I should note that it's not perfect. Every once in a while, I still get stuck with one of the crap jobs. Since reading to the infants is the least predictable and most cerebrally demanding of the crap jobs, it is the one that I get stuck with most often. It's less filthy than cleaning the colostomy bags but no less shitty.

Reading to the infants is absurd. They have no idea what the fuck is going on. Nevertheless, we have to read to them every goddamn day, and all because one of the frumpy middle-aged nurses saw some nonsense article in some New Age parenting magazine. The doctors know that it's bullshit, but they don't say anything. What do they care? They don't have to do it. The hospital peons are the ones burdened with the task. Many of the orderlies are illiterate so they just look at picture books and make it up. No one notices. It's not like they're performing for a discerning audience. Whenever I'm assigned the task, I choose to read children's books that start off with the kids suffering and then end with the kids triumphing over their foes. I only ever read the beginnings.

I was reading from Roald Dahl's *Witches* when Lauren walked by. I read aloud, "A real witch hates children with a red-hot sizzling hatred that is more sizzling and red-hot than any hatred you could possibly imagine." I thought, *If I had a vagina I would be one of these witches.*

Lauren's back was to me, but I could tell that she was listening so I started to perform different voices for the various characters in the book. Anytime a witch spoke I used the cliché cackle voice, when the grandma spoke I used an American/Norwegian vernacular, and when the young boy spoke I used a slightly high-pitched British accent that made my voice crack (a vocal inconsistency that could have been embarrassing if I hadn't played it off as an intentional and ambitious portrayal of a pubescent character). I could tell that Lauren liked my storytelling efforts. Although the menial task she was performing forced her to look down and away from me, I occasionally caught her head tilting in my direction. When she did this, I could see her ear and the upper part of her cheek. Based off the fraction of her face that was visible, it appeared that she was enjoying herself.

After a while Lauren finished her task and stood up. On the way out, she walked on the side of the plastic baby cages closer to me. As the distance between us closed, she started to talk.

"It's nice of you to read to the babies like that," she said. "Most people I hear reading just mumble along in monotone, I like that you add some pizzazz. I know that the babies can't understand, but I think they can feel the positive energies in the air when people really try."

"I agree!" I said. I didn't agree. To be convincing I put on the upbeat face where my eyebrows are raised a bit.

"It's refreshing to see that there are people here who care." As Lauren said this, she continued walking past me. She reached out a hand and rubbed the back of my arm affectionately.

I wanted to flex my triceps as she touched it, but I couldn't. It's hard for me to flex that particular muscle when my arm is bent at the elbow, and since I was holding the *Witches* book, it was impossible for me to do so without it being obvious. Goddamn it, Roald Dahl.

I stopped thinking about my triceps dilemma in time to check out Lauren's ass as she walked through the door. Her scrubs were thin and fell over her skin gently. It was a nice visual.

The rest of the day went by quickly. The spot on the back of my arm where Lauren had touched me stayed warm for the remainder of my shift. Thinking about it gave me a semi—not a painfully hard erection, just a slightly thicker firmness. Although it wasn't a full-blown hard-on, it still muddled my thoughts. As a result, when the other orderlies asked me to go to the bar after work, I agreed. They were excited by my consent. I was not.

"Fuck it," I thought. "I'll just think about the back of my arm."

* * *

When we got to the bar, I ordered a scotch on the rocks. Not the rail scotch but not the high-end scotch either—a single-malt twelve-year, nice but not pretentious. I would have ordered a beer, but the other orderlies were drinking that.

For a while, I successfully tuned out everyone at the table. It wasn't hard to do because they weren't stunning conversationalists. Orderlies are not known for their keen insights or their witty banter. Instead of listening, I thought about the back of my arm, just like I had planned. My triceps still felt toasty which helped my memory seem more vivid. I didn't really remember what Lauren said when she touched me, but I did remember how she looked at me, like I was a pocket of sunshine on a damp and cold day. It was a look that made me feel set apart.

Thoughts of Lauren kept me disengaged from the conversation for a while but not forever. Eventually, I talked. It was an involuntary interjection, a brain fart. By the time I realized that I was speaking, it was too late to stop. It was, however, not too late to say nothing, so that's what I did.

They were talking about baseball when I spoke up, all three arguing about the game's greatest player. Their vocal inflections and hand gestures were cartoonish in their extravagance. It was an absurd dispute, so absurd that I didn't even blame myself for having the mental lapse and jumping in. The lean black orderly was arguing for DiMaggio; the broad old orderly eating bratwurst for Mays; and the Italian orderly adorned with gold chains for Honus Wagner. I wondered if they realized the irony of their choices.

When I first spoke up, I intended to inform the intellectual titans that their entire debate was an exercise in futility. Before uttering a comprehensible word, however, I remembered to whom I was talking. I had to take into account the fact that these men would not understand the word *futility* and that they would probably not understand the word *exercise,* at least as I intended to employ it. I thought about changing the wording, perhaps telling them that their debate was retarded. But this, I concluded, was also not a good option. Telling them that their debate was retarded would inevitably lead to me having to explain why it was retarded, and I did not want to explain. I was not in an explaining mood, and I was really not in an explaining-to-people-with-a-sixth-grade-reading-level mood. Due to their childlike brains, any proper explanation would have taken hours. I couldn't have simply told them that it's impossible to compare players from different eras. I would have had to spell it out for them, describe why it's impossible to compare players from different eras; detail what important changes have taken place — the training, the materials, the coaching, the rules, the diet, the supplements, the exercise physiology, the international nature of the game, the increasingly regimented approach of youth sports, the progressively substantial financial incentive for athletes to succeed, the reactionary understanding of a player's worth based on short-term changes that are overly scrutinized by sports specific media, etc., etc., etc. At the end of such a spiel, they would be staring at me with open mouths and glazed eyes. One of them would probably be drooling. Quite simply, an explication of reality would be beyond them. So, instead of diving into the cerebral deep end of sports dialogue, I chose to say nothing, which is to say nothing of substance, which is to say I spewed bullshit. Rather than diminishing their dialogue through a critical analysis of its fundamental base, I diminished it by being an asshole.

"Ryne Sandberg is the greatest baseball player of all time," I stated.

Ryne Sandberg is not the greatest baseball player of all time. No one would argue that he is, not even Ryne Sandberg. He was, however, really fucking good, just good enough for me to be taken seriously so long as I mentioned him in a serious tone. I was fucking with them.

I argued for Sandberg like he was my only child. I gestured wildly and spoke with as much hyperbole as possible.

After a while, the Italian orderly said, "Come on, the greatest ballplaya of all time is not Ryne Fuckin' Sandberg."

"True," I said. "I don't think his middle name is 'fucking.' That seems unlikely, although I don't actually know his middle name so we could be talking about the same guy." The lean black orderly laughed. The other two did not.

"Didn't he play for the Cubs?" the lean black orderly asked. He had a wry smile. I think he knew what I was doing. "He was pretty damn good. I remember one year his average was over .400 all the way until September. Quite the player that boy was, quite the player." He leaned back in his chair as if to ponder Mr. Sandberg as a serious candidate. This antagonized the other two.

"You've gotta be shittin' me. I barely even remember Sandberg, plus he was a Cub. The best playa of all time couldn't a played for the fuckin' Cubs," the Italian protested.

"Why not," the black orderly replied in a measured calm. "Honus Wagner played for the Pirates."

"But that was back in the day," the Italian said.

"Exactly," the black orderly replied, then he winked at me. I gave him a smile and a little head nod back. The Italian was confused. I was impressed. I didn't think that any of them would catch on to what I was doing. I really didn't think that any of them would make the same point that I originally intended to make. *This guy might be alright,* I thought.

Over the course of the next few minutes, I watched the lean black orderly interact with the others. Usually he shot the shit with them, but every once in a while when they said something moronic he would lean back, grin, and slowly drink his beer. It was like he was having his own inside joke. I figured out from the conversation that his name was Jones. I didn't know that before. Actually, I didn't know any of their names because I didn't think that they were worth knowing. That was a correct assumption for two out of three of them. I also figured out that Jones was a lot older than I originally thought. When he laughed the lines on his face were deep, and when he stopped laughing they didn't quite fade away.

After I figured out a little about Jones, I left the conversation once more. Jones was okay but he couldn't make up for the other two assholes. This time when I sat back in my seat, I thought about Sandra. Thoughts of her kept my mind occupied until it was time to go. Nothing at the table broke my contemplation. When the guys got up to leave Jones had to squeeze me on the shoulder to get my attention.

"It's time to go, son," he said.

I got up and we headed toward the door. Jones and I walked out together, a few yards behind the other two.

"That was fun, messin' with those boys about Sandberg," he said. "A little mean but fun." He laughed and slapped my back.

I was happy as we walked out of the bar.

* * *

Jones and the other two orderlies lived to the east of the hospital; I lived to the west, so I got to walk home alone. Thank God, although I wouldn't have minded talking to Jones for a bit. I wondered how he got to be an orderly. It was probably because he had to get a job straight out of high school to support his single mom and younger siblings. I felt a little ashamed as I considered this hypothesis. It seemed a bit racist. To avoid further contemplation of my white, upper-middle-class guilt, I decided to rehash the night.

I had to admit that Jones surprised me. He was on top of things. As for the other two, well those dickheads only served to reinforce my previously held beliefs. They were genuinely aggravated by my Ryne Sandberg argument. Hilarious. They should have been able to tell that I was trying to antagonize them. Come on, Ryne fucking Sandberg. But I guess I can't hold them accountable for their idiocy. Hyperbole has become a standard form of communication, and consequently it has lost some of its humorous capabilities. People no longer realize when you're exaggerating for comedic effect. That is to say, some people don't realize.

Brad was still up when I got home. He was using scissors and a shot glass to chop up bud. The living room smelled like a FRESH COTTON candle, which meant that Brad had already vaped a bowl.

"Robert's asleep?" I asked.

"Yeah, he said that he had to go to work early tomorrow."

"Do you have to go in early?"

"No, neither does Robert," Brad replied.

There was no judgment in Brad's voice, which was odd because the words he spoke were judgmental. To him it was just stating a reality. As Brad spoke, he used the glass piece at the back end of the vaporizer's whip to scoop the bud out of the shot glass. It looked like good pot, lots of tiny crystals. He plugged the piece into the vaporizer, waited a few seconds, and then took a slow and steady hit. He breathed out as he leaned back on the couch speaking after he exhaled. He did not do the weird froglike talk as he held the smoke in his lungs. We weren't in college anymore, there was no one to impress.

"So what do you think of Hayden?" Brad asked as he offered me the whip. I put my hand up a little and shook my head.

"Sandra's friend?" I asked rhetorically. "She seems pretty cool, and she definitely wants your penis in and/or around her."

"Yeah, she does seem pretty cool and definitely not high maintenance. Plus, she's pretty hot." As Brad said this, he offered me the whip again. I mulled over how drunk I was and decided that the spins could be avoided as long as I only took a couple hits.

"I agree, very fit, and she seems fun," I said, while moving the glass mouthpiece to my lips. Brad was pleased with my positive words. In order to not seem overly excited, he threw in a qualifier.

"She's hot, but she's runner hot. Little boobs, little butt."

"Flat abs and toned thighs," I replied, exhaling a fog.

Brad smiled but then forwarded his hesitation once more. "True, but lately I've been watching those TV shows that are set in the sixties, and I can't get over how fucking sexy those curvy women are. Our grandfathers were onto something. That little bit of thickness and those hourglass bodies, girls like that are a whole different level of sexy. Flat abs and toned thighs can't compete with that shit." Brad said this, but he didn't mean it. He was saying it to disguise how excited he was about Hayden. I couldn't blame him, I do the same thing, most guys do, disguise their early feelings about girls that is. Especially if a girl in their past has shit on them. Enter slowly and get rejected—unfortunate. Enter fast and get rejected—disaster. The latter makes you look like a fool and it makes you feel like a fool, nothing is worse than that.

"Shenanigans," I replied. I didn't want Brad to worry about being foolish so I backed Hayden, at least indirectly. "You're creating a false dichotomy. You're acting as if the situation is an either/or scenario. Either slightly thick, curvy women are hotter, or fit, toned women are hotter, but in reality neither group is categorically hotter than the other. The attractiveness of women must be examined on a case-by-case basis. Plus, if somehow I did buy into your dichotomy I would argue for fit, toned women. Yeah, thick curvy women are hot now but usually not later. The hourglass turns into a blobby-glass. Therefore, if you are seriously considering a lady type it's better if she's not a curvy one."

"That's a fair point, you handsome bastard," he said. "Or maybe I should forget both types of women and get with you. Your ass will stay perky and you got those creamy white man thighs."

"Mmm. I like that idea," I said. "You know I'd treat you right, maybe even braid your taint hair with my tongue."

"No need," Brad said. "I wax that bad boy so the hair is already out of the way." He made a tiger sound and winked at me. We both laughed. Brad took the whip out of the vaporizer and dumped the light brown remnants of cannabis onto a paper towel. It smelled a little like popcorn.

"Alright I'm going to bed, good night lover," I said to Brad, slapping his back as I got up. I walked toward the doorway, and as I exited the room, spoke loudly over my shoulder. "Go for it, man. Hayden's fucking cute."

Brad was happy, I didn't need to see him to know it.

Chapter 5

Charity or the Veil of Impotence

I talked to Jones more over the next few days. He was a sage old bastard. His words didn't require deep contemplation, but they still conveyed substantive ideas. The plain manner in which they were spoken only made them more incisive and judicious. I was increasingly amazed by the fact that he was an upper-middle-aged orderly. What the fuck was he doing? After a few conversations my balls felt heavy enough to ask him about it.

"Why the hell are you here, Jones? You're a smart guy, you could be doing almost anything."

"Ah, it's probably what you would expect, son. I had to get a job straight out of high school to help my mama and my little sisters," he replied. It was what I expected, my hypothesis was correct. This actually made me feel worse and slightly more racist. Jones continued, "By the time that my youngest sister graduated, I was thirty years old. Too old to be a freshman and too old to be an intern, but just old enough to get good benefits from this hospital. By that time, I had already put in twelve years."

"So you just stayed?" I asked this question with a bit too much disappointment in my voice.

"I did, but I don't regret it. I don't know if things would be that different if I had gone and done something else, or if I had went to college. Most college boys I know work for the weekend just like I do. Look at the most competitive residencies at this hospital—dermatology, radiology, anesthesiology. All the ones that work nice set hours. Those docs worked hard early on so that they wouldn't have to later on. Most people just wanna be left to be. College or no college."

Jones had a point, but I didn't like it. I told him he had a point, but didn't tell him that I disliked it. I wanted to process what he said before attempting a rebuttal so I excused myself and went on one of my subterranean snack excursions.

On the way to the basement, I caught sight of Lauren. Once again she was consoling some old, ugly fuck. This one had wildly unkempt, curly hair; a white person afro crossed with the wispy locks of a malnourished bulimic. His scalp peaked through in spots as though it was diseased. Lauren didn't seem to notice his nauseating appearance. Like always, she looked genuinely concerned. Like always, this confounded me. Engrossed by the scene, I watched for a few seconds as she listened to his labored speech and held his withered hand. Their intermingled fingers were a study in contrast. Lauren's were thin, straight, and well manicured while the old man's were swollen, crooked, and riddled with hangnails. His pinkie fingers were particularly bothersome as they bent disconcertingly inward at the last joint. The digits' crooked state had to have been the result of genetics and arthritis working in tandem; there is no way either one could have produced such a deformity on its own. It was a final flourish to the emetic portrait. I shook my head slightly and continued downstairs.

After arriving in the basement, I leisurely strolled over to the vending machines. As usual, I paid with nickels. After the soda fell, I opened it, sipped the liquid that had gathered in the trench around the rim of the can, and then slowly wiggled off the tab. With the soda in one hand and the tab in the other, I meandered over to the oncology unit to provide further support for the fight against leukemia. I was about to drop the scrap of aluminum into the fundraising bin when I saw Lauren turn the corner. She was staring at a chart as she walked down the hall.

As Lauren approached I quickly searched myself for a baggy, locating one in my left pocket. It was filled with candy that I was supposed to give to the kids in the burn unit. I dumped the candy into the trash with my right hand and grabbed a handful of soda tabs out of the leukemia bin with my left. While shoving the tabs into the now empty baggy, I bent over and pretended to tie my shoe. Once Lauren neared, I stood up and extended my arm to drop the baggy of co-opted soda tabs into the charity bin.

"Oh, hey Lauren!" I said in my best surprised voice. She looked up from her chart and turned a smiling face toward me. Certain that I had her attention; I released the baggy into the leukemia bucket.

"Hello, hello!" She replied in an upbeat voice. She glanced at the bin and then went on. "That's so nice of you to give to those kids. Small things like collecting pop tabs really add up and make a difference. It's so easy to save them, but almost no one does it."

"I'm always blown away by that," I said. "No one ever thinks about how big of an impact a little effort makes."

"Exactly." She paused a second and looked at me before going on. "You know, I volunteer at the children's cancer center on Saturdays. It's not a big deal, I just hang out with the kids. You should come sometime."

"I would love to," I replied. "Just give me a time and I'll be there."

She looked at me with warmth, yet I could not tell which positive emotion her face was conveying. "Twelve-thirty," she said. "Will I see you there?"

"I'll be there, twelve-thirty on Saturday," I replied with a grin and a head nod. "I have to run, it's my turn to read to the infants."

"Have fun! Expand those little minds."

"Oh, I will," I said, touching the side of her arm as I headed off.

Unsure as to whether or not Lauren was watching my departure, I broke into a light jog. If she was watching, I wanted her to think that I cared about reaching my reading appointment on time. As soon as I turned the corner, I stopped. Leaning against the wall, I thought briefly about the interaction that just took place and then proceeded to spend fifteen minutes checking baseball scores on my phone. I didn't actually care that I was late. Those little shit bags could sit in silence.

When I finally arrived at the nursery, no one else was there. The entire staff was in the adjacent room looking in through the window in the wall. It felt as if the babies and I were on display. I didn't like it. I did, however, like the solitude that it afforded me. Capitalizing on the opportunity, I walked out of the room, grabbed a men's wellness magazine from the lobby, put it inside a children's picture book, and then returned to the nursery. Since no one was in the room to hear me, I could get away with faking my responsibilities. I read the magazine cover to cover. It was an interesting and surprisingly informative experience. I learned to vary my protein supplements and to be cautious about pulling back a woman's clitoral hood during oral sex. This second bit of news contradicted my previously held clitoral conclusions. I was under the impression that more direct and intense stimulation was always better, but it turns out that it is too much for some women. This was interesting information, and since there was no one to share it with, I read it aloud to the infants. They found it just as captivating as the Roald Dahl book.

By the time I was finished reading, I was also finished working. No one said anything so I just turned those glossy pages of beer ads and scantily clad women until the day was done. On my way to the locker room, I stopped by the gift shop and bought two boxes of buttered rum hard candy and a box of chocolate-covered coconut—stuff kids hate, but I love. I dropped them off at the pediatric section of the burn unit; odds were high that some would be left over for me tomorrow.

Once I got to the locker room, I grabbed my shit and headed toward the back door. It was an emergency exit so the alarm would sound but only for the couple seconds that the door was open. It was worth it. I didn't want to use the main door and risk getting stopped on the way out. As I opened the rear exit, I looked to my left and saw one of the fat old doctors taking a shower. Between his belly and his pubic hair I couldn't make out a penis. Even if he was a grower, his cock was undersized. I wondered if his erection extended beyond his paunch, and if it did, how much of it made it inside his partner—probably not very much. Whoever is on the receiving end of sex with him must feel like they are being stabbed with the first joint of a nail-free thumb. This mental picture vanquished the arousal that the clitoral hood article had given me, so I was forced to walk home contemplating nonsexual thoughts.

On my way home, I noticed more than usual. Unable to drift off into the sweet oblivion of sexual fantasy, my immediate surroundings became more pronounced. In the case of the sun and the sky this was a positive, in the case of the nearby architecture this was a negative. The buildings that I passed annoyed me in a way that they never had before, something about the blandness of their facades. Eventually this frustration drove me indoors.

I entered a pub and ordered an old-fashioned. It seemed an appropriate choice to make at an establishment dominated by dark wood. As the bartender mixed the drink, I sat down on a stool and sent Brad a text that suggested he meet me. The words in my text were spelled properly and all the punctuation was correct. He responded, "c u in a bit."

It was awkward sitting at the bar by myself waiting for Brad. It felt like people were looking at me despite the fact that they weren't. Consequently, I drank a little too fast. When Brad got there, I was on my third.

"What's up, lover; how was your day?" Brad asked as he sat down and ordered.

"It was a day," I replied. "I saw an old guy with an innie penis."

"Innie like a belly button or innie like a dog's where the sword is sheathed?"

"The first one," I said. I would have said "the prior" or "the former," but I was a little drunk.

"That's rough man, poor guy."

"Poor guy? Poor me, it's engrained in my mind. It's going to be one of those nasty pictures that randomly flashes in my brain while I'm masturbating."

Brad laughed. "I have one of those that always reoccurs," he said. "Remember in college when I got John Rawls to sign my copy of *A Theory of Justice*."

"Yeah. You only did that for the extra credit."

"True, but irrelevant to the story. As I talked to him, I couldn't take my eyes off of his hands. They were all veins and liver spots. They were the hands of a corpse—actually they really were the hands of a corpse, he died like a month after that. Anyway, that night one of the field hockey girls was straddling me in nothing but one of those sexy push-up bras and the skirt that went with her uniform. She was playing with my cock, and it was really fucking hot, and then all of the sudden I thought of John Rawls's hands. I imagined those long wrinkly digits wrapped around my dick and my cock just shriveled up."

I laughed. It was a good story. Probably the only time John Rawls ever stole a sexual encounter away from another man.

"I covered it up with the girl," Brad went on. "I lifted her off me, tossed her on the bed, and went down on her. So she was none the wiser, but still, it haunts me."

"That's hilarious. That's a much better flaccid-causing image than mine. Some fat physician in the shower cannot compete with impotence induced by the hands of a philosopher."

"It is pretty funny, but not for me, man." As Brad said this he looked a little past me and shook his head from side to side. He smiled broadly, laughed a little, and then said, "I wish I could go behind his 'veil of ignorance' and forget those bony hands."

We laughed hard.

"That might be the most perverse yet intellectually snobby joke I've ever heard," I said honestly and with a grin. I wasn't surprised that Brad came up with the "veil" bit. He likes cheap beer and football, but he's not dumb. I think that there are a fair amount of guys like that; you just discover it slowly.

In the euphoria of our laughter we ordered a pitcher. At that moment, we didn't care about work in the morning. Furthermore, we knew if we continued to drink quickly, we would not care until our alarms went off the next day. The speed with which Brad and I consumed the pitcher reflected this shared understanding. While we drank we talked about baseball, the wild card race, and then the disadvantage of being a small market team in the American league—designated hitters, what a bunch of shit; the DH is everything that is wrong with America.

After we finished the second pitcher, Brad brought up Hayden. His enthusiasm was less restrained this time. It was as if the words of encouragement that I had given him the previous night, and the alcohol that he had just consumed, were working in tandem to produce a version of Brad that was awash with excitement yet self-possessed.

"I asked her out today," he said with a grin.

"Nice, man," I responded.

"She was standing by the watercooler, just wearing the shit out of this V-necked shirt. So I went up and talked to her. I don't really remember what we talked about, but I made her laugh, and she accidentally snorted a little, and as soon as it happened she covered her mouth and her eyes got real wide. She was surprised and a little embarrassed, but not too embarrassed, and then we both laughed, and she snorted a couple more times without holding back. It was unbelievably fucking cute, and so I looked at her and asked her out."

"Nice, honestly, nice. I'm glad you grew some balls. I could tell that you liked her but weren't doing anything about it. You've just been putting it off, sitting around like an asshole."

"Nah, just waiting for the right moment. If you want to knock it out of the park, you can't swing too early."

"You can't swing too late either," I replied. "Fuck it, whatever you did worked. A celebration drink before we leave." I got the bartender's attention and ordered two shots of hundred-proof peppermint schnapps.

Brad smiled at my order. "You horny bastard, ordering fresh breath shots. You want to sex me up one more time before I'm off the market."

"You bet your ass I do. And you're in for a treat, the minty tingle that the shot leaves in my mouth will feel great on your scrote." We tapped the shot glasses against each other then swallowed the liquid down in one, burning the space between our oral and nasal cavities.

* * *

Brad talked about Hayden the entire way home. I gave my opinion and responded as needed. Really, I just wanted to let him talk. It was good that he wanted to discuss her. She was a smart match.

A few yards from our front door, the topic of conversation suddenly shifted. Brad stopped mid-sentence, put his arm out to halt my progress, and began to talk excitedly about something other than Hayden. His energy was due in part to the alcohol, but it was also a byproduct of genuine enthusiasm. The information that he was sharing made him happy.

"Holy shit, I forgot to tell you. Sandra stopped by today and told me that you should call her. She went out of her way, man. She said that she didn't know how to get a hold of you, so you should get a hold of her, and then she gave me her number to pass on. She was proactive, assertive. Just walked into our office, told me that, and then headed out. It was impressive. Hayden said that she offered to be an intermediary, you know to find out if you liked her, but Sandra said that she would do it. It was really fucking hot. Plus, she looked sexy as hell. She was wearing this tight brown skirt that made her look even more tan, which is impressive because she already has that slightly exotic look. You better call her, she is pretty unbelievable." As Brad said the last sentence he searched his pocket, pulled out her card, and handed it to me.

"Fuck."

Chapter 6

Ambiguity and Insomnia

I don't know if I said, "fuck" or thought *fuck*. I don't suppose it matters, either way it was my initial response to the news about Sandra. I'm not sure what it meant. Fuck is a vague word and I said/thought it in a vague way. Brad would have called me out on my nebulous reaction, but he was either too drunk or too introspective to notice.

I unlocked the front door and we both entered. Inside our house the lights were off, but it was not completely dark. The moonlight trickled in the windows allowing for the space to be negotiated. Brad immediately headed to the refrigerator while I paused to turn on the lights. I had to take the time to hit the switch, as the dull glow from the moon was annoying me. By the time I turned the lights on, Brad was halfway to the kitchen. Once he arrived, he pulled a box of pizza out of the fridge, placed the box on the counter, and lifted himself up to sit beside it. He slowly ate a slice, staring at it as he chewed. The pleasure of eating spread a childlike grin across his face. No self-respecting adult male makes that face. Brad was trashed. I told him good night and headed upstairs. I didn't want to spoil his simple pleasure, and I didn't want him to force me to think. When Brad is blackout drunk he can form surprisingly cogent thoughts and make challenging personal inquiries. I wanted nothing to do with either.

As I headed upstairs, it became apparent that I could dodge Brad's inspection but not my own. My brain refused to let me off that easily. I actively attempted to stop thinking about my reaction to the Sandra news, but it was an effort in futility. I lay down but didn't sleep. The bed got increasingly uncomfortable as my brain became decreasingly satisfied with the ambiguity. The sheets felt damp and the bedsprings aggressive.

I liked Sandra but I had lied to her, really lied to her, about my career. If I tried to date her, I would have to tell her. Fuck. There would be no good time to reveal that little chestnut. "Oh so, by the way, I'm not a world-class architect as much as I'm an orderly." That information would go over swimmingly. It seemed like a problem best avoided.

I moved to the other half of the bed in an effort to readjust and fall asleep. It didn't work. My mind still ran. I kept my eyes closed, but it felt wrong. My feet became uncomfortably warm and sweaty. I pulled the blankets up to expose them, but after a few seconds the sweat turned cool, sending a chill from my toes through to my shoulders. It was awful. It had to stop. I turned to the best natural sleep method in existence.

I pushed down the elastic of my boxers with my right hand and grabbed my cock with the left. I always masturbate with my left. My penis bends slightly to the east, so I hope that through repetitive tugging to the west it will straighten out.

I closed my eyes and thought about Lauren. I imagined her bending over while wearing a pair of light blue scrubs, the thin material allowing for a good view of her perky, but appreciable ass. I gripped my erection and moved the skin back and forth as I thought. I used no lotion. It was relaxation time not mess-making time.

I pictured Lauren catching a glimpse of me as she stood up and then a smirk spreading across her face as she turned to walk in my direction. As she closed the space between us, she winked and then let the back of her hand carelessly brush against my crotch while continuing toward the door. Upon reaching the exit, she looked over her shoulder and then nodded her head to the side: an invitation. I accepted without hesitation. I followed her into a closet where she slammed the door behind me and pushed my body up against it. Her hand grasped my cock over the top of my scrubs while she leaned in and kissed me hard, really hard, so hard my lip began to bleed. The taste of iron didn't abate my arousal. I grabbed her ass and lifted her up. With her legs wrapped around me, I walked to a half-empty table and put her down. She lifted my shirt over my head, and I did the same in turn. She was wearing a silky pink bra. It pushed her tits up and together providing a nice roundness to the tops of her breasts. I looked down at my own shirtless body and was relieved to see that both my scrub bottoms and my boxers were riding low, a few inches above the base of my shaft (I always get worried that a woman will tear off my shirt, see my boxers riding above my belly button, and walk away laughing at the geriatric-like way that my underwear sits). I leaned over Lauren as she lay back on the table. The silky feeling of her bra against my chest made my cock tremble. My kisses worked their way from her mouth down to her neck and then descended toward her breasts. Once I arrived at her bra, I worked my lips across the top of it occasionally slipping my tongue under the fabric. The third time I did this my tongue felt the little bumps that occupy some areolas. She must have been wearing a demi-cut. Down between her breasts and the middle of her taut stomach my soft kisses continued until I arrived at the next level of silky pink. I took my finger and ran it underneath the material, first working across the waist and then, moving lower, from the outside of her leg in. As my finger moved closer to her pussy, the heat and moisture became apparent. I got even harder. Pulling her damp underwear to the side, I used a broad tongue to lick her from bottom to top, slowing briefly near the clit. I then released my finger letting the pink silk cover her once more. I didn't take her underwear off. I wanted to feel its softness against my cock. I moved up, returning my lips to hers. Our bodies now in line, the bottom of my shaft rubbed against the soft material, encompassed by the heat that pulsed through. Lauren's moans rose in volume and her nails inched deeper into my back. Her body shook slightly as she leaned forward. With her lips next to my ear, she whispered, "I need you inside me." Obliging her request, I moved my hand down and once more used my finger to slide the pink silk to the side. She was impossibly wet. I eased into her slowly and with each inch of me that entered her body relaxed more. I moved my hand to her breast as . . .

Nope. It wasn't working. I was tugging at twice the normal speed, but my dick was half its normal firmness. My thumb was pressing up against the first knuckle of my pointer finger. If I am properly aroused the tips of the two barely touch. For better or worse girth is my strong suit.

The insomnia was officially exacerbated. Masturbation, my sleep-inducing stalwart, had failed me. Blue balls, a sweaty left hand, and an even sweatier half-erection, joined ranks with the intrusive bedsprings and the unsettling sheets. As an amalgamation they were a force to be reckoned with, a wakeful, anxiety-inducing force. I attempted to settle into a variety of positions but none of them led to rest. Pillows were flipped and blankets rearranged, but slumber didn't come. My mind repeatedly returned to Sandra. What the fuck did "fuck" mean? Where did it come from? I was vexed not by its etymology but by its intention. As the individual who spoke the word, I should have been privy to this information, yet I was not.

Contemplating my usage of the word fuck made me think about fucking. Then I thought about Sandra. Then I thought about fucking Sandra. I imagined her straddling me, dark black hair falling in front of her shoulders and over her breasts. My cock responded to the new visual instantly. Once more I gripped it, but this time the tip of my pointer finger was barely able to brush against the end of my thumb. I stroked my erection slowly, but the excitement was unbearable. I exploded in under a minute. It came over me quickly. I didn't even have time to press down on my taint to prevent the ejaculate from coming out. I blew the load all over the front of my T-shirt. The most ambitious of which flew up near my collar.

I pulled off the cum-laden cloth and threw it on the floor. Relaxed, my head sunk into the pillow and my body into the mattress. As I closed my eyes a smile spread across my face. Teetering on the brink of sleep I spoke out loud to myself.

"I'm going to ask Sandra out."

Chapter 7

A Question

My alarm went off at its normal time. I felt surprisingly well considering the amount of liquor I had ingested. The only hangover symptom present was the angry grumbling of a belly in need of grease. I hopped in to the shower and washed up, eager to greet the day. I had to go to work, which was unfortunate, but I was excited about the prospect of spending the day contemplating Sandra. The very idea of her filled my stomach with youthful excitement. Conveniently, this also counteracted the liquor's lingering effect.

The butterflies that were occupying my stomach didn't make me feel foolish or naïve, a reaction that they had inspired in the not-so-distant past. Instead, they made me feel the way that they should, like characters in uplifting books and movies. This slight sense of euphoria expedited my morning routine. I was ready to head out well before my normal departure time. As a result, I was slightly taken aback when I got downstairs and found Brad and Robert. They were both standing at the counter, eating cereal. The fourth button of Robert's dress shirt was undone, his tie placed through the opening. Brad's was tossed over his shoulder. Their formal neckwear was safe, properly stowed away from the perilous breakfast food. I looked down at my own shirt, the words INTRAMURAL BROOMBALL CHAMPION emblazoned across the chest. I turned around to go change.

"What are you doing up so early?" Robert asked.

He caught me before I had touched the first step. I finished putting my foot down and pretended to tie my shoe. After a sufficient amount of time playing with the laces, I stepped back down and entered the kitchen.

Brad looked up from his cereal, "Seriously man, why are you

up? I would be using every second available to sleep off this son of a bitch. I'm still burping up that fucking schnapps. This cereal tastes like candy canes."

"Oh, just couldn't sleep," I replied in a chipper voice. Brad looked at me funny. "Beer shits," I added, gesturing toward my belly and grimacing.

Brad paused for a second. His gaze honed in on me as he squinted one eye and pursed his lips. It was a comically inquisitive look, perhaps a knowing one. His face returned to normal as he said, "Me too, I was peeing out of my butthole for like twenty minutes this morning. My feet got all tingly from sitting on the shitter too long."

"Awesome," Robert said. "Well, you forgot to courtesy flush, so I was greeted by your leftovers when I went pee."

Brad smiled. "My bad," he replied to the room at large. I don't think he considered it an actual bad.

"As long as you're up, you might as well walk to the coffee shop with us," Robert said, as he turned back to his cereal. "We're all out, Brad tried to make a pot with the grounds from yesterday, but it tasted like ass."

"It's true, man. I might as well have filled it up with my toilet water from this morning. So, no coffee, you're ready early, might as well come with."

I nodded my head in assent and walked toward the door. I didn't like the idea of strolling alongside well-dressed professionals while sporting the attire of a keg party attendee, but coffee was a necessity. We headed through the front door. On the way out, Brad slapped Robert's ass and then mine. Once we were all outside he turned around and locked the door.

We talked as we headed toward the coffee shop. Baseball was the topic of conversation, the same as the night before. Brad reiterated his thoughts on the designated hitter and small market teams. Robert chimed in showing interest but confusion. As a first-generation American, Robert knows about the sport, but not really. His childhood summers didn't begin with the consumption of hotdogs in the right field cheap seats.

"The guy who plays this position only plays half the game?" Robert queried. "The position is designed to divide the role of one player between two? Why would they do that?" As Robert voiced this confusion, his perplexity struck me as understandable but unacceptable. Yes, the position allows men to succeed while playing only half of the game, but that isn't the issue, that's simply a reality. The issue is that wealthy teams gain an unfair advantage and game management is cheapened by the removal of a weak hitter from the batting order. Musing on how the designated hitter came to be will not change the fact that it is. Although the complaints voiced by Brad and I are unlikely to result in the removal of the designated hitter from professional baseball, they at least speak to the established reality. They're legitimate critiques that could be employed to argue for change. Robert's posited inquires are efforts in futility.

Sometimes I'm struck by the fact that Brad and I operate in a world that is different than Robert's. Not hugely different but slightly different. Maybe that's why I like Brad more, or maybe I like Brad more because he's better to party with; maybe both, or maybe those are the same reason. Either way I count both of them as friends. I simply know that Robert and I can never be as close. What can you do?

About fifty yards away from the coffee shop, we passed some street performers speaking in loud stage voices while gesturing extravagantly. They were standing in an alleyway between two buildings but they spoke as if they were on stage at the Globe. So lucky we were that they deigned us with their words. As we walked by, one of them said something about a corporate noose while glaring at Brad and Robert. Another one set a dollar bill on fire and gave me an affirming head nod. We ignored them but I could tell it bothered the guys and they could tell it bothered me. None of us said anything. Instead, we walked into the coffee shop and looked up at the menu.

The list of drinks was difficult to decipher. Composed in chalk, the words looked as though they were written by a lefty who was unable to raise his palm. The entire menu was smeared due to one person's ineptitude. Christ, how hard is it to make a legible list of options?

I ordered a skim latte because it was impossible to tell whether they had chai. Some woman named Rain took my order; it seemed that her parents named her with the foreknowledge that she would be a barista at an independent coffee shop. We waited too long for our drinks. When mine finally came, I noticed that the insulating sleeve surrounding it had been used before. It had been recycled but not through the proper channels. Unsanitary. As we sat down and sipped our coffee, I told the guys how fantastic this place was. Inwardly I was wishing that it were a chain with a clear menu and brand-new coffee sleeves. I wanted to like it but did not.

After a few minutes Sandra walked through the door. I was surprised and as a consequence gawked a bit. Brad watched me watching her. After a couple of seconds, I regained cognizance of my behavior and looked back down. Brad was grinning. He knew she would meet us here. As we waited for Sandra to join us, I continued to watch her out of my periphery. She stared up at the menu for a bit and then ordered a black coffee. Rain handed it to her. She took the cup, looked down at it disapprovingly, then turned around and joined us.

Sandra spoke as she pulled up a chair, "This place has a nice ambience and everything, but this coffee sleeve looks like it used to be around a homeless man's begging cup and the girl that's working reeks of patchouli. I know it's boring, but can we go to Starbucks next time?"

Brad said, "Sounds good, I love their caramel drink things."

I said, "Do you want to go out sometime?"

Chapter 8

An Answer

Sandra was not taken aback by the suddenness of my question.

"Sure," she replied, without missing a beat.

Brad made a "Woooooo" sound. It was the reaction that a middle-school boy would have had. Although it was silly, I was glad that Brad did it. It took all the balls that I could muster to ask Sandra out and I was glad that my friend recognized the gutsiness of my action. In a way it also made her recognize the gutsiness of my action. Maybe it wasn't a silly sound to make.

I blushed a bit and smiled a lot. I wanted to play it cool, but I couldn't hide my delight. Sandra looked at me warmly. She was pleased by the sincerity of my reaction.

"Friday?" I asked.

"Friday is perfect," she replied while sitting down in the chair that she had pulled up next to me.

We made plans for seven and decided on Italian and then something fun. We all debated about which Italian place was best. It was a good topic of conversation. It pertained to our date but was general enough for everyone to discuss. After reaching a consensus on the restaurant, we all got up and headed off to work. I squeezed Sandra's wrist as we parted.

On the walk to the hospital my steps were lighter than normal. I covered half the distance in a dazed euphoria only regaining awareness when I looked up and realized that I was two blocks past my normal turn. As I retraced the steps of my detour, the euphoria moved from my head to my chest. I still felt nice, but I thought a little more clearly. I got a bit nervous contemplating the date. There is the unhealthy nervous, where you're apprehensive because you don't want to say something to upset your date, and there is the healthy nervous, where you're confident in saying what comes to mind but scared that you may have bad breath when you go to kiss her. I was suffering from the halitosis nervous. My awareness of the nervousness enlivened my stride even more. I arrived at the hospital, changed, and went about my business without much knowledge of the fact that I was going about my business. It was one o'clock before I was even remotely aware of my own proceedings. The half a day I spent on autopilot is a testament to the cognitively demanding nature of my job. I would have been able to finish my entire shift in that fashion if Jones hadn't shaken me out of it.

"What's up with you?" he asked.

"Huh?" I replied.

"You've been acting off all day, staring into the distance, and breathing out your mouth, and working hard. What's that about? You haven't even taken any of your bullshit breaks. The ones where you take twenty minutes to do a simple task."

"Just distracted."

"By what, a lady?" Jones said through a smile. "You smitten for some girl?"

"Smitten? Christ, Jones, what is this 1955. Yeah, I'm smitten for some girl. I want to take her out to the malt shop so we can share a chocolate shake while she is wrapped in my letterman sweater." My words could have been interpreted as friendly teasing or derisive mocking. My tone intentionally tended toward the latter. Maybe my reply was disagreeable because I was angry that he turned off my autopilot, or maybe because I was a bit disconcerted by another's recognition of my smitten-ness. Either way, Jones was unfazed by the harshness of my retort. Actually, he brightened as I spoke.

"So, do you think she is as keen on you as you are on her?" He asked through an increasingly larger grin. Jones was giving me shit, but there was also an excitement in his inquiry.

"Yes and no," I said. The reality of these words fully formed in my head as I spoke them. From the moment I blew my load while masturbating to thoughts of Sandra, I knew that I had to ask her out. The cum that she had inspired me to ejaculate was the final factor leading me to that definitive conclusion.

For the few hours between the decision to ask Sandra out and the actual asking out of Sandra I had a single-minded focus on the task. Unfortunately, now that the task was accomplished, and the elation of her positive response had worn off, my initial trepidation toward dating her hit me once more. The anxiety that it induced was amplified tenfold compared to the first time I felt it. My butt cheeks got tight and my shoulders contracted up and back. Jones saw this physical and mental shift.

"Relax, friend," he said. "I was just giving you a hard time. I didn't mean to make you all worried."

". . ." I replied.

"Damn, son. What's the problem? What the hell does 'yes and no' mean? Does she like you? Are you gonna throw up?" In response to my lack of response, Jones decided to bombard me with questions. It seemed a poor tactic, but it worked.

"The problem is I lied to her. 'Yes and no' means she likes me but only the modified version of me that she knows. So, I don't know if she actually likes me or not. And I don't know if I'm going to throw up. It's a possibility." My stomach wasn't lurching but the overwhelmingly salty liquid that portends vomit was coming from under my tongue and the sides of my mouth.

"Sit down and breathe," Jones said as he wheeled over a stool. "Calm yourself and tell me what the deal is, because right now you're talking like a mad man."

I did as instructed.

"This girl, Sandra, she agreed to go out with me Friday night. She's incredibly sexy with this deep brown skin and impossibly black hair and super perky breasts and . . ."

"Yeah, this girl is sexy, I got that, but there's more 'cause you wouldn't be this messed up if she was just some looker."

"Well yes, she does have appeal beyond her looks, but it's

irrelevant because the minute that she finds out I'm an orderly it's all over."

"What does she think you are, a Kennedy?"

"An architect."

"Ahhh, I see," Jones said. "That is a predicament." After a few seconds' pause he spoke up again. "Well friend, if you want my advice I would just tell her. She'll either accept it or she won't, but either way you'll know. Then you'll stop feeling like shit. It's like a Band-Aid son, rip that son of a bitch off."

I nodded in agreement. Jones got up off the stool, slapped my back, and departed. His advice was incredibly simple, bordering on cliché, but it made me feel a little better. There was something in his voice that indicated he was not giving a canned response, something suggesting that he understood the complexity of the situation and the full spectrum of possible options. His advice to be forthright was a product of deliberation and experience. It wasn't a default answer.

I sat on the stool with my head down meditating on Jones' guidance. When I finally looked up from the ground, I saw Lauren. She was re-tying her scrubs while exiting one of the geriatric's rooms. Her stomach was exposed, nice and toned. She caught a glimpse of me as she looked up and waved happily. I replied in the same fashion adding a smile.

"See you on Saturday!" she said from across the room, her words spoken with a bit too much volume.

"Super excited!" I replied, matching her loudness.

Lauren bounded off around the corner. With her ponytail still in sight, my mind once again began to mull over ways to present Sandra with the truth. Over the course of the afternoon, I imagined a myriad of ways to deliver the unpleasant message. By the time the workday was done, the pretend version of myself had told the pretend version of Sandra that he was an orderly over fifty times in over thirty ways. Unfortunately, under repeated scrutiny none of these confessions played out to an agreeable end. Pretend Sandra always left.

By the time I started the walk back home, the idea of continuing to lie about my occupation had risen to the top of the list of possible actions. The more this conclusion settled in, the more my shoulders relaxed. A headache that I was unaware I had subsided. With each step I took toward home, I breathed more easily. The path forward was clear. The lie was my compass.

Once I resolved myself to sticking with the fiction, my trip home became quite enjoyable. I grinned at passersby and gave change to a homeless man that was kind enough to hold up a sign that told me he would use the money for food. I was pleased that he kept me in the dark regarding his actual expenditures and because of this rewarded him with all of the coins in my pocket. The derelict next to him was holding up a piece of cardboard that read, "Need money for booze." His paper cup was empty, which pleased me.

Eventually, I turned onto a block with significantly less people, a block I usually didn't walk down. This stretch of macadam provided fewer recipients for my smiles so my eyes began to move upward. As the trajectory of my gaze changed, the awe of the structures that comprised the city washed over me.

I paused to appreciate the shadows cast by the decorative embellishments of the older buildings and stared unabashedly at the swirling façade of one of the city's more recent architectural additions. The billowing metal face of the new structure held my attention for a while, but gradually I grew tired of its gaudiness and looked away. I'm not opposed to aesthetics for aesthetics' sake, but I am opposed to a lack of subtlety. I wanted the building to please me, but I didn't want the building to tell me that it aimed to please me. Unfortunately, the new building couldn't help itself. It threw its beauty in my face. That annoyed me. In an effort to combat my irritation, I tried to think about buildings that were done well; *8 House* in Copenhagen came to mind.

Bjarke Ingels Groups did it right when they created *8 House*.

They manipulated for beauty but they did it in an understated manner. This actuality is exemplified by the way that slight distortions in the design allow for more of the structure to face in an agreeable direction. The building's pulchritude is achieved in a sagacious fashion, and therein lies its greatness.

Thinking about *8 House* assuaged my irritation. It also made me feel better about the decision to continue lying about my career. By the time I arrived home, I was completely prepared to see Sandra and a bit frustrated that I had to wait another day to do so.

Chapter 9

Salmon and Seuss

Work on Friday was the standard amount of awful. I wheeled some new mothers out of the hospital as they cooed to their spawn, cleaned up some vomit near the NNICU, and emptied a couple of bedpans. The only worthwhile part of the day came when I got to look down Lauren's shirt as she leaned over the old codger with the gnarled pinkie fingers. Her breasts looked perfect, and I was able to stare at them for ten to fifteen seconds before getting distracted. Eventually, my eyes were pulled away by the erection springing forth from the ancient fuck she was helping. Although I was pissed that he ruined my visual, I was simultaneously amazed, blown away by the fact that Lauren's tits could reanimate the dead. Combined, the visual stimulation of Lauren's chest and the admiration for her chest's restorative capabilities provided roughly ninety seconds of pleasure in an otherwise perfectly miserable day.

The workday would have been more enjoyable if I had daydreamed about Sandra, but I intentionally abstained from such thoughts. I worried that if I spent too much time contemplating our date I would talk myself out of continuing the lie. I didn't want that to happen, and as a consequence, work was as painful as always. Maybe a little worse since Jones had the day off.

On the walk home, I was careful to avoid the route that goes by the building with the swirling façade. I also concentrated on not concentrating on Sandra. It was a difficult task that slowed my pace.

By the time I walked in the front door, Brad and Robert had already loaded up the vaporizer. They offered me the whip, but I declined. I was worried that my angst over the planned deception would hinder my ability to control the high. There was a seventy-five percent chance the pot would relax me and a twenty-five percent chance it would make me more anxious. I didn't like those odds. In lieu of weed, I grabbed a beer, popping the cap off on the banister on my way upstairs.

The lager was borderline freezing. Its cold presence in my empty belly served as a reminder of how little I had eaten. Ignoring my stomach's request to turn back toward the kitchen, I headed to the bathroom, turned on the shower, took a sip of beer, and then stuck my hand under the faucet to check the water temperature. There was a stark contrast between the steamy liquid coming down on my palm and the cold beer sloshing around in my belly; it was a bit disconcerting, like I was in two places at once. Eager to make my body completely warm, I pulled my hand out from under the water and got undressed.

While pulling down my boxers, I caught a glimpse of myself in the mirror and was surprised to see that my pubes were not as well manicured as I thought. Although they looked good from above, they appeared a bit patchy when viewed straight on. I weighed my longing to get into the warm water against my desire to have well groomed genitals for Sandra, ultimately deciding that the visual appeal of my junk was more important.

I took my electric clippers out of the drawer and grabbed an unused trash bag from under the sink. I laid the trash bag down on the ground, straddled it, and proceeded to trim. Per usual, I went slowly, top to bottom, left to right, careful to push my dick as far away from the cutting as possible. The grooming went off without a hitch, save a minor nick to my taint. Fortunately, that didn't matter as no sex acts performed on a first date would result in her looking too closely at that part of my body.

While in the shower, I let the water descend directly onto my crotch in an effort to wash away the last of the shaved pubes. With all the distracting hair gone, my penis was significantly larger. Well, it wasn't, but it appeared to be. I wanted to see how big it looked hard and contemplated rubbing one out but decided to refrain. I was fearful it would make me underperform with Sandra. Conventional wisdom suggests that masturbating before hooking up increases your longevity, but I have found the opposite to be true.

After the shower I got dressed and went downstairs to the kitchen. Robert and Brad were eating wings and potato chips with onion dip. I declined their offer to share and opened the fridge in the hopes of finding food with a more pleasing aroma. The options were sparse. I resigned myself to eating a carton of blackberries and then headed out the door. As I departed, Brad told me that I looked "fuckable" and Robert wished me luck.

On the way to Sandra's, I swung by a gas station and picked up orange mints and a diet soda. I drank the soda quickly in an effort to combat the dry mouth I felt coming on. The drink achieved the desired aim, but it also made me belch. The belches smelled like beer so I ate orange mints until they smelled like orange mints. I fixated on my breath the entire way to her house, my anxiety reaching its zenith as I knocked on her door.

"Hey," Sandra said, answering with a smile. "Hold on one second I just have to grab my bag."

I smiled and nodded but didn't say anything. My concern over my breath kept my mouth shut. I watched Sandra turn the corner then breathed into my hand and inhaled. It smelled like oranges but I wasn't sure if that was because my breath smelled like oranges or because my hand smelled like oranges. I remembered that somebody once told me that if you lick your finger and smell it you can tell whether or not you have bad breath. I tried it. It didn't work the first time so I tried again. The second time I put my finger closer to my nostril. After a couple of deep inhalations I realized that if Sandra walked in it would look like I was picking my nose so I quickly lowered my hand. I was still worrying when she returned to the room. As Sandra walked toward me, I looked up at her face for the first time since I had arrived. At that moment, my worries ceased to be. The very word *worry* became a foreign concept to my mind.

I didn't say anything as I looked at her. Perhaps that said more than I could have hoped to say.

Sandra spoke up, "Smells good in here, like oranges. Ready to go?"

I shook my head, took her hand in mine, and we walked out the door.

* * *

Sandra ordered the salmon. It was a selection that pleased me. Women that are aware of their weight and want you to know that they are aware of their weight order side salads; women that want to stay thin but don't want to throw it in your face order lean meat. I want the woman that I'm with to be fit, but I don't want her to constantly remind me of what it takes to be that way. I also ordered the salmon. I'm opposed to double standards.

"Good choice," Sandra said. "My sister always gives me shit when I order salmon at a nice restaurant. She says that no matter how talented the chef is salmon always taste like salmon, so if I want to truly enjoy the gourmet experience, I should select a dinner that allows the kitchen to showcase its talent."

"Is that true, does salmon always taste the same regardless of how it's prepared?"

"I don't know, but who cares. I like the taste of salmon. I'll eat it on a boat with a goat, in the rain on a train. Anywhere. It's delicious."

"I appreciate your fervor for the fish on that dish. I would not, could not mock your fish wish."

I immediately regretted my decision to channel Seuss. Sandra's reference was cute; mine was childish and redundant. Following my rhyme, I kept my head down for a few seconds. I wanted to take a moment and commit to memory a picture of how Sandra looked at me prior to those words leaving my mouth. Before I raised my head, she spoke.

"Holy shit, you're a huge nerd."

My eyes looked up at a grin, the same one she gave me before we kissed, her tongue extending just beyond her two front teeth.

"I love it! And if I'm not mistaken that was a rhyme of your own composition, a little free style. You've been holding out on me."

"Well, I didn't want to show off," I replied with a grin that matched hers. "Plus, some women feel intimidated by my lyrical prowess, and I didn't want to scare you off with my genius."

"A wise choice, if you had versified like that on the night we met I would have scampered away, awestruck and weak-kneed." She laughed softly while taking a sip of gin. She continued talking as she set her glass back down on the table. "I do have to say, it's rare to find a guy who will play along with a *Green Eggs and Ham* reference. Do you really like Dr. Seuss or were you just being an ass?"

"All of the above."

"Good answer."

"What about you? You weren't referencing *Sam I Am* in some insufferably ironic way were you?"

"No, no, I really do love Dr. Seuss and I definitely don't reference things ironically or wear clothes ironically or any of that nonsense. Well, that's not totally true. One time in college I wore a Sheryl Crowe shirt. I thought it would impress my uber hip roommate."

"Did it?"

"No, actually one of my other friends that was less hip but infinitely more fun saw me wearing the Sheryl Crowe shirt and the irony was lost on her. She just thought I liked Sheryl Crowe and believing that we had a shared interest asked me if I wanted to go see her live that weekend."

"That's pretty funny, what are the odds of Sheryl Crowe being in town that weekend?"

"I know, crazy."

"So did you go?"

"Of course I went. I had no desire to explain to her that my clothing was not in line with my actual musical taste. The idea of telling her that my shirt was mocking her made me feel like a bitch. Anyway, I ended up having a lot of fun at the concert."

"Fun? At the Sheryl Crow concert?" I said, more snidely than I intended.

"Yeah, fun at the Sheryl Crow concert, you ass," she replied, adding a smile and a punch. "And even though I ended up enjoying myself I still learned my lesson. Now I only wear things and buy things that I actually like. It's too exhausting to try and be yourself by not being yourself."

Outwardly, I smiled in agreement with Sandra's conclusion. Inwardly, I felt a bit nauseated, or guilty, or both. I mulled over using the opportunity to tell her the truth about my profession, but when I went to open my mouth I couldn't. My jaw and my ass cheeks clinched up simultaneously. Thankfully, Sandra was taking another sip of gin as I swallowed the words that wouldn't come out. She noticed nothing.

"So, back to this Seuss business," she said. "Do you have a favorite?"

I was surprised to find out that I did. "*And To Think That I Saw It on Mulberry Street* is definitely my number one." The speed and vehemence of my reply was a testament to the fact that it was an honest opinion. It was one of those rare moments when the two people taking part in a dialogue learn a personal fact about one of the interlocutors at exactly the same time. I wanted to elaborate on my assertion, but I couldn't. I knew that *Mulberry Street* was my favorite Dr. Seuss book, but I didn't know why.

"That's the one where the kid imagines that he sees all these fantastic things on his walk home, right?"

"Right, but when Marco, that's the kid's name, when Marco

tells his dad what he saw he only tells him what he actually saw. Just a horse and a wagon." As I said this, I realized why I love the book.

"Well it's not *The Sneetches* but it's pretty good," Sandra said, ignorant to my inner epiphany. "Plus the fact that you even have a favorite Dr. Seuss book is pretty respectable. Any other favorite authors from your childhood?"

"Roald Dahl, for sure."

"Awesome," Sandra grinned. "He wrote so many good ones, especially *Witches*, a classic. Sometimes when I'm feeling kind of bitchy and I'm around some petulant child or crying baby I think about those witches. Maybe they were onto something."

"I was just thinking that a couple days ago when I was reading that book to the babies."

Sandra looked at me quizzically. "What babies? Why were you reading to babies?"

"Well," I said, and then paused to take a drink of scotch. "Sometimes I volunteer at the children's cancer center during my free time. Actually, I'm going there tomorrow." This was the first time I had directly lied to Sandra all night, in fact it was the first time I had lied to her at all. Brad had fibbed about the architect thing, I just didn't correct him. The lie made me feel like shit. I'm not sure why, it wasn't even a sizable one. After all, I was going to volunteer tomorrow, I just wasn't volunteering when I read Roald Dahl to those babies.

"Oh," Sandra said, looking surprised and then pensive. She paused for a second. I hoped that she was not considering going with me. I didn't want her and Lauren to meet. Lauren would spoil my ruse. Also, I would have to choose to focus my attention on one of them, which would almost certainly kill my chances with the other. I wanted to avoid any situation that would force me into such a decision. I really liked talking to Sandra, but I also really liked looking at Lauren's ass and still possessed a longing to play with it some day.

Sandra broke her brief spell of thoughtful silence. Her words brought my mind back to the conversation. It had begun to drift toward thoughts of Lauren, Sandra, and I having a threesome.

"Okay," she said. "So I don't want to sound like a heartless bitch, but that sort of volunteering sounds like a nightmare. I mean I really respect you for doing it, but there is no way I could ever do that. It would make me terribly depressed, and I think I would resent those poor kids as a result. Sorry if that makes you hate me."

"No, no, it doesn't make me hate you at all. Actually I'm impressed with your honesty. I think a large number of people share your sentiment, they just lack the chutzpah to admit it."

"Wow, that's not the response I was expecting."

"Oh yeah, what were you expecting?"

"I don't know, usually when I tell guys something along those lines they make me feel like a horrible person."

"Well, those guys are assholes, and I would guess that none of them are spending their free time down at the pediatric oncology unit or mentoring underprivileged youth."

"That's true," Sandra said, as if relieved of a burden.

"Plus it's not like you're wishing ill for those kids, you just recognize that volunteering at some place like that would have a somber impact on your life and, consequently, the lives of those around you, so you devote your time elsewhere. I bet you even donate money to St. Jude's or something because you wish you felt differently."

"Ha, that's absolutely correct."

"Yeah, well then you're doing more than about ninety percent of those dicks that called you a horrible person and you have more integrity than all of them."

"Thanks," Sandra said. It was a heartfelt thanks, her face was bright and appreciative.

I felt warm as I looked at her. Unfortunately, as my eyes returned to my plate the warmth left. Cognizance of my own hypocrisy filled the vacancy. I stared jealously at the salmon. It was a constant, no matter what. Julia Childs could flambé the shit out of that orange fish and it would still taste the same. Goddamn it, I had less integrity than a fucking fish, a dead one at that.

I looked up, prepared to set things straight. "Sandra, I'm not an . . ."

"Not what?"

"Not sure we should go to the movie. I heard it was pretentiously vague in an effort to make up for the fact that it has no substance."

"So, basically really crappy."

"Ha, yeah, so basically really crappy."

"No problem let's go get ice cream or something instead. I need a dessert to cleanse my palate, otherwise this salmon is going to be sticking with me."

"Yeah," I said, "fucking salmon."

* * *

We held hands on the way to the ice cream shop. It made me excited and anxious. After a couple blocks of walking hand in hand, I began to swing our arms in an exaggerated fashion. I wanted to be cute and a little funny. I also wanted her to know that I liked holding her hand without letting her know how much I liked holding her hand. Sandra saw right through it. My lighthearted effort to mask the intensity of my feelings failed. Once again, I felt like a Little Leaguer trying to strike out Ty Cobb.

"It's funny," she said quizzically, "when you're young and you first start to like someone of the opposite sex, or the same sex I suppose, I don't know, I'll have to ask my gay friends. Anyway, when you're young and you start to take an interest in someone, the first physical thing you do is hold hands. But then, once you're older, holding hands becomes a huge deal. Now it's usually one of the last things you do with someone. I mean I have certainly had sex with a lot of people that I haven't held hands with."

"A lot, huh?"

"Yeah a lot, you ass. Don't act holier than thou. I know you've slept with some girls that you would never hold hands with."

"Nah," I shook my head in disagreement while smiling knowingly in affirmation. Of course she was right. There are a number of women that I've slept with that I've never, and will never, hold hands with. Actually, there are a couple of women that I've had sex with that I never really looked at and hope never to look at in the future.

At the ice cream shop we both ordered sherbet, she got orange and I got peach, a novelty. After each of us had consumed our respective kiddy scoops we walked back to the car. We held hands again, but this time I didn't swing our arms wildly. When we arrived at her house, I got out of the car quickly so that I could open her door, a minor attempt at chivalry. As I pulled the handle on her side of the hybrid, I became momentarily concerned that my action would be perceived as benevolent sexism. Fortunately, my fears were allayed as Sandra popped out of the car cheerily.

"Such a gentleman," she said.

"It's true," I replied. "I have impeccable manners, akin to that of British royalty."

"And so modest."

"Well, it's hard to be modest when you're so obviously fantastic at something."

"Indeed," she said, while offering her hand to me. A limp wrist and extended arm indicated that she wished to be escorted to the door. It was a bit of faux propriety and it was quite endearing. Her action revealed that my bout of chivalry was not insulting but also not required. I felt foolish for being concerned about opening a door. I had no desire to be with a woman who would find serious fault in such an action, so I shouldn't have worried about it. I was glad to see Sandra was not such a woman.

Actually, that might have been something I already knew.

At the door I put an arm around her. With my hand on the small of her back I brought her in close. Looking down into her eyes, I raised my hand and brushed her hair behind her ear. I was preparing to make my closing move. Then it became clear that I didn't have to. Sandra didn't wait to be kissed. She rose on tiptoes and brought her lips to mine. Once again they were soft but not greasy. We kissed for a long time, and although I held her tighter with each passing minute, I didn't make a move toward her breasts or her crotch. I didn't even think about it. Her lips were a lot to take in on their own. Eventually, we paused.

"We should do this again tomorrow," she said, while looking up into my eyes.

"We don't have to be done tonight," I said, or perhaps implored.

"Ha, I know we don't, but I want to rile you up a little more before we go there."

"You coy minx."

"Yeah, I know," she said, while turning toward the door. As she stepped inside, the back of her hand brushed against the erection suppressed in my jeans. "So tomorrow? Lunch? Or dinner again?"

"Yeah. Wait. Shit. I can't, I have to do that volunteer work."

I was worried that Sandra would interpret this as a rejection or as an effort to play courting games, but she didn't.

"Sunday then," she stated brightly. "We should go to a ballgame. You can buy me a beer and some Cracker Jacks, we'll have a quintessential all-American summer night."

"Sounds perfect."

"Yeah, it does," she said, while closing the door.

The grin that I had already come to adore was spread across her face.

Chapter 10

Clown Shoes

Lauren greeted me cheerily as I walked into the children's cancer center. She was wearing a red ball on her nose and oversized shoes on her feet. A caricature of what a pediatric oncology volunteer should be.

"Wow, you look great. You're going all out," I said. She was not going all out. Her head and her feet were that of a clown, but her body was still that of a woman. Thank God. I had no desire to spend the day looking at her in a ridiculous costume.

After we had exchanged a few pleasantries, Lauren took a spare red ball out of her pocket and placed it on my nose. She then turned and pointed to an extra pair of oversized shoes sitting in the corner and informed me that I could use them for the day. I acted as though I was excited to wear the clown gear. I was not.

It was difficult to put on the gigantic shoes. Their openings were disproportionately tiny and their laces were stiff and unmanageable. I spent roughly half a minute trying to bend the unyielding strings to my will but was unsuccessful. The bulbous addition to my face inhibited my vision and the laces were too stubborn to knot up blind. I quit and left the laces untied.

As I looked up from the improperly secured shoes, I saw Lauren walking toward a group of children sitting cross-legged on the floor. Her steps were labored due to the oversized nature of her footwear. The children laughed as she made her way toward them. I looked at her ass as she went. Those comical strides were keeping it fit.

"Hello again, friends," Lauren said to the gaggle of little humans on the floor. "As you all know, my name is Socko the clown and this is my friend Glauco." Her finger rose to indicate my presence.

I thought Glauco was a shit clown name, but I chose to keep silent on the matter. Instead of objecting to my new moniker, I waved like an imbecile. The kids waved back. After a couple of wrist wags, they returned their attention to Lauren. The children were clearly unimpressed by Glauco. I was appreciative of their disregard since I had no idea what I was supposed to do. I probably would have just kept on waving at them.

Once the audience's attention was turned away, I began to head toward Lauren. There was an empty space adjacent to her that was clearly left open for me. I made my way to the vacant spot rather quickly, surprised by how well I walked in the oversize shoes. Occasionally my toe would drag causing the excess sole to bend back for a while and then flip forward quickly as I pulled my leg through. Other than that, my stride was impressively routine.

At the conclusion of my relatively dignified walk, I settled in next to Lauren. I smiled at her; she smiled back and then turned her head forward. I did the same and at that moment my smile evaporated.

I looked out onto a mass of expectant faces and for the first time realized that they were expectant of us. This shouldn't have surprised me, but it did. I had no idea what Lauren and I were supposed to do, and the group clearly thought that we were supposed to do something. My fears mounted quickly but were laid to rest with equal speed. The instant that Lauren opened her mouth it was made apparent that I didn't need to know what to do because I didn't need to do anything. Socko was a one-woman show. She made balloon animals, told age-appropriate jokes, performed magic tricks, impersonated cartoons, put on a play with shadow puppets, everything. Every once in a while I held something for her. That was it. That was the extent of my contribution.

As a consequence of my limited role in the production, I found it somewhat difficult to stay focused. Lauren was clearly a gifted children's entertainer, but she was still a children's entertainer. The content of her performance was geared toward a prepubescent audience. Since my balls dropped long ago, I didn't find the show engaging and, as such, my mind began to wander.

At first this was fine, I thought about baseball and remembered that the College World Series was coming up. I considered whether I could get to Omaha this year and decided that I lacked the funds. Thinking about Omaha made me think about my cousin Duncan who works at the state university there, not a bad school considering that it's in Nebraska. I couldn't remember the school's mascot, the Bulls maybe. I wondered why the Bulls didn't have a better baseball team with the College World Series right in their backyard. This was, however, flawed logic, which I quickly realized, and returned my thoughts to the subject of my cousin. Thinking about Duncan made me think about Scotland because Duncan is the most Scottish name in existence, never mind the fact that Duncan's parents are German. Musings on Scotland turned to musings on scotch because scotch is wonderful and it's from Scotland. Thinking about scotch made me realize that I wanted some, and then it made me realize that I needed some. I was surprised by this compulsion. The contents occupying my stream of consciousness were far from heavy. Indeed, they were fairly trivial. Nevertheless, they seemed to be inducing a depression worthy of drink.

For a short while, I sat perplexed in my and by my own sadness. Then it dawned on me. It was not the contents of my ruminations that were bothering me but the contents occupying my visual plane. The scene that was laid out in front of me was void of joy, nothing but a clump of sick children, surrounded by the parents of sick children, surrounded by hospital equipment. Although the parents were not bald or emaciated, they looked just as ill as their kids. Their malady was different, but their degree of pain was not. I suppose that Lauren brought a bit of light to the landscape, but it wasn't nearly enough, a candle next to a black hole. In its entirety, it was an extremely bleak portrait. So bleak that mere passive observation of it was driving me to drink. I needed to escape.

I waited until Lauren started something for which she didn't need the minimal assistance that I was providing. As soon as she began, I headed for freedom, my eye on a safe haven in the back of the room, a spot where I could busy myself with tasks that would not require that I stare at Death's underage waiting room.

The first few movements of my departure were executed with remarkable stealth and great ease. Unfortunately, the ease was short lived. The clown shoes made sure of that. As I went to take my first sidestep away from the group, it became clear that the cumbersome footwear would resist my exit every inch of the way. Comprehension of this actuality almost led me to sit back down . . . almost. Instead, I soldiered on, willfully ignoring the fact that furtiveness and clown shoes are mutually exclusive. Moving on with my exit strategy, I lifted my foot high into the air in an effort to get the entirety of the shoe off the ground. I did not succeed. My hip prevented the necessary range of motion. Despite this failure, I tried again and again and then a couple more times. Finally, on the fifth or sixth attempt, I succeeded in lifting the whole shoe. Now, free to execute a lateral move, I took a step out to the side. My foot moved surreptitiously through the air and landed softly on the ground. I then repeated the maneuver with my trailing foot. Once it had come quietly to rest, I looked up at the audience to see if their attention was drawn. It was not; their eyes were still fixed on Socko. Emboldened by the triumph of my first clandestine shuffle, I made a second and then a third. They were just as successful as the first. Unfortunately, my fourth was not.

The fourth shuffle began well enough, and ended okay, but in the middle it didn't go so well. A third of the way through executing the movement my hip flexor cramped. The pain was immense. It demanded that I return my foot to its point of origin, but I refused to comply. Gritting my teeth, I continued moving to the side, but now with my leg slightly out stretched to accommodate the pain. The new leg position changed the trajectory of my stride. As my foot moved through the air, it became apparent that the revised flight pattern was directly in line with one of the children. I tried to straighten my leg more, in order to raise the shoe up and over her head, but my hip would not allow it. My knee was as high as it could go, and my leg was as straight as it could be. I considered warning the small child but did not. I did nothing but watch. I watched as my clown loafer slowly smacked the sick girl across the face—first coming into contact with her cheek, then slowly dragging across her face and over her nose, and then snapping a bit as the tip of it departed from the corner of her mouth. As I set the offending foot down on the ground, the terminal child looked up at me. An odd and confused look spread across her face. It was the look of someone who had been bitch slapped, in slow motion, by a clown shoe.

Staring into the girl's face, I matched her expression exactly, and while maintaining eye contact, continued to move slowly away. Mute in her disbelief, the child said nothing. I also remained silent and when I looked up at the audience, it was clear that no one else had seen what happened. After one more side step, I had enough space to turn and walk straight toward the back of the room. I did exactly that, only dragging the toe of my shoe once along the way.

All in all it was a pretty inconspicuous exit. Only one person noticed me.

* * *

The back of the room was much better than the front. Despair was still in the air, but it was no longer in my eye line. The change in location improved my mood and after a couple of minutes I began looking around for a way to busy myself. I would have sat and looked out the window for the remainder of my volunteer hours, but I didn't want Lauren or the parents to think that I was shirking all responsibility.

After a cursory glance around the room, I noticed that the toy area in the corner was in disarray so I walked over and began to clean up. It was a little gross, but it was better than staring at the half dead. I organized the bookshelf, picked up the crayons, put the dolls and action figures into a chest, and put the board games away, placing the majority of the game pieces into the correct boxes. Some of the toys were a bit wet, as if they had been sneezed or drooled on, so I made a mental note to use hand sanitizer once I was done. Fifteen or twenty minutes later, the corner looked neat and tidy save for a collection of plastic farm animals that were piled up in a dark corner. I had intentionally avoided the agriculture-themed toys because they looked partic-ularly disgusting, but since I had cleaned everything else up, I decided to finish the job.

One by one I returned the unhygienic plastic animals to their model barn. As I performed the chore, I continually reminded myself that cancer is not contagious. It was the only way I could stomach the task. As a strange kind of reward for a job well done, I found a small gold ring inside the last of the animals that I put away. It was not a particularly fancy piece of jewelry, but it was fancy enough that it shouldn't have been rattling around inside a bronze-colored toy horse. I thought about keeping the ring but decided that it would be better to give it to Lauren. She would either accept it as a gift or say how kind it was for me to return it and then hand it into the lost-and-found. No matter what she chose to do with the horses' stomach contents, I would look good. I put the ring in my pocket for safekeeping and then panned over the room in search of another way to stay busy. As I looked around, Lauren caught my eye and waved me over. Begrudgingly, I acquiesced to her hand gesture.

Once again I found myself in front of the sickly audience. This time it was even worse than it was thirty minutes prior. My chair had been pushed away forcing me to sit cross-legged on the ground with the children. The little girl that I had slapped in the face with the clown shoe was scowling at me.

"And here to wrap up the festivities for the day is Glauco," Lauren said. "He's going to read you a classic."

I smiled and waved at the children. All but one of them smiled and waved back. Lauren handed me *To Think That I Saw It on Mulberry Street*. I smiled at her and said, "Good choice."

"I don't love it, but the kids and parents do," she replied.

I took the book from her hand and nodded. Before I started to read, I looked once more into the withered faces in front of me. It was odd; all the emaciated little humans sat in the same cross-legged pose that I was in. I felt like a yoga instructor at Auschwitz. At first this thought depressed me, but then I decided that those unfortunate souls would have enjoyed a yoga lesson. It wouldn't have been as welcome as food, but it would have been better than the alternative. It would have distracted them from their reality. This thought cheered me, allowing me to read to the children with remarkable pep. When I finished the story the kids pleaded for an encore and I obliged, repeating the tale of Marco and his imagination and his mundane honesty.

* * *

"You did a really great job," Lauren said, as the crowd dispersed.

"Thanks, I was trying, but I'm not nearly as talented as you."

"Oh, well thank you," she replied, her face slightly blushed. "But I'm honestly not that talented, I've just been doing this for a while, long enough to hone a few basic skills."

"Don't underestimate yourself, it was very good."

"Well, I'm glad you were impressed. Did you have a favorite part?"

I thought for a second. "Your shadow puppets were pretty great, you had the kids and the parents entranced." It was true, she had created shadowed images on the wall, the likes of which I had never seen.

"You weren't entranced?"

"I was for a bit, but then I remembered that I was supposed to be contributing, not just watching, so I got back to tidying up."

"And you did a great job, the place looks spotless and the kids loved your story."

"Ahh, it was nothing," I said. I didn't really know how to react to the compliment. It seemed like bullshit. I hadn't done anything worthy of praise. I had cleaned up and read a book aloud. Any literate, able-bodied person could have done exactly the same thing. Unsure of what to say, I became a bit fidgety. I didn't want Lauren to notice so I grabbed the ring out of my pocket in order to provide myself with a talking point.

"I found this ring while I was cleaning up. I'm not really sure what to do with it, do you want it?"

Lauren took the small gold circle from my hand and examined it closely. As she stared at it her face seemed to reveal something. What it revealed I don't know.

"Wow, this is my ring," she said, her eyes fixed on the object. "I lost it a while ago. I can't believe you found it."

"Fantastic! What are the odds of that," I replied. I was excited, finding a treasured item long since lost had to increase my chances of sleeping with her. I watched Lauren expectantly, anticipating some childlike jubilance, some hugs, some jumping up and down. No such excitement occurred. Her face held its initial reaction. It continued to evince something, but what that was remained unclear.

"I'm really glad you found this, but, you know, I actually don't think that I need it anymore," she said flatly. The ring was then slid back into my palm. "You should keep it."

Unsure of what to do with such a response, I returned the

object to my pocket. After a couple of seconds of awkward silence, Lauren spoke up again, her face and her voice regaining their usual angelic quality.

"You truly were wonderful today. You should come again next week, I'm sure the kids would love it and the adults as well."

"I think I can swing that."

"Excellent, and come a few minutes early so I can introduce you to some of the parents, a number of them are quite remarkable. This is the best children's cancer center in the region, so some pretty impressive people bring their kids here."

I threw in a "sounds good" but I don't think Lauren heard me as her words continued on unimpeded.

"I would introduce you now, but unfortunately I have to run. I told Abe I would watch a movie with him tonight, and since he goes to bed at seven, and it's four-thirty now, I'm already pushing it."

"Abe, Abe who?"

"Just a patient at the hospital. We've grown kind of close over the past few weeks and he's not doing very well right now, so I'm trying to make sure that I see him for at least a few minutes every day," Lauren paused for a second to compose herself. It seemed a bit theatrical. "You know, just in case he slips away."

"Well, that's incredibly kind," I said, while squeezing her upper arm consolingly. It was firm, none of that underarm blubber that most women have.

"You're sweet."

"Well, it's the truth. I would love to go with you, but unfortunately I have another commitment." I didn't really have another commitment, at least not a significant one, but I certainly wasn't going to spend the rest of my day off at work. Plus, I was fairly certain that Abe was that old fuck with the right-angled pinkie fingers and the half-ass alopecia. His appearance made me a little sick to my stomach, and I had no desire to look at him voluntarily.

"I completely understand. Well, I will see you next weekend for sure and probably at work before that. I'll try and sneak away sometime this week and come read to the infants with you," Lauren said. She then met my eyes, gave me a beauty queen smile, kissed me on the cheek, and walked away. Per usual, I watched her ass as she strolled. I was staring at it when she suddenly stopped, turned around, and walked back toward me. I averted my gaze as she turned, I don't think she caught me gawking. After she had closed the distance between us, she spoke, her voice rather bashful.

"I hope this isn't too forward of me, but I was wondering if, maybe, after we're done volunteering next week, if you would like to, I don't know, maybe hang out or grab a drink? It's just, I mean, I don't normally ask guys out, but you seem so nice, and I thought . . ."

"I would love to," I interjected, relieving her of the task of finishing the sentence. She was cute. It reminded me of being asked to the Sadie Hawkins dance in ninth grade. It didn't seem like a doctor asking out an orderly.

"Excellent," she replied, then bounded off toward the door. Lauren's departure was consistent with the delivery of her query, the buoyant demeanor of a love-struck freshman. I watched her until she was out of sight.

Once Lauren was no longer in front of me, I became aware of the fact that I had no desire to go on a date with her. I had said yes because it seemed the obvious answer. It was, however, the wrong answer. From the first time I saw Lauren until the moment before she asked me out I had wanted to date her, but that was no longer the case. I liked the looks of Lauren and I liked the idea of Lauren, but I didn't like Lauren. I certainly didn't want to be with Lauren. Her kindness, breasts, ass, and face made this a difficult truth to realize when she was in the room, but it was a truth nonetheless. It was a truth that I might never have known if it weren't for Sandra. I had lied to Sandra and I hadn't lied to

Lauren, yet I knew that I was more honest with the former. When I talked to Sandra I was more myself than I had ever been before. With her, I was even more myself than I ever was by myself. I could deceive my own mind and feel relatively little discomfort, yet when I deceived Sandra's I felt increased anguish with each passing moment. This, coupled with the fact that Sandra is only slightly less hot than Lauren, elucidated the path forward. It also shined some light on the path that I had traveled.

* * *

After Lauren left, I walked over to the corner where I had taken off my regular shoes. On the way I accidentally flung a plastic farm animal through the air. It was a little toy pig. I'm not sure how it had escaped the clean-up, but it had, and as a result it became the unsuspecting victim of my gargantuan footwear.

The fake swine was sent airborne when the tip of one of my shoes sprang forward and caught it underneath its little corkscrew tail. The piglet moved through the atmosphere at a remarkable clip, as if it had come off the bat of Roger Marris. Before the toy was able to make its way back to earth it caught one of the youngest children in the head. The little girl let out a wail that commanded the attention of the entire room. The parents looked at the sniveling child rubbing her head and then at the pig. Having made the connection, they began to look around the room for the culpable party. At that point, I walked over to the child that I had slapped in the face with my clown shoe earlier that day.

"That was not very nice," I said to the little girl, as I escorted her over to the crying child. "You know we don't throw toys here. Why don't you apologize."

Utterly bewildered, the first victim of my clown shoes looked into the eyes of the second victim of my clown shoes and said, "I'm sorry."

In between sobs, the injured party accepted the girl's apology. The situation resolved, I slid off the oversized loafers, put on my regular shoes, and headed out the door.

"See you next weekend," I said.

A chorus of cheery good-byes came in response.

Chapter 11

Bismuth Milk and Ginger Ale

I couldn't decide what baseball hat to wear to the game/date. I was worried that if I wore the relaxed fit cap with the weathered and bent bill, Sandra would think I was too much of a bro. If, on the other hand, I wore the structured hat with the crisp, flat brim, she would think I was a recording artist wannabe. After a few minutes of deliberation, I decided to err on the side of bro.

I have no idea why I was so worried about my hat. Except for Seuss's cat no one was ever defined by their hat. I suppose it could have been that by obsessing over headwear, I was preventing myself from thinking about the imminent confession—triviality providing an escape from substantiality. That had to have been it.

True, I had decided to come clean with Sandra before and nothing had come of it, but this time was different. The nausea, indigestion, and diarrhea that I had been experiencing since making the decision served as a testament to this fact. The consumption of three quarters of a bottle of bismuth milk had done little to abate the symptoms, and in an odd way, their resilience provided me with confirmation that I was actually going to tell her the truth.

Emboldened by my ailments, I headed out of the house. I felt confident in my chosen course of action and moved with a sense of purpose that was reflective of that confidence. I ran into Robert and Brad on the way to my car. They both had coffee cups in their hands. Robert had a financial newspaper under his arm.

"Damn, you already went to the coffee shop," I said. "What made you assholes so industrious this morning?"

"You know my asshole is always industrious," Brad replied. "Shitting, sex, getting bleached, my asshole is a workaholic."

Robert laughed in spite of himself and then answered my question. "We both got assigned to this new client so we have to get ourselves up to speed before we meet with them tomorrow."

Robert's innocuous statement bruised my confidence. It reminded me how removed I was from the world of worthwhile employment. People with real jobs had to get "up to speed" on things. No one ever had to get "up to speed" on emptying colostomy bags. The bookie in my head changed the odds on Sandra giving me a chance from three-to-one to five-to-one. The alteration to the line must have been visible on my face.

"What's wrong, man? You look bad," Robert asked.

"Nothing, I'm just a little nervous for my date with Sandra. Well, I'm not nervous for the date, I'm nervous about telling her that I'm a glorified janitor."

"She doesn't know?" Robert said, somewhat taken aback. "That's a little shady, man."

"Ah, he wasn't being shady, I was being shady," Brad interjected. "I'm sorry, bud, I shouldn't have told her you were an architect. I was just trying to help get you laid. If I had known you were really interested I wouldn't have done it."

I was impressed with Brad's contrition. I don't think he would have expressed such a sentiment a couple of weeks ago. Hayden had changed him, they had yet to go on a real date, but she had changed him.

Inspired by Brad's maturity, I responded in kind. "No it isn't your fault, I could have come clean, or immediately qualified your statement, and I chose not to. So really, it's my fault. Plus you're not a fucking soothsayer, how were you supposed to know I would end up liking her. The odds were much higher that I would have been turned on, but annoyed by her. In which case, I would have been very appreciative of the fact that you helped me get laid."

"All right then," Brad said, with an approving head nod. "Well good luck, man. If she rejects you, I'll ease your pain with an over-the-pants hand job."

"I'll hold you to that. Can Robert join in? Maybe tweak my nips a bit."

"You guys are so fucking weird," Robert said, with a smile and a headshake.

I got into my car and drove off toward a verdict.

* * *

I stopped and got some ginger ale on the way to Sandra's. I hoped that the effervescence of the soda would succeed where the pink bismuth had failed. It didn't really work. It just shifted the problem upward. In between the futile sips of pop, I rehearsed my confession. It didn't sound good, and I couldn't make it sound better. The more flowery I made the delivery the more I realized that the beauty of the composition could not overpower the content of the message. Additionally, the closer I came to her house, the more I realized that I would be incapable of magnificent oration. My nerves and my stomach made it clear that they would not allow for grandiloquence.

By the time I pulled into Sandra's driveway, the decision had been made to tell her the truth as immediately and succinctly as possible. It was the only way I could actually do it. I got out of the car and walked to her door as quickly as one can without going into a jog. The tension in my chest and the nerves in my stomach increased as the distance to her door decreased; I noticed the ill effects of the inverse relationship but ignored them, choosing instead to power through. I knocked on the door three times and then took a step back to ready myself. Sounds emanating from inside indicated that Sandra was coming, but I was unsure how quickly. It was difficult to determine her progress, as I couldn't decipher between the sounds of her footsteps, the heartbeat in my ears, and the odd groans escaping my stomach.

By the time the door started to open, the cacophony of noises, the slew of digestive problems, and the random patches of sweat had rendered me nearly incapacitated. Barely able to function, the idea of talking was almost incomprehensible. I did it anyways. I had to.

Interrupting her greeting before it began, I blurted out in a rapid staccato, "Sandra, I'm not really an architect. I want to be, but I'm not. I'm an orderly. I do menial and often disgusting labor at the hospital." I paused for a second, breathed deeply, and then spoke up again, this time in an apologetic and significantly less stilted tone. "I'm sorry I lied, I'm really sorry." I looked her directly in the eye as I delivered the last words, and upon their completion, threw up.

Chapter 12

Get Shit Done

It was a pretty mild regurgitation, just a little amber liquid dribbling over my lips and down my chin; embarrassing nonetheless. I brought my hands up to cover my mouth and muttered out an apology.

The parade of expressions that had adorned my face in the short time since Sandra opened the door must have been a ridiculous sight. Anxiety, into relief, into remorse, into confusion, into surprise, into puking, into embarrassment, Jesus Christ, I probably looked like a schizophrenic. If I had been in Sandra's shoes I would have slammed the door in my face. I would have slammed it out of anger and out of fear. Anger that I had been lied to and fear that the person in front of me had experienced a mental break. Fortunately for me, I was not in Sandra's shoes, Sandra was in Sandra's shoes, and she chose to laugh. She laughed against her better judgment, but she laughed.

"Holy shit, you're a fucking mess," she said. I nodded, my hands still cupping a little vomit. "Well come on in, you asshole. I'll grab you a towel." The way Sandra said "asshole" revealed irritation but also amusement. This, coupled with her reluctant laughter, indicated that the opportunity for us still existed.

"I'm so sorry," I pleaded, as Sandra returned with the towel. "I know what I did was horrible, and I feel really fucking shitty about it." The apology contained more swear words than I would have liked; articulation was still proving to be elusive.

"Put the towel under your chin and follow me to the bathroom," Sandra said. She had composed herself and adopted a less amused tone. I did as I was told and then, once we had arrived at the bathroom, stood to await further instructions. I must have looked pathetic.

"Clean yourself up and brush your teeth, then we'll talk. There is a new toothbrush in the bottom drawer. Please throw that puke towel in the outside garbage."

After she left, I turned the tap on with my elbow and then washed my hands and face. The soap replaced the aroma of vomit with the aroma of a moonlit path. Up until that moment, I had never smelled a moonlit path. As it turns out, regardless of where it's located, a moonlit path smells faintly of lavender.

With my skin now regurgitation free and pleasing to the nostrils, I moved onto my teeth. I opened the bottom drawer and pulled out the packaged toothbrush and a tube of toothpaste. I opened the brush, applied the paste, and proceeded with my normal oral hygiene routine. The bristles on the new brush were firmer than I was used to, but they cleaned efficiently enough. Once the brushing was completed, I gargled with some water and then brushed again. I wanted to make sure that if the opportunity for intimacy presented itself, I was ready. Such hopes were presumptuous, but Sandra's initial reaction had infused me with some optimism.

I left the bathroom and headed to the garage. I had never been to that part of her house before but I knew where to go. Sandra's place was decorated in a quirky fashion and it had some interesting spaces, but the general layout was fairly standard. As such, it was easy to navigate. After putting the vomit towel into the appropriate receptacle, I walked to the living room.

Sandra was seated on the edge of a large cushioned chair. Her arms and legs were crossed. Her eyebrows were raised and her lips were slightly pursed. The expression was not a happy one. It was not an enraged or distraught one either. She looked at me the way I looked at my sister the night she got her stomach pumped. On my sister's twentieth birthday, she had too much vodka too fast. When I picked her up from the hospital, I was thirty-three percent pissed, thirty-three percent concerned, thirty-three percent amused, and one percent glad that she owed me. That's how Sandra looked at me.

"Are you alright?" she asked. The same query and the same tone that I had used on my sister.

"Yeah, a little queasy, but yeah."

"Good, well then, as long as you can talk without throwing up you can explain why you made a conscious effort to deceive me."

". . ." I replied while rubbing my palms on my thighs.

". . ." Sandra countered, her eyebrows rising another half inch.

I lifted my hands off my legs and then spoke up. "I honestly didn't set out to deceive you, it's just, well, I don't know. We were at the bar that first night and you were so interesting and clever and sexy, and I was captivated. I normally prevent myself from being captivated, but with you, I couldn't help it. Anyway, I really wanted to have a chance with you, and when you asked me what I did for a living, I saw that chance evaporate. I mean I know that girls like you, not that I've ever met a girl like you, but girls like you do not date orderlies. Still, I was going to tell you the truth, but then Brad interrupted and said I was an architect"—I sped up at this point, because I didn't want it to seem as though I was blame shifting. The pace of my words remained quick until they placed responsibility squarely upon my shoulders—"and when he said it I saw my chance with you rematerialize. So, I went with it. It's not his fault. He was just trying to help me out. He knows that I'm embarrassed about my work so, you know. But that's beside the point. I should have spoken up immediately, but I chose not to, and then I meant to tell you on our date, but failed there as well. That night, every time I opened my mouth, I froze up. I felt like a coward, and an asshole, and then I got jealous of the salmon, and of Marco and—"

"Wait, what?"

"Huh?" I replied, coming to from my own rambling.

"Salmon and Marco? What are you talking . . . wait . . . no . . . I think I get it. You were jealous of Marco from *Mulberry Street* because he told the truth even though it was boring."

"Wow, exactly. That was amazing." I paused for a second to appreciate her ability to deduce the motivation behind my envy of a fictional character. "And I was jealous of the salmon because it has the integrity to stay the same no matter what the situation."

"Fair enough," she said, with a slight grin.

"Yeah, well, anyway. I'm truly sorry, and I totally understand if you never want to see me again. I mean I'm an orderly, and I acted like a total ass-shit, so yeah." I faded out. I couldn't believe that the word *ass-shit* left my mouth. I suppose it was appropriate that my confession ended with a recess-worthy expletive. The entire oration had been delivered at a sixth-grade level.

Sandra sat silently for a second. I tried to do the same but fidgeted.

"Well," she finally spoke up, "what you did was pretty shitty. At best it was a deceptive omission caused by insecurity, and at worst it was a nasty ruse used to try and get me into bed. Based on my knowledge of guys I would guess the latter," she paused and looked at me knowingly.

I shifted in my chair and mumbled something inaudible.

"Yeah, well regardless of your intention, you owe me an apology."

"I am sorry, so sorry. And, if I'm honest, part of me did lie because I wanted to get you into bed. But I think the primary motivation behind my fabrication was that I was scared by how much I was drawn to you."

Sandra gave a disbelieving smirk.

"No, I know that sounds like some bullshit line that an unfaithful douche would feed his insecure girlfriend, but it's true." There was pleading in my voice, I was embarrassed by it but I continued. "If I really try and objectively analyze my behavior I would say that, due to a bad experience in the past, I'm hesitant to get into a relationship with someone I feel strongly about, and I could tell right away that I felt strongly about you. Actually, I think the lie was part of an effort to feel less, or to put obstacles in my own way, so that it would be more difficult to act on my feelings."

"Why would you want to feel less? Don't you want to feel strongly about the person you're with? Why would you even be in a relationship with someone you didn't feel strongly about?"

"I don't know, because it's safe, because you can control it. If you feel strongly, and the other person doesn't, then there is a decent chance that they will abuse that asymmetry."

"I understand that, but it's crap. It's weakness. Cowardice. You can't stop yourself from feeling really good because you are worried that it could eventually lead to you feeling really bad. So what if you end up getting shit on by someone that you really care about. So what if you have to get out of a relationship because you love them more than they love you. Better to have tried and failed than to never have tried at all. I know that's a cliché but that doesn't mean it lacks validity. You can't sit around and lie to yourself about how you feel to avoid potential discomfort."

"No?"

"No! In fact, I would venture to say that such behavior would ultimately lead to more discomfort. Denying yourself the truth about yourself. Hedging every relationship decision you make. What could induce more anxiety and depression than that?"

"That's a fair point," I confessed, my tail firmly between my legs.

"Yeah, it's a fair point!" Sandra replied. "No, actually it's not just a fair point. It's more than a fair point. It's just correct!" The volume of her voice increased with each word.

Pausing in the wake of her assertion, Sandra inhaled slowly, exhaled even more slowly, and then repeated the process. Her calming breaths proved effective. The next words she spoke were delivered in a completely different tone. Calm and sincere replaced frustrated and firm. Perhaps, a hint of frustration remained.

"Listen," she said. "I don't like to mess around so here's the bottom line. I'm upset with you for deceiving me. Also, I think that your efforts to avoid relationships with people you care about makes you either a bit of a masochist or a bit of a pussy, which is something you need to figure out. That being said, I really like you. I like you in spite of your fuck-ups."

"Yeah?"

"Yeah, and I am glad that you came clean."

"That's fantastic! And, in case I haven't made it clear already, I really like you as well." The eagerness in my voice was palpable. I wasn't ashamed. It was liberating. I charged ahead. "So then, do you want to be together now? I mean officially together?"

"We'll see," she replied, smiling at my unfiltered excitement. "How about we go on a few dates and then talk about it."

"That sounds good. A few dates is all I'll need. I'm going to woo the shit out of you. You're definitely going to want me as your boyfriend."

"Alright then, commence wooing. I expect my heart to be aflutter by the time we get to the game."

"Of course, my lady," I stood and offered her my arm. She accepted in a jovial fashion, and we headed out the door.

As we departed, I mulled over what had just transpired. Sandra's reaction to my deception was the best I could have hoped for. I would have been disappointed if she had agreed to be my girlfriend immediately after learning of my misdeeds. It would have compromised her integrity. As it was, her measured response maintained my respect, my interest, and my desire.

* * *

I bought us tickets for the right field bleachers. We sat down four rows up from the first base line. Sandra got us the upgrade.

As soon as we entered the ballpark she made her way to a railing, stood up on the first rung, and surveyed the stadium like a meerkat scouting the savannah. After identifying her target location she hopped down, grabbed my hand, and took off at a determined clip. Adeptly maneuvering through the crowd, she brought us to the entrance of the desired location in under a minute. I expected her to continue through the gateway without pause, but she didn't. Instead, she stopped, readopted the meerkat pose, and panned the crowd. I assumed it was an attempt to locate the stadium employee in charge of checking tickets so that we could then avoid the stadium employee in charge of checking tickets. I was half right. Sandra was on the lookout for the usher but she wasn't trying to covertly sneak around him. She was trying to make her way toward him.

"Hey!" she said, tapping the usher on the shoulder.

"He-hey." The usher responded. He started the word annoyed and ended it happy. A remarkable feat considering there were only three letters to work with. I suppose Sandra should be credited with the accomplishment as her appearance inspired the quick shift in sentiment.

"So, I was hoping you could help us out."

"Okay beautiful, how can I help you out?"

"Well we," she said pulling me over, "were hoping to get an upgrade, and we were hoping you could help make that happen."

I thought it was a mistake to pull me over. Feminine wiles were her best tools, and my presence rendered them useless.

"And why should I do that?" he retorted, his tone back to its annoyed state.

Sandra continued on unfazed. "Well, because you look like an actual baseball fan."

"Yeah," he replied with a grin. Sandra's assertion seemed to amuse, intrigue, and flatter him. I was impressed with the fluidity of the man's emotions, and with his ability to convey a lot with a little. Also, he really did look like a baseball fan.

"Yeah," Sandra said. "And as an actual baseball fan, you know that this game is going to be amazing. I mean two Cy Young winners at the top of their game supported by the two best offenses in the National League, ridiculous. And who is sitting in your section right now? A bunch of yuppies that are only here because it's corporate day at the ballpark and their employer gave them free drink tickets. I mean, they don't even know who the fuck Roy Halladay is, and they don't care, and as a baseball fan you know that's a tragedy. So, I think that you want to help us out because you want at least a couple of actual fans sitting above the home dugout to watch this epic game."

"Alright," he said with a smile. "I'm impressed with your lady balls, so I'll hook you and your friend up."

Laughing a little to himself, the usher escorted us to the best available spots. As I slid passed him, and into the three-hundred-dollar seat, he handed me some drink tickets that had been dropped by one of the yuppies. Before departing he slapped me on the back and imparted some friendly man-to-man advice.

"Hold on to her, you lucky bastard."

I looked him in the eye, smiled, and said, "I will."

I already knew that I was lucky to be with Sandra. I didn't need to have that confirmed by a random stadium employee. I didn't mind it either. Awareness of your own accomplishments, and your own good fortune, doesn't make you indifferent to compliments. They are nice to hear. I would like to think that I would have complimented a stranger and his girlfriend in the same way.

As the game went on, Sandra continued to impress me. In the second inning, she snagged a foul ball that had ricocheted off the back of a terrified businessman cowering in the first row. In the fourth, she politely asked a beer guy for two tall boys, and when he ignored her, she loudly and assertively repeated the order. This resulted in her receiving service before the well-dressed executive three rows down. In the fifth, we were put on the kiss cam. She gave a bright smile, waved to the big screen, turned my hat around, and kissed me with an appropriate amount of tongue. During the seventh inning stretch her abs peaked out as she extended her arms upward, the faint indentation down the middle revealing just the right amount of tone. In the eighth, she snuck the beer guy a twenty and he snuck us two after-hours tall boys. In the top of the ninth, she called me out on some bullshit. She wasn't shy about it.

"I'm calling you out on some bullshit," she said.

"Oh, yeah?" I replied. Turning my head toward her, I revealed an amused smile. She didn't see it. Her eyes were fixed on the game, the rim of her tall boy resting against her lips as she waited for a pitch to be delivered. The batter took a strike then she took a drink. After placing the can in a cup holder, she placed her focus onto me.

"Yeah, bullshit," she said. "It's bullshit that you aren't an architect."

"Well, that's not really fair. I can't just wish myself into being an architect," I replied, a bit defensively.

"No. You can, however, work at trying to become an architect."

"But . . ."

"Yeah, but it's a ton of school, but the economy is in the toilet, but no one is building, but no firms are hiring . . ."

"Well, I have the school done," I interjected defensively.

"So what Brad said wasn't all crap? The little green house you designed was for real?"

"Yeah," I said, with a slight nod of my head.

"Well, what the fuck? Then how are you not an architect?"

"Well, I mean I'm employed as an orderly, that's my job. Which means that I'm not an architect."

"Are you still trying to find a job as an architect?"

I shook my head. It was a sheepish response.

"Are you still working on your own? Designing buildings? Entering competitions?"

This time my sheepish head shake was accompanied with a nearly inaudible, "No." I felt emasculated, but I didn't defend myself. I deserved the chastising words. I was responding like a little bitch, but it was the best response I could give. Forwarding a retort to Sandra's rebuke would have only increased my little bitch quotient. Sometimes you deserve a verbal lashing.

Sandra's assertiveness was unaffected by my contrite head wagging. The vehemence with which she spoke did not abate. Perhaps a more rallying tone was adopted.

"Well, it's time to get it together. The best way to get shit done, is to get shit done. So start doing." She paused for a second and then continued with less volume but no less verve. "Listen, I'm not trying to sell you some bootstrap hyperbole. I know that it's a crap time to be starting a career in architecture. Huge forces that are outside of your control are hindering your career path and, honestly, you might not succeed no matter how hard you try. That being said, trying is better than not trying."

I responded with an unintelligible sound, a "hmmmm" or "ummmm," that was intentionally noncommittal. I wanted to be annoyed but wasn't. Sandra's words were a bit preachy, but they weren't bullshit. She wasn't selling some rudimentary "hard work equals success" dictum. I could have dismissed that without thought. Instead, she advocated for individual effort with no promise of results. It didn't seem like an original idea, but I had never heard it before.

The rest of the game passed in silence. The quiet wasn't awkward it was considerate, like Sandra wanted to give me time. She watched the game as I thought. After ten minutes or so Halladay finished his complete game with a strikeout. As the dugouts emptied Sandra returned her attention to me. Introspection was still on my face.

"Relax," she said, while playfully pushing me on the shoulder. "I wasn't being profound I was just telling you what I thought."

"I know," I replied with a smile. Maybe I didn't.

She polished off the last of her beer and then said with a smirk. "But, as long as you are in a contemplative mood, let me lay two more truth bombs on you. One, as long as you're trying to be an architect, you're an architect, I don't give a shit what your primary source of income is, alright?"

"Alright," I said. "And two?"

"Two, I don't give head to blue-collar workers, so if that's something you're interested in then you should sort your shit out."

"Fair enough," I replied. *This girl is fucking awesome,* I thought.

Chapter 13

P-PAD

"You puked? Like you actually expelled the contents of your stomach right in front of her? Oh dear god, that's good." As Brad spoke he bounced a little on the balls of his feet.

It was Monday morning and the coffee shop line was extraordinarily long. That didn't matter to Brad. Neither a lack of caffeine nor a slow line could dampen his mood. One of his best friends had puked on himself in front of a smoking hot girl to whom he had just confessed an unpleasant truth. Brad had just been breast-fed enough joke fodder for a year. The fact that Sandra didn't reject me after I threw up made it even better. Since it wasn't a sore subject, Brad could start making fun of me immediately, no waiting a week for my wounds to heal.

"Oh, my god," Brad went on with a smile. "Maybe I shouldn't be making fun of you. Maybe you have a problem. Do you think you're bulimic? What brought it on? Did one of the other cheerleaders say that you needed to be a base and not a flyer?"

The woman that was ahead of us in line gave an involuntary chuckle. Robert laughed as well, his brilliantly white teeth highlighting his grin.

"It wasn't even bad," I said. "It was like a mild regurgitation."

"Is that your defense? 'There wasn't that much vomit.' Seriously, come on, man. Any vomit is too much vomit. Plus you weren't even drunk or sick, you just puked for no reason. Spontaneous vomitus."

"Yeah," Robert chimed in. "And technically you can't even claim it was regurgitation. Regurgitation serves a purpose, vomiting doesn't. Mother birds regurgitate food for their chicks, they don't puke into their babies' mouths. So, unless you were trying to provide Sandra with some nourishment, you can't claim it was a mild regurgitation." He used air quotes around the last two words he spoke.

I didn't respond. It was over. Robert rarely banters, so you know that when he enters the shit-giving fray, all is lost. You will never live the incident down. He is the harbinger of one's fate as the butt of enduring mockery.

Fuck it, I thought, as I contemplated my future ridicule. Everyone has to take a turn in the pillory. Plus, if you own it, getting lampooned isn't that bad. I suppose that it's easy to have a positive outlook when you're dating a beautiful and intelligent woman.

Brad took advantage of my failure to respond. "So, what I surmise from Robert's presentation on the semantics of puke is that unless you and Sandra are birds masquerading as humans, you cannot claim regurgitation as an out. You just straight up vomited in her face."

Robert spoke up again as we stepped forward in line, his eyes locked on his smartphone. "Wikipedia confirms the difference between vomiting and regurgitation."

"That makes it an undeniable fact," Brad commentated.

As Brad testified to the reliability of Web-based encyclopedia entries, Robert muttered, "Oh, shit." It was a reaction to the information on his phone. A second passed, he composed himself and then adopted a sarcastic voice. "Actually, I'm seriously concerned for you. This new spontaneous vomitus problem you have, coupled with your lactose intolerance, might lead to stercoraceous emesis."

"Ohhh that is very troubling," Brad said, feigning concern, as well as knowledge of the term *stercoraceous emesis*. Brad loves it when Robert gets in on the shit dispensing, so he is always eager to encourage him.

"Mmmm, Brad, it is very troubling. Very troubling indeed," Robert continued. "It seems a distinct possibility that if our friend here continues to throw up randomly in front of hot women, he will eventually start vomiting up fecal matter."

"Indeed," Brad said, with a contemplative finger to his mouth. "I should have seen it myself. He is displaying telltale signs of early stage poop-puking syndrome."

"Mmmm, Brad, I believe Poop-Puking Ass-Mouth Disease is the technical term. P-PAD for short."

"Of course, right you are Robert, Poop-Puking Ass-Mouth Disease. Very serious business."

"Very serious," echoed Robert.

"So," Brad said, turning to me with an impressively realistic bedside manner. "Are you concerned about how your P-PAD problem will affect your love life?"

"You guys are assholes," I said, with a begrudging smile.

"Judging by that reaction, Brad, I would say that it already has."

"I agree with your conclusion, Robert. So then the real question is when did the P-PAD emission take place?"

"There is no good time for a P-PAD emission," Robert faux empathized.

"No there is not, but some times are worse than others."

I shook my head.

"Brad, his silent head nodding seems to indicate that it happened during one of the worst times."

"Unfortunately, Robert, I think you're correct. The obvious conclusion is that he poop-puked during sex. What position were you in? Cowgirl? Doggy-style? Missionary? Oh, I hope it wasn't missionary."

"I hate you guys," I said. My amused face showed that I didn't.

"Oh, Jesus." Robert continued his mock empathy. "It appears it was missionary. You poor, poor man, you poop-puked right on her, didn't you?"

"And the poor girl, too," Brad added.

"Yes, of course, the poor girl," Robert agreed. "I suppose the silver lining is that you eat a lot of oatmeal, so it was probably solid."

"That is fortunate, maybe just one little solid turd, blooop, right onto her chest. Not a big deal at all. Just flick it off and you're back in business."

We finally stepped up to the counter as Brad finished his thought on stool removal. When we ordered our drinks, Robert told the cashier that my name was P-PAD. A minute later, the barista put my Americano on the counter and announced the name loudly. Half of the shop stared as I retrieved my drink. Fortunately, by the time I returned to our table the topic of conversation had shifted away from fecal vomiting. The boys had decided to take mercy on me.

The remainder of our time at the coffee shop was spent talking about obese flight attendants. Brad was less harsh than normal. Probably because he knew that I was on the look out for an opportunity to counter. He likely, and accurately, suspected that the delivery of any overly crass comment would result in my reminiscence of his drunken college days. Twenty-year-old Brad had no qualms about copulating with the corpulent and I have no qualms about bringing that up when he has me down in the count. Giving your buddies shit is like adult league sports. It's friendly fun, and you don't want to hurt anybody, but you still play to win.

On the way out of the coffee shop, Robert grabbed my shoulder. "But seriously man," he said, "congrats about Sandra." Brad nodded in agreement and then slapped me on the ass. The walk to the hospital went quickly.

* * *

Work went well that day. Well, it didn't actually go well, in actuality it was the standard amount of awful. I had to lend hygienic assistance to babies and fat people and old people, just like I always do. Still, at the end of the day I felt better than normal. The tedium and degradation of the job was the same, but the effect that it had on me was not. In the past, there were days when successful mental vacations had made the workday bearable. Such days, however, always ended with a harsh return to reality, an abrupt awareness of the fact that nothing in my life had actually changed. This time it was different. Sandra was real. Well, I suppose that most of the things I daydreamed about were real, but Sandra was really real. She was a tangible part of my life that was aware of who I was. She had also reminded me of who I could be.

During lunch I sketched out some ideas for buildings. I had lost some of my drawing ability, but I had enough talent left to know that it was not gone for good. I also knew that the buildings I was sketching would never be constructed. Knowledge of that actuality, however, did not hinder my satisfaction. It was enough to be doing something.

Enthralled, I worked for three straight hours. My lunch break ended, but I didn't notice so I didn't stop. I wouldn't have stopped even if I had noticed. Eventually, Jones had to come and get me.

"Looks good," he said.

"Huh? Oh, thanks," I replied, regaining awareness of my surroundings.

"I like this one." He pointed at one of the more completed sketches. "Why is it raised like that?"

"It's a flood house," I replied, my enthusiasm unsuppressed. "There are these guys out in Colorado that design doomsday dwellings. One of their houses looks kind of like this. I don't know. I liked the idea, so I sketched out my own. Actually, I don't even care if it can withstand floodwater, I just like the way it looks."

"It does look impressive," Jones said, positivity in his voice.

The compliment was genuine, as was the pride that I felt as a result. I thanked Jones, but he waved it off.

"Don't thank me, son. The work is good so you deserve to be told that it's good. But this," he said, holding up the sketches, "is not enough. This needs to be the beginning. You need to keep working on this," he waved the sketches again. "So you don't have to work like this," he gestured at our surroundings.

I nodded.

"For real," Jones said.

"For real," I replied with the solemnity that was due.

Jones deemed my response acceptable and moved on. "So who tossed a firecracker under your ass?"

At first I couldn't make sense of his query; after a second, intelligibility dawned on me.

"Sandra," I said with a grin. "Sandra got me moving." As her name departed my lips, my ears felt warm and my cheeks flushed. It was a sensation I hadn't felt in ages. I couldn't place it. I wasn't embarrassed, and I wasn't looking to boast, and I wasn't infatuated, I was, I don't know.

"Smitten," Jones said. "You're smitten boy."

"You're right," I said. "I suppose that word's not outdated."

"Damn right it's not," he grinned back at me. "Well, I've never met the girl but she put your head on straight, so she's alright by me."

"I'll let her know."

"You better, the Jones seal of approval is an honor. It's a pretty big deal to get endorsed by an old orderly."

He delivered the line tongue-in-cheek, but I answered with sincerity.

"Yeah," I said, "it is."

I headed off to do the work I had ignored.

* * *

I contemplated Jones's motivational words as I emptied bedpans.

His efforts to encourage my escape from a career as an orderly seemed incongruous with some of his previous statements. I remember him saying that he didn't regret his career as an orderly, that things wouldn't have been that different if he had gone to college, that people just wanted to be. Who knows, maybe he was lying to himself then. Maybe he was lying to me now. Maybe he wasn't lying at all.

"Fuck it," I said to myself after half an hour of consideration.

I caught sight of Lauren as I roused from my contemplative state. She was leaning against the door frame of a patient's room. I looked over her shoulder to see with whom she was speaking. Some codger was nodding his head enthusiastically at the sound of her chipper voice. He had armpit hair growing out of his ears, so I suspect that the specific words she used were lost on him. After a few seconds, she gave a jovial wave and departed.

Having bid adieu to armpit ears, Lauren turned her attention to the chart she was holding. She stared at it as she walked toward me. I stared at her. The intensity with which she was examining the chart ensured that I wouldn't be caught gawking. Although I had fallen for Sandra, I still liked looking at Lauren. A parade of homes tour is not off limits to those that love their house.

I watched Lauren's breasts as she closed the distance between us, and her ass as she moved away. The entire time her eyes remained fixed on the papers in her hand. About ten yards past me her focus finally broke, something on her pants momentarily captured her attention. It must have been a stain. She sidestepped over to a water fountain, pulled a napkin from her pocket, dampened the napkin, and began to scrub.

Lauren's commitment to the stain removal was tenuous at best. The bulk of her attention remained on the papers, as she absentmindedly wiped her thigh. About a minute into this multitasking, a concerned expression fleeted across her face. She tossed the napkin into a bin and jogged back toward the room from which she had come. The bouncy strides put her breasts and ass on display. It was an impressive show that I watched until it concluded with her arrival at the patient's door. I expected her to jog right into the room, but she didn't. Instead she paused to collect herself, only entering after meticulously readjusting her top and hair as well as the papers in her hand.

Lauren began talking to armpit ears with her standard amount of cheer. I caught the beginning of their conversation, something about him forgetting to sign something; I don't know, I quickly became bored. Uninterested in eavesdropping, my thoughts drifted toward my enduring fascination with Lauren's good heart. She actually took the time to make herself presentable before going in to see this ancient fuck with woodland creatures in his ears. It truly blew my mind. I used to feel bad about the fact that I didn't want to help people the way that Lauren helps people. That guilt might have resulted in some excessive cynicism and some knee-jerk reactions. It may have even led me to adopt false stances to avoid self-reproach. Maybe that was wrong. Maybe it is possible to admire someone's efforts without feeling bad about having a lack of desire to do the same.

Such waves of understanding washed over me as I stood outside the patient's room. They seemed both familiar and foreign. I think in the past I had produced them, but up until that point, I had never felt them. It was refreshing. I was smiling to myself when Lauren walked out of the room.

"Oh, hey!" she said, surprised. "I didn't see you. Have you been standing there a while?"

"Just a few minutes," I said. My response must have been delivered with a spacey air. Lauren looked slightly concerned. No, perplexed.

"Uh. Okay. Well . . ." she began.

"You know I really do admire all of the work that you do," I interrupted. "You're thoughtful and selfless and the world is a better place because of your efforts."

"Thank you," she replied. The prototype of a bashful grin spread across her face, all traces of puzzlement and concern vanished.

"You're welcome," I said. "Actually, I should have told you that a long time ago."

"Well, you did. If I remember correctly you've given me quite a few flattering compliments in the past."

"Yeah?"

"Yeah."

She was right of course. Ever since we met I had given Lauren compliments in abundance. They were, however, never sincere. This time it was different. I had no ulterior motive, no hidden cynicism, and no envy of her altruism. For the first time, my compliment was given in earnest. Of course, I didn't tell her that.

"Well, as I was standing here, I was struck by the full extent of your exceptionality. You are a truly amazing person, and I wanted to let you know that . . . again," I finished lamely.

Lauren looked at me as if she had discovered something new. She opened her mouth to speak but refrained after a second's pause. Unable to find the right words, she gave me an intrigued look, squeezed my arm, and departed. The squeeze seemed to convey something that her previous touches had not, something undeniably positive. Had she touched me in such a fashion a week previously I would have been irrepressibly excited. That was no longer the case. I was pleased that she had been moved by my compliment, but I felt indifference toward the promise of her affection. Sandra had shown me what was possible, and Lauren's appeal had declined accordingly.

Chapter 14

Two Great Weeks or SARS and Spoons

Over the course of the next two weeks, Sandra and I spent a lot of time together. On Tuesday of the first week we went for a run. Sandra's exercise ensemble was perfect. The bulk of her hair was pulled back in a ponytail, the strands that couldn't reach tamed by a colorful, extra-wide headband. I liked the headband. It combined flair and functionality. Her tank top was made out of the newest wicking material, her shorts out of retro, bird's-eye mesh. They were short but not obnoxiously short. She didn't look like an attention whore—the type that run in their underwear in an effort to boost their confidence through the accumulation of gaping male eyes—but she also didn't look like one of those overly serious I-train-too-hard-to-care-what-I-look-like types. What a bunch of bullshit that is.

After our run, we walked and talked. It started as a cooldown but turned into a two-hour stroll along the river. It ended with us making out on her doorstep. We were both salty and slightly disheveled from our run. Somehow that made the experience more intimate.

* * *

On Thursday morning, she met the boys and I for coffee. We went to Starbucks rather than the local coffee shop that reuses hot beverage sleeves. I was pleased with the change of venue. My preference for the chain coffee shop no longer embarrassed me. Starbucks' menu is legible, the service is fast, and the staff is not comprised of judgmental pricks that are too cool to try. It makes sense that I prefer it. Really, it's just nice to get a latte without being patronized by haughty baristas debating the Velvet

Underground. Sandra expressed a similar sentiment.

"I'm glad we came here," she said, as we sat around the table at Starbucks. "That other place makes me feel like an asshole. I ask for a plastic spoon and they look at me like I'm a monster. I mean I respect their effort to be green, but that doesn't mean I want to stir my coffee with a spoon that has been sitting in a mug on the condiments table for hours and hours. A spoon is not clean just because it's residing in an old coffee cup marked CLEAN. I've seen people scratch their backs with those spoons. I've seen little shits balance them on their nose. Disgusting. That's just asking to get sick."

"I believe that's how SARS got started," I said, teasingly. It was an effort to goad Sandra about the vehemence of her diatribe.

"Yeah," Brad added. "I'm pretty sure that SARS is a coffee-spoon-borne illness."

"It wouldn't surprise me," Sandra said, taking the razzing in stride. "Probably AIDS, too, coffee shops and AIDS got big around the same time. I bet there is a cause-and-effect relationship there."

"You should probably inform the CDC of your findings," I added.

Brad and Robert smiled at Sandra. Their grins indicated that they were impressed with her ability to both give shit and take it. Their approving looks were important to me.

"Plus, to get to that other coffee shop you have to pass by those self-righteous street performers," Sandra continued. "Last time I walked by them, they told me that I was a corporate zombie slaving away for paper. I told them that it's not paper, it's money, and that I don't slave away, I contribute to society."

"They told Brad and I that we were wearing corporate nooses," Robert tossed in as an aside. His tone was intentionally casual. I could tell that the remark had bothered him. The disguised disconcertion in Robert's voice was not lost on Sandra.

"Yeah, well those guys are fucking assholes," Sandra said

assertively. She said it to the table at large, but you could tell that she was trying to assure Robert in particular. In actuality she assured all of us. "I'm sure they have some legitimate gripes," she went on. "But they aren't actually doing anything about it. They're standing on a street corner making people feel bad. That's not helping, and it's not contributing positively to society, it's just being a whiney douche."

"They probably use the communal coffee spoons to itch their genitals," Brad added.

"Oh yeah," Sandra said. "And those fuckers are loaded with SARS."

* * *

We went to another ball game on Friday. Improving on her previous effort, Sandra cajoled the usher into giving us front row seats on the third base line. In the bottom of the fourth a foul ball rolled along the ground in front of us. Sandra had me hold her by the legs so that she could lean out and pull it in. It was an impressive score. The fans surrounding us gave her a round of applause, and in response, she gave a playful bow. On the way out of the stadium, she gave the ball to a little girl who was wearing a backward ball cap and her dad's glove. The girl was elated. She thanked Sandra and then turned around to show her father. The amount of happiness that was generated by Sandra's small act of kindness was impressive. The fact that the little girl had manners and was appreciative of a used baseball was encouraging.

* * *

That Saturday I called off my volunteer plans/date with Lauren. I had never canceled a date before, well at least not a date with someone attractive, so I was a little nervous to call. In order to combat my nerves, I drank four beers in quick succession. It proved to be an effective technique. When I called Lauren, I was apologetic but direct. I told her that she did amazing work but that it wasn't for me. I also told her that she was smart, caring, and beautiful, but that I had met someone, and because of that, could not go out with her. Lauren handled it gracefully and wished me luck on my new relationship.

Pleased with how well the conversation went, I had two more beers to celebrate. I followed the beers up with a nap and followed the nap with a run. I jogged until the app on my phone told me that I had burned as many calories as I had drunk earlier that day. Sandra might be willing to date an orderly but certainly not a fat orderly.

* * *

The following Wednesday Sandra and I went to see her sister's improv group. The show was mediocre, but the performers had fun, so the audience had fun. Everyone that was on stage did a good job of owning their cheese-ball lines and minor mistakes, which relieved the audience of the burden of angst that typically saddles amateur theater patrons. It's hard to be entertained by someone if you're fretting for them.

After the show, I met Sandra's sister Nina. She was affable and smart and seemed less self-involved than the average college student. She was definitely less self-involved than I was in college, possibly less self-involved than I am now. Although she had many of the offbeat quirks that are common among theater majors, she didn't seem overly dramatic. Instead, Nina possessed a healthy recognition of the difference between performing and living. She also demonstrated a get-shit-done attitude akin to that of her sister. Such a mindset precludes the fostering of dramatic tendencies.

Once the show finished, the three of us got coffee. Sandra and

I ordered decaf. Nina ordered regular. Our beverage choices revealed the clear disparity between the partying habits of people in their early twenties and those in their late twenties.

We discussed a variety of topics as we sat around a high-top table in the corner of the shop. It became clear, over the course of our conversation, that Sandra and Nina were close. They spoke like friends, like they would seek out the company of one another even if they weren't related. As I watched them, I was struck by how uncommon that is.

After an hour or so, Nina headed out, she wanted to take a shower before going to a party. Sandra got up at the same time.

"I could tell you that I'm going to the bathroom, but that would be bullshit," Sandra said. "So I'll skip the ruse and just let you know that I'm going to talk about you with my sister."

"Sometimes I wish you were more frank," I replied.

She winked at me and headed toward the door with Nina. I watched them as they walked away, so did the male employee refilling the milk pitchers, and the businessman texting on his smartphone, and the hipster waiting at the counter, and the cute lesbian ruffling her pixie cut. Sandra typically receives a few glances but not that many. I suspect that the increased attention was due to the fact that she was walking with her sister.

While neither Sandra nor Nina are astoundingly beautiful, they are both pretty, and in different ways. Their faces are similar but their bodies are not. Sandra has perky, medium-size breasts on a lithe yet toned frame. Nina, on the other hand, has large breasts and a fair-sized ass, a slightly thick but fit hourglass. When walking side by side, they're a live visual representation of the entire spectrum of alluring female body types. In my experience, it's rare to see such different forms of beauty side-by-side, and based off of the inordinate number of eyes on them, my experience is reflective of the norm.

As I watched Sandra and Nina say their good-byes, I made a mental note to tell Brad about the experience. The sisters served as a perfect case study for our debate on female body types—athletic versus curvaceous. The similarity of their faces and their relatively equal overall beauty effectively isolates their bodies as the only physical difference between them. As such, when standing next to one another, they afford observers the opportunity to learn exactly which habitus they find most appealing.

On second thought, perhaps that's why so many people were looking at them. After all, it seems unlikely that Brad and I are the only people that have ever deliberated that issue. Half of the onlookers were likely using the unique opportunity to conclude the debate for themselves. The woman in the pixie cut was probably thinking, "Now I know which one I prefer, curvaceous. I'll have to tell Daniella or Holly or Portia . . ." I don't know. Those are just the names that came to mind when I imagined an unknown, hot lesbian.

As for me, Sandra and Nina confirmed the conclusion that I had reached when discussing the topic with Brad. A lithe but toned body definitely wins out. Sandra's athletic beauty has staying power. "Actually," I thought, as she headed back toward our table, "Sandra has staying power."

"So what's the verdict?" I asked as she slid back into her seat. "Did Nina approve?

"Meh, she thinks you're alright," she replied with a coy smile.

On our walk back to the car Sandra pulled a piece of paper off of one of the campus bulletin boards. The flier provided details on an upcoming architecture competition. The winning design would become the new central library, the hallmark structure for a major metropolitan area.

"You should do this," she said, in a matter-of-fact tone.

"I will," I responded.

It was not the answer I would have given a few weeks before.

* * *

The following day, I called in sick to work. Instead of doing menial labor at the hospital, I started to design a building. The next day I did the same. While drawing I considered all of the shitty bedpans, dirty colostomy bags, and old folks in wheel-chairs that must have been stacking up without me. Perhaps they were all being backlogged into the same space, gross.

By Friday night, I had some sketches of a building that were fairly impressive. I brought them over to Sandra's so that I could show her before our date.

"Nice," she said enthusiastically.

"Yeah? You really like them?" There was more sensitivity in my voice than I would have liked.

"Yeah, I do. You know that I don't pull punches. If I thought it was shit, I would tell you it was shit. That's something you better get accustomed to. I'm sure that, in the future, you'll design plenty of buildings that I'll find less than impressive."

"Well, I'll be prepared for the constructive criticism."

"Oh, I won't constructively criticize. I will rip you a new asshole."

"Looking forward to it," I said with a grin.

I really was looking forward to it. The thought of a future in which I was with Sandra and designing buildings made me happy. Then I realized that at that moment, I was with Sandra and I was designing a building. That made me even happier.

"So, what does the interior plan look like?" she asked.

"I haven't thought about it in too much detail."

"Yeah, you should probably do that."

"Eh."

"Eh?" Sandra repeated indignantly. "Eh, is the wrong answer. Yeah, I definitely should, is the right one. The interior is just as important as the exterior. No, scratch that, interior architecture is more important. Who gives a shit if the exterior of a building is breathtaking if the interior is unlivable?"

"The hordes of people that walk by but don't go in," I said.

Sandra paused.

"Fair enough," she said, a couple seconds later. "Let's say that they are both important."

"I suppose," I replied, acting as though I were humoring her.

Sandra thought that I was joking but she wasn't positive. Her confusion was warranted. I intended for the comment to come out in an obviously sarcastic tone, but it didn't. Probably because up until that moment in time, I had held a view that was not in total agreement with the one she expressed. But of course she was right, both exterior and interior are important, both aesthetics and functionality. Actually, I shouldn't say, "of course." Many of the world's most famous buildings obsess over one or the other. No one feels moved by the beauty of Chicago's "form follows function" skyscrapers, and no one fawns over the efficiency of Denver's visually striking art museum. Maybe Sandra's comment was more insightful than it seemed, maybe she is an architecture genius whose talent has been lying dormant, or maybe she's just a person that unknowingly called bullshit on all the famous architects who can't see the forest for the trees.

The insightful yet ordinary nature of Sandra's critique ran through my head as she left the room to grab a purse. When she returned, I made sure to clearly express myself.

"You really are right," I said. "They're both important."

"Fucking right," she said.

Somehow Sandra made the expletive-laden response charming. I held out my hand, she took it, and we headed out for dinner.

There was a thirty-minute wait at the restaurant. We sat down at the bar to pass the time. Our stomachs were empty, so the couple of drinks we consumed had an impact. We were on our second when some slightly overweight white guy sat down next to us. He was wearing a short-sleeve dress shirt, and in doing so indicated that the entire concept of formal attire was foreign to him. The shirt showed off his pasty arms and put his understated tattoo on display, an artfully crafted Jesus fish filled in with the stars and stripes, GOD BLESS AMERICA was written in poor cursive underneath. His presence at the restaurant made me question its quality. The tattoo on his arm made me question my nationality. Afraid that he might accuse Sandra of being an Islamic terrorist, I suggested that we go elsewhere. Sandra agreed. On the way out, she said something in French. I thought it sounded vaguely threatening. The xenophobic evangelical thought it sounded like the final scream of a jihadist suicide bomber. Startled, he slopped his tomato juice and beer all over himself. No doubt he considered his clothes another victim of Al Qaeda.

"Was that French?" I asked as we stepped outside.

"Yeah," Sandra said, with a laugh. "But that asshole probably thinks that the Middle East is a country, so I doubt that he can tell the difference between French and Arabic."

"Well played, madam, what did you say? Die infidel scum?"

"No, I asked him to point me toward the restroom."

"So he wasn't much help."

"No, kind of a dick."

I looked over at Sandra with a grin on my face. "You're awesome," I said, and wrapped my arm around her shoulders. I left it there while we walked to the next restaurant. Sandra was wearing heels so my arm was positioned at an awkwardly high angle. It should have been uncomfortable, but it wasn't. It was right. The rest of the night was right. The food was mediocre, the waiter was unfriendly, and the weather turned cold, but the night was right. Sandra made it so. Her thoughts, laughter, and honest beauty made it so. Her fascination with the world, her appreciation for what she had, and her desire to do more made it so. Her sharp tongue, her playfulness, and her subtle kindness made it so.

We had sex that night. We didn't fuck and we didn't make love, we had sex. There was none of the exaggerated sentimentality of making love, yet there was more than the raw physicality of fucking. Not that either of us were opposed to fucking. It just didn't seem like the right thing to do that first time, something more needed to be conveyed.

Sandra's breasts turned out to be better than I had imagined. They are, I discovered, full but not excessively large. They have proportionate and well-placed areolas, at the center of which reside nipples that stand out in the cold but have the decency to become less pronounced in other climates. No matter what position she's in, they maintain their high quality, moving naturally yet always keeping their general shape. They don't fall into her armpits when she lies down, and they don't hang like a warm ball sack when she bends over. They stay high and bounce softly when she's on top and disperse evenly when she's on her back.

The first five minutes of our sexual encounter were great, the next seven were good, and the last three were amazing. The first five were great because I was having sex with a beautiful woman, and it is great to have sex with a beautiful woman. The middle seven were good, as opposed to great, because in order to prevent myself from ejaculating I had to spend a significant portion of the time trying to remember how many seasons it took Hank Aaron to break the career home run record. The last three were amazing because Sandra had already cum so I didn't have to restrain my excitement. As I came she pulled down gently on my balls, which amplified my pleasure. After I came I still wanted to be there.

Sandra slept in one of my dress shirts. I had always wanted a woman to do that but none ever had. She breathed heavily as she slept but she didn't snore. When we woke up in the morning, we had sex again. After we had sex, we ate breakfast. After we ate breakfast, we fucked. Even when we fucked there was something more.

* * *

That afternoon we hung out with Robert and Brad. We bought some beer and went to the park. It was a warm summer day and we imbibed at a rate that was appropriate to the season and climate. Our drinking was punctuated with a couple games of wiffle ball and an occasional toss of the Frisbee. It was evident that Sandra was not well versed in the art of Frisbee, but she joined in anyway. Her willingness to take part despite her deficient skill served as further proof of her remarkableness.

Hayden met up with us on our way home. Brad didn't hide his enthusiasm for her arrival. Sandra thought it was cute. I thought it was refreshing. It was nice to see Brad act how he wanted to act, rather than how he thought he was supposed to act. Brad has spent many years as the loud cool guy. It's an image that he deserves and enjoys, but it's also an image that has, on occasion, stifled him. Somehow Hayden made him realize that he could be that guy without constantly being that guy. Maybe she said something that opened his eyes or maybe it was just a byproduct of her presence, either way it made me like her.

That night we drank some wine, vaped a bowl, and played some cards. Nothing serious, we all just chipped in a couple bucks. Sandra never bluffed but she still did pretty well, she paid attention to the cards and only bet when she had a chance. She didn't walk away with the most money, but she was close. I don't know why I paid attention to the way that she played cards. It was just something that I picked up on. I also noticed how she tucks her hair behind her left ear when she is interested in a story, and how she pushes against the tip of her nose when she is concentrating. Both quirks are adorable. Such endearing mannerisms are what allow her to come across as cute even though she has a sharp tongue and a foul mouth.

After the card game we all retired for the night. Sandra held my hand as we walked to my room. I was still a little high so I was a bit nervous about having sex. True, cannabis normally makes sex better, but sometimes it makes me self-conscious about my naked body and my ridiculous intercourse faces. Fortunately with Sandra, I only experienced the positive effects. We came at the same time, which is a notable feat considering I didn't distract my mind with baseball statistics. She laid her head on my chest after we finished.

As we drifted off to sleep, I muttered, "I love you."

I could say that it was a sentiment that had been induced by weed, beer, and post-coital bliss, but that would be a lie. It was a sentiment inspired by Sandra and it was a sentiment that she returned without hesitation.

Chapter 15

Disappointed

On Monday Lauren and I fucked. I wished that we didn't, but we did. It happened rather suddenly like something out of a porn film.

Abe, that ancient fuck with the eating disorder hair and the crooked pinkie fingers, had just died. Lauren seemed fairly upset, so I helped her to clean up his room. There was a fair amount to do. Old distorted digits had been knocking on death's door for quite some time, and as a result, his room had accumulated an abnormally large number of personal effects. Pictures, handwritten letters, novels, and children's drawings littered the walls and tables. I was picking up a stack of books that included *Mother Night* and *The Republic* along with a slew of mindless thrillers when I noticed a fresh bouquet of flowers sitting on the windowsill. They looked expensive and had yet to reach full bloom. I gently fingered through the arrangement in search of a card but was unable to find one. It seemed a shame to throw them out, so I suggested that we move them into the room down the hall.

"That old lady loves flowers," I said. "These will make her day."

Lauren looked at me as though I were the picture of thoughtfulness and compassion. "That's so sweet," she said.

"Oh . . . well . . . uh . . . you know," I replied suavely.

She walked over and hugged me tightly. It was like I had provided her with the exact words of comfort that she longed to hear. After a few seconds' embrace she looked up at me. There was a smile on her face. A smile that erased the sadness from moments before; puffy eyes were the only trace of grief that remained. She removed her hands from around my waist and wiped the remnants of tears from her eyes. I patted her on the shoulder and then turned to go. As I stepped away, she grabbed my wrist, turned me around with a gentle pull, and then brought me closer with a firmer one. The second tug of my arm made it clear that I would be cum-ing, not going.

Lauren led the way to a supply closet and my dick followed. It was rewarded with her pussy, and then her mouth, and then her pussy again. Despite all of the attention, my penis was disappointed. It was as if Lauren was something that he thought he should like so he pretended to like—the sexual equivalent of a William Burroughs novel. Lauren came twice before he was able to dribble out a nominal amount of semen.

I tried to convince myself that my cock's apathy was the result of a shortcoming in Lauren's physical appearance. "Her breasts bounced in an oddly uniform way," I told myself. "So it makes sense that my penis was less than enthused." It was bullshit. A few weeks before, I would have found the unusually consistent boob movement to be a turn-on. My dick wasn't dissatisfied with Lauren, it was dissatisfied with me. No, it was disappointed with me. No, I was disappointed with myself.

Lauren wasn't disappointed. "Oh, my god," she said. "That was amazing."

"Yeah," I replied. *Amazingly fucking stupid,* I thought.

* * *

Wracked with anxiety and guilt, I spent the next couple of hours shitting out liquid, a physical manifestation of my distraught emotional state. As I peed out of my butthole, I childishly hoped that the incident with Lauren was a dream. The futility and immaturity of this wishful thinking became apparent to me as I wiped my ass. By the time I was done washing my hands my mindset had completely changed course. Useless fretting had given way to proactive solution seeking. I had fucked up and I felt bad about it, but guilt-induced paralysis would do nothing to help the situation. It needed to be confronted head on.

I walked out of the bathroom and began my search for Lauren. It didn't take long. She was inside a glass conference room with a slew of imperious-looking fifty-somethings—probably a bunch of administrators. I waited around the corner until their meeting was over. Lauren was the last one to come out. She caught sight of me as I walked determinedly in her direction. Before I was able to utter a syllable, she suggested that we grab a coffee. I agreed and we headed off toward the cafeteria. We, however, didn't stop at the cafeteria and we didn't stop at the Starbucks down the street. It wasn't until we arrived at the judgmental street performers that I realized we were headed for the independent coffee shop with the previously used insulating sleeves and the dirty "clean" spoons. Lauren would be the type to legitimately prefer that sort of establishment, not because it increases her hip factor, or because it allows her to look disapprovingly at others, but because she cares about humanity and the world and believes that by patronizing such an establishment she is positively contributing to the betterment of the earth and its inhabitants.

Lauren was dressed in a crisp, professional ensemble, and as a result, she faced immediate criticism from the street performers that we had to pass to get to the shop. After they informed Lauren of her status as a slave to the establishment, they moved on to broader topics. A diatribe on corporate greed was followed by a soliloquy on the ontology of money. I don't know why we stayed and watched, but we did. In order to provide a dramatic conclusion to their exposition on the man-made nature of currency, two of the performers ripped five-dollar bills in half and dropped the pieces onto the ground. As the torn pieces fell, the performers informed onlookers that the bills are nothing but paper. They followed this theatricality by silently staring into the audience, acting as though they had ripped blindfolds from everyone's eyes. Who knows, maybe they had. A number of people had gathered and they were all raptly staring.

After a few seconds passed, Lauren stepped on to the makeshift wooden platform that served as their stage.

"You're right," she said, as she leaned over and picked up the torn five-dollar bills. "It's nothing but paper."

The performers were surprised by her action and even more surprised when she turned and walked away quietly. As she stepped off the stage, she caught my eye and nodded her head toward our destination. I followed her nonverbal cue.

Lauren dug around in her purse as we made our way down the last block before the coffee shop. A few feet away from the door, she pulled out a roll of penny stamps and removed four of them. With the stamps stuck to the tips of her fingers Lauren lined up the edges of the torn bills. Once she was pleased with their alignment, she took the stamps and taped them back together. Inside the shop she used one of the refurbished bills to pay for our coffee and placed the other into a collection bucket for a local charity. Her actions amused me, and I wanted to tell her as much, but I didn't get the chance. As soon as we sat down, she began to apologize for what had happened earlier that day.

"I'm so incredibly sorry," she said. "I should not have acted that way. You told me that you were not interested, yet I made a move on you anyway."

"Oh . . . well . . . that's okay," I replied slowly, taken aback by her apology. I had planned on being the one to regretfully acknowledge my behavior. I still should have. I should have matched Lauren's apology with one of my own, but I didn't. I made a conscious effort to stop myself. If Lauren felt that responsibility rested solely on her shoulders, she would be more likely to put the event behind us, and I would be more likely to come out of the situation unscathed. It wasn't the noblest thing to do, but it was the most prudent.

I let Lauren continue to talk. She explained how, even though she had grown close to many patients that had passed away, their deaths still hit her hard. Elaborating on the subject, she discussed the emotional distress that she felt after Abe's passing and then proceeded to offer it up as an explanation, but not an excuse, for her behavior. She was emotionally jarred and slept with me in order to feel comfort. Comfort from someone she knew had a kind heart. She used my reading to the infants, donating of soda tabs, volunteering at the children's cancer center, and willingness to help her clean Abe's room as evidence of my caring nature. I refrained from correcting her.

After she finished apologizing and explaining, she moved on to other topics. I continued to listen. With each word she spoke, our sexual encounter moved farther into the past, so each time she suggested we get back to work I encouraged her to continue talking. The more that she could associate me with conversation and work and volunteering, the less likely she would be to associate me with fucking—and the less that she thought about me when she thought about fucking the better. It would reduce the likelihood of her making a big deal out of our romp in the closet. I didn't want my life to be fucked because I fucked her.

We ended up talking for over an hour. Halfway through, I went and got us more to drink, we both switched from coffee to skim lattes. The barista was the type of fat person that attributes their weight problem to all skinny people. I don't understand those chub monsters, they act as though they were held down and force-fed by a cross-country team. Needless to say, I watched her closely as she prepared our drinks. I wanted to ensure that our cups were filled with skim and not whole. She saw that I was watching and prepared our drinks the way that I ordered them.

By the time Lauren and I were done with our lattes, the fuck in the closet seemed like it had never happened. I couldn't have asked for our conversation to go any better. The problem had been addressed and put to rest, and Lauren had taken responsibility for the whole thing. She wasn't upset with me, and she wasn't going to make a scene, and she wasn't going to try and pursue a relationship. She was going to set the incident aside and continue on as friends. Well, work friends. I didn't want to run the risk of interacting with her outside of the hospital.

We walked back to the hospital and said friendly good-byes. She headed off to another administrator's meeting, and I made my way to the break room. I didn't want to go back to work yet. I still needed to mull over what I was going to tell Sandra— maybe everything, maybe nothing. The classy way in which Lauren had handled the situation left every door open to me. I could proceed as I saw fit.

* * *

Jones found me in the break room. "I didn't come and get you earlier because I thought you were designing buildings," he said. "But now I see that you're just sitting on your backside. Get back to work you lazy ass."

Rather than doing as I was instructed, I told Jones what had happened over the course of the day. There were two reasons I decided to confide in him. One, I valued his opinion, and two, I didn't want to go back to work. Cleaning up other people's shit would not help me resolve my own.

I thought Jones would suggest I tell Sandra, but he didn't. Actually, he didn't suggest anything, he just discussed.

"That's a tough one," he said. "I'm not a fan of lying, but it has a time and a place and it's not just when it's obvious. Everyone knows that you should lie if, say you're a member of the Underground Railroad talking to a slaver, or if your mother-in-law asks for your opinion on her nasty meat loaf. But, it's a lot less clear if you should lie in order to, I don't know, protect your friend who committed a minor crime, or change some rich guy's will so that a charity gets his money rather than his snotty, alcoholic kids. You know what I mean?"

"Yeah," I said, as I stared at the wall in contemplation. Jones was making a classic consequentialist argument. I had heard similar ones made numerous times before. Still, it was nice to hear his thoughts and it was nice to know that he didn't think the answer was cut and dry.

"I guess you have to decide what will be the best for everybody in the long run," he said. "But do me a favor, think about it while you're wheeling out some of these old folks and pregnant ladies. They're stacking up."

"Of course," I replied, my mind still elsewhere.

On his way out the door, Jones gave me a reassuring pat on the back. At that point, I was struck by the fact that his reassuring pats and no-nonsense life advice had become a common occurrence. "Christ, I need to get my shit together," I thought. Shaking my head in frustration with myself, I headed off to the line of wheelchairs.

One by one I removed the geriatrics and the new moms. By the time I was done, I had decided to tell Sandra about the indiscretion. I would call it an indiscretion. It sounded better than a fuck.

Chapter 16

Coming Clean

Sandra and I went out that night. We ate seafood, and talked about recent Supreme Court rulings and the current state of the Catholic Church. We also discussed what blackberries do to your poop; it's not fun to be intellectual all the time.

I didn't confess to Sandra right away because I didn't want to. I wanted more time and there would be no more time once I informed her of my indiscretion. Still, it needed to be done, and I resolved to do it before the night concluded. Actually, I decided that I would do it before we had sex, a laudable decision considering how ridiculously beautiful she looked and how bad I wanted to see her tits again.

After dinner we went for a walk. I asked her about work and her reply was interesting because her job is worthwhile. Then I asked her about her sister and she told me an entertaining story about how Nina and her friends got drunk and snuck into one of the academic buildings to steal a professor's laser pointer. Evidently, it was an object that was universally despised.

I smiled and laughed as Sandra told the story, but I did so in a half-hearted fashion. The weight of the impending confession hampered my enjoyment. My weak attempts at enthusiasm didn't fool her. She could tell that something was wrong. When she inquired as to what it was, I changed the subject. I wasn't ready to lose her. Instead of telling Sandra about Lauren, I asked her which house she would be in at Hogwarts. Anyone who is the least bit nerdy has spent a fair amount of time considering this question and, in my experience, is eager to tell someone about the conclusion that they have reached.

"I know that this is an evasive maneuver," Sandra said. "But I want to answer anyway. We'll come back to your odd behavior."

I knew that Sandra would answer the Harry Potter question. A) It is a fun question to answer and B) she has little patience for moodiness and, as such, was apt to choose an amusing hypothetical over a conversation about, what appeared to be, an unjustified case of melancholy. If you have a real problem, Sandra will go to great lengths to help. If you're angsting over something petty, she'll instruct you to get your shit together.

Ravenclaw ended up being Sandra's house of choice. I was pleased she didn't choose Hufflepuff. Those who choose Hufflepuff tend to be naively optimistic. I also chose Ravenclaw. Mainly because I value intelligence, but partly because Cho Chang is a member of that house and in my imagination she is a twenty-something Japanese gravure model. I willingly ignore the fact that Hogwarts is for eleven- to eighteen-year-olds.

The conversation was silly, but it was not stupid. It was comforting, like a threadbare quilt. And like a threadbare quilt, I didn't want to let it go. So, I didn't. I brought up another Harry Potter hypothetical and then one more. The discussion proved to be a powerful distraction. Sandra forgot about my malaise and so did I. Perhaps she forgot because I did. Either way, the mood lightened.

As we continued walking we made our way into one of those wealthy old neighborhoods that are located remarkably near the parts of town with hip nightlife. The comfort and safety of a suburban neighborhood a stone's throw from the culture and excitement of the city, ideal. Plus, people that live in such neighborhoods can drink as much as they want, free of the concerns that come along with a commute to the bar.

Looking up at the houses, I was struck by the fact that this sort of neighborhood would soon be within Sandra's reach, whereas for me, it remained an unattainable fantasy. Even if my attempt to become an architect proved successful, it would be years before I had anything resembling a respectable income and many more years before I could seriously consider moving into an idyllic location such as this. Sandra was the only thing that made the world around me seem plausible.

This thought reawakened my anxiety. The angst and depression over my imminent confession reasserted its dominance over my mind. In an attempt to forestall its progress, I took Sandra by the hand and jogged off toward the beautiful homes. She asked what we were doing, and I told her that she would see. I looked back at her as we made our way between two of the houses and saw that a smile was spread across her face.

Behind the homes, we found two lavish swimming pools, their surface reflecting the moonlight. Without a word, I took off my clothes and dove into the one on our right. Sandra did the same. I was pleased to catch a glimpse of her naked body before she jumped in, her breasts looking even better in the soft light.

Sandra swam up to me and wrapped her arms around my neck. She looked good in the water. That may not seem like a big deal, but it is. Swimming often points out aesthetic deficiencies. Wet faces make fine facial hair more evident, slicked back hair reveals the true size of foreheads, physical motions separate those that are toned from those that are merely thin, and, of course, most makeup comes off in the water.

Part of me wished that the water had revealed a physical shortcoming in Sandra. The time to tell her about my indiscretion was closing in, and I preferred the idea of relaying that information to someone with a gargantuan forehead. It's easier to tell ugly truths to ugly people.

I held my arms around Sandra's toned body, and looked down into her dark-skinned, dark-eyed, and hair-free face. I pushed a wet strand of hair off her appropriately sized forehead and kissed her softly on the lips. The soft kiss turned into a passionate kiss, which turned into a carnal kiss. I grabbed her right breast hard and she put her hand between my legs. She ran her middle finger from my asshole, over my taint, and then up the seam of my scrote and the bottom of my shaft. When she made it to the head of my cock I grabbed her hand. I stopped her because I had to. I had promised myself that I would tell her before we had sex and there was little doubt that we were about to have sex—awesome, weightless, pool sex. The thought of it made my cock throb. Roughly translated, that meant my penis was telling me to put off the confession until after the awesome, weightless, pool sex. I told my penis to shut the fuck up. Sandra deserved to know and she needed to know immediately, or at least, I needed to tell her immediately.

I took a second to compose myself, and then with the confession perched on my lips, looked down into her eyes.

"Sandra," I said. "I would like you to be my girlfriend. Officially, me and you. As in you would have to introduce me as your boyfriend, and maybe meet my parents, and introduce me to your parents, and all of that business."

It was genius. I didn't know that I was going to say it until I said it, so it was unconscious genius, but it was genius nonetheless. A proactive move and a perfect solution, it addressed the problem without addressing the problem. It established that moment in the pool as the inception of our relationship and in the process excused any behavior that took place prior. If Sandra agreed to the relationship, then the fuck in the closet would become nothing more than a fuck in the closet— a poor choice, yes, but not an indiscretion. I was exploiting a loophole, but it still eased my conscious.

Sandra grinned, amused by my request.

"You're cute," she said. "And, yeah, I suppose I'll let you be my boyfriend." She winked as she delivered the last line.

At that moment I made a vow to myself. Never again would I do something that could hurt Sandra or something that could jeopardize our relationship. It's a promise that I have kept and a promise that I'll continue to keep.

After we made it official we fucked. It was awesome. The weightlessness that the water provided more than compensated for the natural lubrication that it removed.

Chapter 17

Rightness

The next three months were the best of my life. I'm not being hyperbolic. They were literally the best three months of my life. Sandra and I went to plays and sporting events and movies and a music festival. Her tastes proved to be as eclectic as mine. Few people derive the same amount of enjoyment from chili dogs in the left field bleachers as they do pinot noir before theater in the round. Sandra and I both turned out to be part of that few.

Over the course of those months, we spent time by ourselves, we spent time together, we spent time with friends, and we spent time with family. We were comfortable in every setting. Neither of us melodramatically yearned for the other when we were apart. We did, however, get shit done so that when we were able to spend time with each other our minds were not preoccupied with work. When we were together we were ourselves. Unencumbered, unfiltered, and unapologetically ourselves. When we were with friends, we were with friends. We didn't act like a couple that had been forced to spend a romantic evening in close proximity to people we knew. When we were with our families, we were with our families. We didn't sneak off in pursuit of alone time. We had conversations after dinner, played board games around the kitchen table, and watched public television in the family room.

Real love allows for solitude and for company, it doesn't demand constant and uninterrupted togetherness. Uninterrupted togetherness is a sign of infatuation and infatuation fades. It also annoys. No one would have wanted to hang out with Romeo and Juliet as they waxed on about each other's celestial qualities. In real life that sort of shit makes people want to throw up, or drown the annoying couple, or throw up while drowning the annoying couple. Had Romeo and Juliet been real, and had they survived their own stupidity, their lives would have turned out horribly. Those allegedly star-crossed lovers would have lost all of their friends and family due to their obnoxious behavior. As a result, they would have grown resentful of one another. Not resentful enough to break up but resentful enough to be discontent. In forty years' time they would have ended up bitching at each other from their respective recliners as some old person solved a mystery on the television—or the 1400s equivalent of that.

The healthy and genuine nature of the relationship between Sandra and I was apparent not only to us but to everyone around us. This was a first. In the past, I had been in a relationship that everyone disapproved of, a relationship that my family approved of but my friends disapproved of, a relationship that my friends approved of but my family disapproved of, and a relationship that my family and friends approved of but I found completely intolerable. The relationship between Sandra and I was the first time that everyone was on board. It felt good.

I think that Sandra's friends and family felt the same way. Of course they were skeptical at first. My status as an orderly didn't instill them with great confidence. Fortunately, the rightness of our relationship did. Sandra and I were good together, it was a fact that was impossible to deny. Still, I made sure that everyone knew that I was working toward a career in architecture, just in case our obvious compatibility was not enough to overcome my vocational shortcomings.

In addition to making me seem more worthy of Sandra, my architectural efforts also made me feel more worthy of Sandra. They also made me feel more worthy of life and they made life seem more worthwhile. Working on my design for the new central library gave me a sense of self-confidence and purpose that I hadn't felt since I took my final step off the mound. Although I was not actually an architect, I was working toward becoming one and that was enough.

* * *

Within ten weeks of Sandra's initial encouragement, I had finished my design for the new central library. I was proud of it. Although it wasn't good enough to win, it was good enough to compete. It showed that I had potential and potential is all that I needed.

Sandra went with me to submit my proposed design. After I handed it in, we went out for a celebratory dinner. Sandra said that she was proud of me, and I told her that I couldn't have done it without her. She tried to wave off the acknowledgment.

"No, no. I didn't do anything," she said. "You're the one that worked hard."

"True but you're the one that inspired me to do it and the one that reminded me why I should. If it weren't for you, I would have never designed that building, actually, both you and Jones. You two showed me how and why, or at least reminded me of what I used to know."

"Well, I'm glad I could help," Sandra said with a smile and a tip of her glass. "And I'm excited to meet this Jones guy. If he's in the same inspirational category as me he must be pretty awesome."

"He is," I confirmed.

"Now enough of this sentimental business," Sandra said, transitioning from a celebratory and sentimental tone to a celebratory and rowdy tone. "Let's get shit-faced."

And we did. We finished two bottles of wine at dinner and then bought another at a convenience store on our way home. A block from my townhouse we stopped at a playground and got on the swings. The combination of the youthful activity and the adult beverage resulted in optimistic contemplation and discussion of the future. It was the sort of experience you share with your close friends the summer before college. The sort of experience that I thought was a thing of the past.

The next day we slept in late. When we woke up, we went to a greasy diner and ate the sort of horrible food that tastes wonderful when you're hungover. Rejuvenated, we picked up Robert and Brad and Hayden and beer, and then went down to the waterfront. We spent the day casually drinking and dicking around. It was unsophisticated and frivolous and perfect. That night Sandra and I fucked. Afterward, she laid her head on my lap while we watched a cheesy but cute romantic comedy and slowly drifted off to sleep.

The following morning we ate cereal in bed. Halfway through the bowl, Sandra asked me what I was designing next. Her tone suggested that my continuing in architecture was a foregone conclusion. I loved that her tone suggested that.

"I have a few ideas," I replied. I was being modest. I had more than a few.

Chapter 18

Spine Semen

I was in with the infants when I got the call. They seemed unfazed by the interruption. It was as if they were indifferent to the article on sustainable design strategy that I was reading to them. Tiny jerks. It wouldn't kill them to show a little gratitude every once in a while.

The call was a good one. I was informed that my design had been chosen as a finalist for the new central library competition. My heart rate increased and my ears got warm as my mind processed the information. The rest of the call passed in a blur. I had to ask the person on the other end of the line to repeat the date, time, and location of the finalists' gala. The caller was happy to do so. I believe she was amused by my obvious surprise and excitement. It seemed novel to her. The other finalists must have been well-known architects that received the news in a calm and measured fashion. Indeed, they probably didn't even take the call themselves. Their secretaries likely wrote down the information and passed it on to them later. Fuck it, I wasn't a famous architect, I could be elated and I could let my voice reflect that emotion.

After she hung up, I stayed on the line until the screen on my phone flashed and changed to sleep mode. I wanted to make sure that I didn't accidentally hang up on her. Confident that the call had come to an end, I looked around for someone with whom I could share the good news. The babies were the first people to enter my eye line. There was no way that I was going to tell them first, not after the way they had just acted. Then I saw the old broad shouldered orderly walking beside the Italian orderly with the fake tan. The fact that I knew them only by physical appearance and not by name indicated that they were also unworthy of my good news. Next, I noticed Lauren. Despite the incident in the closet we had remained acquaintance-friends, talking for a few minutes whenever we crossed paths. My overwhelming feelings toward Sandra, along with the handful of stress-eating pounds that Lauren had gained following her recent promotion, made it easy to keep our relationship platonic. Because of our amiable, albeit brief and infrequent conversations, I considered telling Lauren my good news but after a second of deliberation decided against it. She was also an undeserving audience. Having decided that no one in my immediate vicinity was worth telling, I jogged off to find Jones and pulled Sandra's number up on my phone.

Jones offered his congratulations by slapping my back, buying me a beer, and talking in a heartfelt tone about how impressed he was with my determined effort to change the trajectory of my life. That night Sandra congratulated me in a similar fashion. The only real difference was that after Sandra conveyed her praise she put on lingerie, tied me to a bed, and then kept me on the brink of orgasm for ninety minutes. When I finally came, it felt like I was pouring out semen from a secret reserve in my spine.

Chapter 19

The Manatee in the Corner or an Opportunity to Stare

The finalists' dinner was on a Friday. I tried to get the day off from work, but my request was denied. According to the administrator that scheduled the orderlies, I was an "indispensable part of hospital operations." Clearly he had never seen me work. If he had he would have known that I was very dispensable. In fact, sometimes I actively hindered hospital operations.

At first I was annoyed by the denial of my request, it seemed unreasonable. Then I realized that it might be a blessing in disguise. If I spent the day at home, my nerves would destroy me. Anxiety would almost certainly lead me to either overeat or under eat, neither of which would be good. Overeating would result in uncomfortably tight pants, excessive ass perspiration, and gas concerns. Under eating would result in odd stomach noises, hunger-nausea (an ailment that has never made sense to me), and unreasonable grouchiness. Going to work, on the other hand, would make the day seem routine, and in turn, my digestive system would stay in working order.

As it turned out, work was the better option—for the first seven hours, anyway. During the eighth and final hour it became very clear that it was the worst option. Sandra's thoughtfulness served as the catalyst for the negative change, that and my own paranoia.

* * *

I was wheeling a fat woman down the hallway of the bariatric unit when I spotted Sandra. I caught a glimpse of her through the small rectangular windows of the department's double doors.

She was waiting in line at an information desk wearing a form-fitting, chocolate-colored dress. It was a visual that would have aroused me at any time, but one that really aroused me at that time. Having spent the previous three hours with the grotesquely obese, my standards had been lowered which meant that the sudden glimpse of my beautiful girlfriend in a sexy ensemble sent my cock skyward.

With a deft hand I quickly slid my erection into the waistband of my scrubs. I didn't want anyone to see me sporting a hard-on, and I really didn't want anyone to see me sporting a hard-on as I pushed around a half-ton woman with thinning hair and decaying teeth—the former a side effect of her gastric bypass, the latter a side effect of her massive high fructose corn syrup consumption.

My stiff cock properly hidden, I wheeled the manatee-sized woman into the nearest vacant room, abandoned her in the corner farthest from the door, and headed out toward the lobby to greet Sandra. The fat woman yelled when she realized what I was doing. Her protestations, however, were short lived as she quickly became winded and stopped; resigning herself to the corner until help arrived. With determination like that I wonder how she became so large?

I walked toward the double doors with gaiety in my stride and a grin on my face. I was touched by the fact that Sandra took off early so that she could pick me up from work. It was a markedly different reaction from the one I had when my last girlfriend acted in a similar fashion. I considered her to be desperate and needy, whereas I considered Sandra to be thoughtful and supportive. Actions are important, but they don't stand alone, they are indelibly marked by those that perform them and those that observe them.

As I pushed open the door I noticed that Robert, Brad, Hayden, and Nina were also there. Unlike Sandra, they were dressed for the bar not for a high-end dinner party. Sandra must have told everyone to come out for a good luck drink before the event, further proof of her thoughtfulness and my good fortune.

I was delighted with the presence of my friends, and after taking two or three steps into the lobby, I opened my mouth to greet them in a tone that reflected my positive feelings. The greeting, however, didn't reach their ears, indeed, it didn't even leave my mouth. It died in my throat, snuffed out by the sound of Lauren calling my name from behind the doors that I had just passed through.

* * *

Reason would suggest that the predicament I faced was not an extremely difficult one. Although the woman I loved was in my line of sight and the woman I quasi-cheated on her with was beckoning me from yards away, the potential for actual danger was relatively low. Indeed, I could have resolved the entire problem by turning around at the sound of Lauren's call, walking back to her, and asking her what she needed. Had I done so, Lauren would have stopped hailing me, and Sandra would have noticed nothing other than me talking to a coworker.

Alas, I did not resolve the situation by responding to Lauren in a routine manner. Instead, I attempted to avoid the problem by feigning deafness and hiding behind a pair of fat conjoined twins. Well, there wasn't a pair of fat conjoined twins; that would be ridiculous. There was just the one. Or two. I don't know. It's hard to explain. There were not four total people; there was just two, the pair of conjoined twins. Is that right? Fuck it. Either way I couldn't have chosen a more inconspicuous hiding place.

Anne Frank would be jealous, I thought to myself, as I peeked out over the connected part of their portly bellies. *Too soon?* I wondered, as I slid toward the nearest closet in an attempt to get away from the worst hiding spot ever. *Probably*, I concluded as I eased the door closed, *but still funny*.

Once I was safely hidden, I took a second to appreciate the fact that I had just taken refuge behind fat conjoined twins. Having properly acknowledged that unique moment in human history, I turned my attention toward the events unfolding in front of me. From the safe confines of the closet, I peered out into the lobby; a spectator, divorced from yet tied to all that was taking place.

Oddly enough, the first thing I observed was neither Sandra nor Lauren nor my friends, but rather the crowd of people that was slowly filtering into the rows of collapsible chairs that had been set up facing the far wall of the lobby. A First Friday performance I concluded, fortunate.

On the first Friday of every month a small show is put on in the lobby of the hospital. It began as an attempt to raise spirits and build community, and by all accounts, it has succeeded in this aim. Unfortunately, it has also succeeded in annoying the shit out of me. The hospital masses might adore the performances, but I typically find them to be mindless drivel unworthy of attention. Not this time, however, this time I was pleased to see that a show was taking place. It would draw a large crowd to the lobby and focus attention in one direction, both realities that would help me to avoid detection.

Comforted by the additional cover that the performance provided, I opened the closet door a little wider in an attempt to locate Sandra. I caught sight of her as she turned away from the information desk and toward our friends. I wanted to watch her ass as she walked over to them, but refrained. I needed to locate Lauren, provide myself with visual confirmation of her whereabouts to ensure that she was nowhere near Sandra.

I was concerned that if Lauren and Sandra came close to one another they might talk, and if they talked they might talk about me, and if they talked about me they might talk about sleeping with me, and if they did that then things might turn ugly. Perhaps it was an irrational concern but it was a concern nonetheless.

I spotted Lauren standing in front of the double doors to the bariatric unit. Her head slowly moving from left to right, scanning the lobby. I assumed that she was searching for me, and for a terrifying moment, when her gaze seemed to linger on the closet in which I hid, I thought that she had succeeded. Fortunately, my concern was short lived. Lauren's eyes didn't remain fixed on my hiding spot, but instead continued with their survey of the room. The nearly imperceptible break in her visual scan, I decided, a figment of my imagination.

Having averted detection by Lauren, I returned focus to my other concern. Sandra was standing around talking to our friends. She wasn't, as I had expected, heading out of the lobby in search of me. The information desk employee must have agreed to track me down for her, a generous act that was likely inspired by Sandra's generous cleavage.

The continued presence of both Sandra and Lauren in the same room increased my anxiety to unprecedented levels. I had hoped that one of them would depart quickly, but now it looked as though both would remain indefinitely. Sandra would wait until the guy from the information desk found me, an event that seemed unlikely, and Lauren looked as though she would continue her search until it proved successful. Indeed, when I shifted my attention back to Lauren I found that the intensity of her hunting had increased. She was still scanning the room, but was now employing a roving method, slowly walking around the lobby as she searched. Her determination made it seem as though my sudden disappearance had served as an affront to her senses and that the only way to restore order to her universe was to establish my whereabouts.

The next few minutes passed with my attention constantly shifting between Sandra and Lauren. I fell into a rotation in which I would watch Lauren for twenty seconds, and then steal a glance at Sandra, then return my attention to Lauren for another twenty. I wanted to spend more time looking at Sandra but I couldn't. Lauren was the bigger threat.

The system proved effective and the rhythmic nature of it began to alleviate some of my unease. My heart rate had almost returned to normal when something began to encroach sideways into my line of sight. Taken aback, I almost yelped at the appearance of the massive entity. Stifling the exclamation, I moved deeper into the closet as the unidentified being continued to slide in front of the opening in the door. I use the word "slide" liberally, the movement was actually more akin to the scuttling of an injured crustacean or to be more precise, the ungainly shuffle of morbidly obese conjoined twins. The latter description is the most accurate because the unidentified entity was, in fact, the morbidly obese conjoined twins.

Having identified the mystery being, I took a second to consider how the least stealthy people in the world had managed to surreptitiously appear a mere foot from my face. There was no explanation. It was astounding.

After the awe I felt over the furtiveness of the conjoined twins wore off, my anxiety returned. Once again, the need to locate both Sandra and Lauren became paramount. I moved back to the front of the closet and commenced efforts to reestablish visual contact. I stood on my tiptoes and got down on my knees, but it was to no avail, I couldn't see beyond the twins. They were the human equivalent of blackout curtains and they weren't moving.

I was about to give up and move back to the deeper, more comfortable, recesses of the closet when a hand wrapped itself around the door and began to inch it open. It was the twins, or perhaps it was just one of the twins. No, it couldn't be just one of the twins . . . could it? Can a conjoined twin act alone? No. Maybe. I don't know. Either way, they (I'm sticking with the plural) were easing the door open, and as they were doing so my asshole was getting tighter and my eyes wider, a useless involuntary reaction to my impending discovery.

With my last couple of seconds I frantically scanned the closet for a hiding spot. There was none. I was going to be revealed. The fat conjoined twins were going to ruin my life. They were going to expose me to the lobby and everyone in it. Sandra and Lauren and my friends were going to spot me, converge on me, ask me questions, hard questions, questions like, "Why were you hiding in a closet?" Answers that hid the truth would not come easy. No, it dawned on me, they would not come at all. Sandra was going to find out.

Resigned to my fate, I put on a smile, straightened out my shirt, and stood up tall. If I had to greet disaster I wanted to do it with dignity. And I would have done it with dignity, if I had needed to, but as it turned out, I didn't.

A second before I came into view, the door stopped moving. It stayed there. Immobile, stationary, left alone a third of the way open. It was as if the twins had changed their mind (minds?). As if they had decided against opening the closet. No, that wasn't it. If they had changed their mind the door would have closed again and it didn't. It remained motionless and there was no indication that its position would be altered. It seemed as though the twins had always intended to open it partway, to make it slightly more ajar.

The motivation behind this action was unclear. What was clear, however, is that I was fortunate. I remained hidden and the new positioning of the door allowed me to see out. I had to get down on my hands and knees to do so, but still.

After adopting the requisite four-legged stance, I quickly regained sight of Lauren. She was still roving the lobby, headed slowly in my direction. Her meandering pace indicated that she was still unaware of my location. I was still safe.

Having acquired Lauren's whereabouts, I turned my attention toward Sandra. I had to shuffle around on all fours to regain sight of her. I didn't move too quickly. It hurt my knees when I moved fast, and the situation didn't seem to warrant pain-inducing urgency. Lauren was the urgent threat and she had been located. Sandra's whereabouts were less of a concern. She wasn't searching for me, she was waiting for me, and she had people to communicate with while she waited. I was confident that when I spotted her, she would still be standing around talking to our friends. My confidence was ill founded.

Sandra had turned away from the group and was walking toward the information desk when I regained sight of her. She had a slightly annoyed look on her face, a what-the-hell-is-taking-so-long look, but not a what-the-fuck-is-taking-so-long look. It was an expression that I found troublesome.

Sandra has no patience for ineptitude. If she thought that the guy at the information desk was failing to perform the simple task for which he had volunteered, she would let him know. Although the expression of her displeasure would not be extremely loud it would be firm, and as a result, it would grab people's attention. I didn't want my absence brought to people's attention. I needed to stop her.

My brain was frantically searching for a way to prevent Sandra from reaching the information desk when a line of sick children, headed to the First Friday show, made her change course. Her new route, I quickly realized, was going to take her right by the closet in which I hid. It was also going to bring her into contact with Lauren. I couldn't be sure, because one of the twin's four ass cheeks was obscuring my view, but it looked like their paths were going to cross immediately in front of me. Well, immediately in front of the fat conjoined twins, who were immediately in front of the closet door, which was immediately in front of me.

"Fucking shit," I said to myself.

As I muttered the word "shit" a fart was expelled from somewhere amongst the myriad of butt cheeks in front of my face. Having done what they came to do, the twins closed the closet door.

* * *

I assessed the situation and decided that things were not going well for me. The aim of my evasive maneuvers was to prevent Sandra and Lauren from coming into contact with one another, and as I knelt on all fours, in a dark supply closet, breathing in the gas expelled from the anus (ani?) of conjoined twins, it became clear that I was going to fail to achieve said aim. Sandra and Lauren were about to cross paths a mere three or four yards from where I hid. Nothing but a closet door, and fat twins joined at the belly, separated me from the impending disaster. All of my efforts to avoid detection would soon be exposed as futile.

Of course, statistically speaking, there was a good chance that Sandra and Lauren would walk by one another without a word. Indeed, that was the probable outcome. Nevertheless, it was clear to me that they were going to interact. I knew it in the pit of my stomach. My stomach was right.

"Are you okay?" I heard Lauren ask, the sound of her voice muffled by the closet door and the labored breathing of four fat, Siamese lungs. In response to her voice I knelt down further, placing my ear near the crack at the bottom of the door. I was hoping to hear an unfamiliar voice respond to her query, but my hope was in vain.

"Huh? Oh, yes," Sandra replied, slightly surprised by the expression of interest and concern from a stranger. "Just a little annoyed. The guy at the information desk said that he was going to get someone for me and it has been fifteen minutes or so, and I haven't heard anything."

"Well, maybe I can help you," Lauren offered with her standard amount of sprightliness.

"It's kind of you to offer Doctor, but I'm sure you have more important things to do. I can get this sorted out," Sandra said. She was right. It was kind of Lauren to offer. She was abandoning her own search to help a random stranger with a frustrated look on her face. She was displaying ridiculous kindness, unparalleled generosity. I wanted to punch her in the face.

"No, really, it's not a problem," Lauren warmly insisted. "Who are you looking for? Maybe I know where they're at."

Jesus Fucking Christ, they had talked for less than thirty seconds and my name was already on the tip of their tongues. My future with Sandra was over. I was about to hear its death. Then, suddenly, I grabbed the doorknob of the closet, opened it swiftly into the asses of the conjoined twins, and then closed it again. It was not an unconscious action, but it was so impulsive that it might as well have been. It was also brilliant.

From behind the closed door I heard the odd sounds of morbidly obese conjoined twins tumbling over. It was unlike anything I had ever heard before. Lauren responded instantly.

"Oh my goodness, are y'all alright?" Her immediate use of the plural contraction indicated that she would never dream of referring to the conjoined fatties as one entity.

"Erghhh," one of them replied.

"Ughhh," the other interrupted.

Genius struck me again as the twins attempted to drown out each other's moans of pain. Acting on inspiration I scanned the supply closet once more, found a surgeon's cap and mask, and put them on. As soon as I heard Sandra say, "I'll go get someone." I eased the door open, covertly slid out, and walked away. No one noticed. All eyes were on the twins. I knew they would be. Everyone wanted to gape at them, but for fear of being rude, no one ever did. Now that they were writhing and wailing on the ground, it was okay to stare so stare people did. I even watched over my shoulder as I walked away. It was an amazing sight.

* * *

Sandra was successful in her search for assistance. She came back with two orderlies and a nurse. Lauren directed the reinforcements. She informed them of what had happened, instructed them on how to help the twins to their feet, and then advised

147

them on how to assist the twins into the nearest vacant room. It was quite impressive. Lauren seemed like an expert on the matter. I use the word seemed because no one is actually an expert at moving fat conjoined twins, not even fat conjoined twins. In fact Lauren appeared to know more than they did. From my new hiding spot, I could see one of their faces and it looked like he was taking mental notes as she talked.

Lauren ended up escorting the twins all the way into the room. As soon as she was out of sight, I took off the surgical mask and cap and walked casually over to Sandra and the rest of my friends.

"There you are!" Sandra said, as she caught sight of me approaching.

I smiled brightly and waved. Before I could offer any verbal greetings, Brad interjected. "Holy shit, man, you just missed the craziest thing ever."

I responded without pause. "Really? What happened?"

Chapter 20

Avoiding Arrogance, Acknowledging Achievements

Brad talked about the fat conjoined twins all the way to the bar. He is a raconteur so it was entertaining. After two glasses of wine Sandra and I headed off to the gala. Her idea to get drinks with friends was a good one. It suppressed my nerves, or rather, it kept them suppressed. The incident with the twins had served as the initial suppressing force. It's hard to be concerned about an impending formal dinner when grotesquely obese conjoined twins are hindering your efforts to spy on a conversation that could potentially ruin your life.

Unfortunately, even with the positive effects of our pre-dinner drinks, I was still overawed when I walked into the gala. It was a lavish affair. Lavish enough to make me realize that up until this moment, I had never been to a truly lavish affair. Counted among the attendees were numerous influential politicians, important business executives, and a handful of architects whose work I had studied in school. It was clear to me that I didn't belong.

Sandra noticed the expression on my face and offered some encouragement.

"Relax," she said. "Don't let the tuxedos and ice sculptures and people serving foie gras intimidate you. You belong here. In fact, you belong here more than anybody else, save, maybe, the other finalists. All of this pomp is nothing more than positive feedback from powerful people. They liked what you did and this is the way that they know how to show it."

I didn't know if I believed everything that Sandra said, but I knew that she did, and that was enough. Sandra's consistently candid demeanor gives weight to her words, and as a result, when she provides assurance you feel assured. I took a deep breath, thanked Sandra for the vote of confidence, and then kissed her on the cheek.

"No need to thank me," she said. "I'm just telling you the truth."

"Maybe, but it's still nice to hear," I said. As I replied, I took her hand in mine. With our fingers interlocked, I looked around the room once more. It was different, or at least it felt different. Although I remained slightly uncomfortable, I no longer felt like an impostor.

As the night rolled on, numerous people came up to congratulate me. Sandra consistently reinforced their expressions of approval. Usually she did this by giving me a look of proud affection as I accepted their praise. If, however, I tried to wave off someone's approval she adopted a more direct approach, which is to say, she called bullshit. Bullshit on my refusal to accept credit when credit was due.

At one point she said, "If you do something worthwhile be proud of it. Be appreciative, but be proud. Arrogant assholes are obnoxious, but so are people that refuse to acknowledge their own achievements."

Her point was well taken, and after an hour of receiving compliments, I found the middle ground that she suggested I adopt—happily accepting people's praise without acting as though I was entitled to it.

It's odd how long it took me to get that down. It should have been easy, the sentiment I sought to express was the sentiment that I truly felt, and nevertheless, it proved elusive. On one occasion I came across as cocky, on another falsely modest, and, three or four times, as though I were completely unworthy of commendation. Fortunately, the most important conversation of the night didn't come until after I found my stride.

* * *

When Soren Holm came up and complimented me, I gracefully accepted his praise. Of course, when I delivered my composed response, I didn't know that I was talking to one of the most famous architects in the world. Thank God he didn't introduce himself right away. If I had known with whom I was talking, I would have fucked it up. I would have come across as either arrogant or insecure or both—that may seem impossible but I would have found a way. As it was, I made an excellent first impression, the success of which kept me feeling comfortable even after I learned to whom I was talking. By the end of our conversation, Soren had offered me a job. It wasn't an extremely high-ranking job, but it wasn't an entry-level job either. It was a job I would have thought impossible a few months prior. I accepted the position in a composed fashion. I maintained that composure as Soren elaborated on the position and the projects that I would be working on. I forewent all composure the second that he bid us adieu. Sandra joined in with me. We clasped hands and squealed through unsuppressed grins. The people around us probably thought that I had been named head cheerleader. Fuck it. I didn't care. I was happy, and Sandra was happy for me.

On the way out of the gala, we stopped by the room that displayed the top five entries. I had avoided it on the way in, afraid that I would find my design laughably inferior to the others. But now, on the way out, having been accompanied all night by a beautiful and smart woman that believed in me, having been congratulated dozens of times by successful people, and having been offered a job by a world-class architect, I found the confidence to look. The confidence to walk into a room where my work sat alongside designs that had been created by some of the best.

As I led us into the room, Sandra said, "Holy shit. How did we miss this? We should have come here right away."

"Yeah," I replied. I didn't tell her that I saw it on the way in. I didn't want her to know about my cowardice. Obviously, Sandra knew that prior to dating her I had been a bit of a defeatist, that I had been afraid to try and afraid to fail, that I had dwelled in the morass of compliance rather than proactively seeking solutions. But I had changed, or at least, I was changing, and I wanted her to see that, so I pretended that I had also overlooked the room.

Sandra and I looked at the designs for a few minutes. We didn't talk we just looked. I was happy with what I saw. My design was not the best, but it wasn't the worst. I would have ranked it third, better than the collegiate gothic design and the I.M. Pei derivative, worse than the new neoclassical design, and definitely worse than Soren's sustainable neomodern master-piece.

Sandra ended our quiet assessment of the various designs with an upbeat comment. "Wow, awesome babe, you should be so proud."

The unadulterated positivity in her voice gave me pause. I thought, for a second, that she was going to tell me that my design was the best. I would have been disappointed if she had because it would have been a lie. A lie that would have made me question her blunt honesty, which is an attribute of hers that I adore. Fortunately, Sandra didn't tell me that mine was the best.

"Your design is on par with almost all of these," she said. "I would rank it third, maybe tied for second. I mean that's amazing, these are solid entries from great architects. Not to mention the fact that you are just starting out or the fact that you just recently stopped being a lazy asshole."

"Thanks beautiful," I said, with a flattered smile, accepting the compliment but not acting as though I were entitled to it. It was a response that came naturally.

Sandra looked up at me, raised herself onto her tiptoes, and kissed me. It was a quick and simple kiss that showed both love and contentment. We walked out of the gala hand in hand.

Chapter 21

Fat Synonyms

Corpulent is an odd word. Before I worked at the hospital, I always considered it an unnecessary and pompous adjective. As far as I could tell it served only one purpose, namely, to assist pedantic assholes in their never ending search for words that make the person that they are talking to feel like an ignorant douche. After I started working at the hospital, however, I realized that corpulent is, in fact, a useful word. This realization struck me the first time that I stepped foot in the bariatric unit. When you are in a bariatric unit, "fat" and "obese" just don't cut it. Sometimes you need another word, and sometimes you are in a situation in which that other word cannot be derogatory slang. In such cases, corpulent proves quite useful. I have typically used it to describe the impeccably dressed or well-coiffed fatties. The ones who think that by being impeccably dressed or well coiffed, people will somehow overlook the fact that they weigh as much as a baby whale. That's not an exaggeration. A newborn killer whale tips the scales at roughly four hundred and so do most of the gastric bypass patients. Nevertheless, physicians and hospital administrators don't like when low-level employees vocalize such realities. They prefer that large marine mammal compar-isons be kept to a minimum. As such, words like corpulent come in handy. Let me amend that statement. Words like corpulent used to come in handy. Thankfully, that is no longer the case.

Ever since I handed the hospital my two-week notice I started calling a spade a spade. The days of referring to a patient as "that corpulent woman giving me difficulties," are over. Now, if some baby-whale-sized bitch is acting like an impudent cunt I say, "Listen baby whale bitch, stop acting like an impudent cunt." This new approach has greatly increased my job satisfaction;

however, I do question its long-term tenability. Occasionally, I get the impression that if I was not quitting my behavior might become an issue. Alas, we will never know for certain as tomorrow is my last day.

* * *

I spent my final day as an orderly splitting time between the maternity ward and the bariatric unit. It seemed appropriate, a delightful end to a delightful job. One might think that since it was my last day I found these places more bearable. Such a person would, however, be mistaken. My level of despise remained unaltered. Babies and fatties frustrated and annoyed me in the same way that they always had.

At one point, I daydreamed about starving the bariatric patients. It was pretty hilarious—morbid, but hilarious. Think about it, when asked for a cause of death the pathologist would have to look down at the grotesquely obese corpse and say, "starvation." There's no way he could keep a straight face.

Of course, I don't actually want the baby-whale-sized humans to die. For that matter, I don't want the baby-human-sized humans to die either. All I really want is to not have to deal with them. Thankfully, as an employed architect, I won't have to. Throughout my last day, I frequently reminded myself of this actuality. It proved effective in buoying my spirits. The babies and the fatties might have annoyed me in the same way that they always had but the impact of that annoyance was different. I felt less stifled by it, less imposed upon.

Thanks to the new job, I now had a way out, a clear solution, and, more important, I now had knowledge of the fact that solutions can be sought, that action can be taken. That may not seem like a groundbreaking insight, but it is, or at least it is to me. It's something that I knew but something that I had forgotten. It's something that Sandra reminded me of, and it's something that made the future look brighter.

At lunch I shared my insight with Jones. I felt like it was something that he may have forgotten or, perhaps, something that he never knew. Although Jones is a smart guy, it seemed possible that this particular insight could have eluded him. He grew up poor, and sometimes, such circumstances make it difficult to see the value of seeking solutions.

As it turned out, my first inclination was correct, it was something that he had known but forgotten . . . kind of.

"I guess that I didn't really forget," Jones said, in between bites of his sandwich. "It's more like I gave up on the idea. You see, back when I was younger I tried to take action, to change things, to make things better for myself, and when I did, I failed. Actually, I failed a bunch of times. I failed at being a musician and I failed when I tried to start my own restaurant and I failed at a few other things and eventually I got negative. I stopped trying to fix and I started excusing and justifying." Jones shook his head as though he was ashamed of the memory. I was about to offer some words of comfort when his expression suddenly brightened, and he spoke up again. "But then you came along and changed that."

"Really!" I said, flattered by the thought that I had motivated Jones. "You felt inspired by the work I put into designing the library?"

"No, boy," he said, through a grin. "You inspired me well before that."

"Yeah?" A confused look made its way onto my face.

"Yeah," Jones replied, still grinning. "The first time that we had a beer together, the first night we really met, I suppose that's when you started to inspire me. When you started to revive my belief in taking action."

". . ." My confused face replied.

"Yeah, you see, that night I realized that you were a smart guy, that you could be doing something, and right away I said to myself, I said, 'What the hell is that boy doing working as an orderly?' I was so confused. I couldn't figure it out. I couldn't understand why someone who could be doing something substantial was working such a crap job, and I'll tell you something, it bothered me. It bothered me for a week until eventually I thought about things a little differently. I thought, 'Wait. That boy's no different than me. We're both smart, we're both able. So when I sit and wonder why he's working as an orderly, I'm really wondering why I'm working as an orderly?' I mean I knew why I started, but I didn't know why I was still doing it. Sure, I had told myself the same bullshit that I told you. That by the time I finished helping my sisters out it was too late to leave the job, that my benefits were too good and I was too old to change careers, but deep down I knew that was some bullshit. The truth is that I was working as an orderly because I wasn't trying to do anything else, because it was easier to use my smarts to justify my inaction rather than use them to take action, and when I saw you doing the same thing, it made me stop and think, and all that thinking made realize that I was acting like a fool. You see, I saw you pissing away your talent and it made me realize that I wanted to stop pissing away mine. That's how you inspired me."

"Oh," I replied. My tone didn't imply anything, it couldn't have. In order to imply something I would have had to know how I felt about what Jones had just said and I had no idea how I felt.

"Listen, friend," Jones responded. "I'm not trying to be a son of a bitch, I'm just telling you the truth."

"No, I know. Actually, you know what?"

"What's that?"

"I appreciate it," I said. It was the truth. I did appreciate it. "It makes me feel better about where I'm at and where I'm going and it makes me realize that there is some sort of inherent worth in taking action."

"Right you are, son. And you're on track now. You got back on track way quicker than I did."

"Thanks, Jones," I paused for a second to let him know I meant it. "Alright, so what are you doing? What problem are you seeking a solution for? Are you trying to get out of here, pursue a new career?"

"Sure am, friend," Jones replied. He spent the next fifteen minutes telling me about how he was going back to school and getting back into music. He was excited, and I was excited for him.

* * *

After lunch I went to the nursery and read to the infants. It was my final performance so I decided to mix things up.

"You have brains in your head," I said to the babies, or rather, I read to the babies. Dr. Seuss is the one that said it. I just read what Seuss said. Actually I read what he wrote, although I'm sure that at some point he said it, but that's beside the point.

"You have brains in your head," I read aloud. "You have feet in your shoes. You can steer yourself any direction you choose. You're on your own. And you know what you know. And you are the one who'll decide where to go."

Lauren came into the room as I read. I think she listened to me for a while, but I can't say for sure because I didn't pay her much attention. I might not have noticed her at all if it weren't for her breasts. They looked even larger than normal. They demanded the attention of everyone in the room. She must have bought one of those super-lift bras, the ones that make small-breasted women look curvaceous and make large-breasted women look like they'll have back problems in their thirties. Anyway, I was thankful that by the time I finished the book she was gone.

When I left the nursery, I noticed Jones setting up chairs for a First Friday performance. It seemed odd considering it wasn't the

first Friday of the month. When I asked him about the irregu-
larity, he informed me that the hospital administration had
decided to start putting them on twice a month, providing me
with yet another reason to be happy about leaving.

Fueled by the knowledge that I would never have to set up for
a First Friday again, I diligently assisted Jones. By the time we
finished, it was nearly time to go. By the time we walked to the
locker room, changed, and drank the half-pint of whiskey that
Jones had brought to congratulate me, it was time to go.

A sense of relief and excitement washed over me as I walked
toward the hospital exit for the last time. These feelings gave way
to unfiltered delight when I caught sight of Sandra heading into
the hospital with a cumbersome present in her hands.

I could tell that the package that she was carrying would
prevent her from using the revolving door and that it would
make it difficult for her to press the handicap button. As such, I
started to jog forward so that I could open the door for her. I
slowed when I noticed that a kind person was already doing so.
I slowed even more when I noticed that the kind person holding
the door had huge tits. I stopped when it became clear that the
kind person with the huge tits was Lauren.

Chapter 22

Learn from Your Mistakes

Having learned from the conjoined twins incident, I paused for a second to collect myself. I had no desire to repeat my previous mistake. If you end up crouched in a supply closet inhaling the farts of fat Siamese twins once, shame on them. If you end up crouched in a supply closet inhaling the farts of fat Siamese twins twice, shame on you.

As I organized my thoughts, Sandra successfully maneuvered into the building. She rested the awkwardly shaped package on the ground and then expressed her appreciation for the assistance with the door. Lauren waved off the words of thanks or, at least, she appeared to. I can't say for sure as I was not within earshot.

After exchanging pleasantries, it looked, for one glorious second, like Lauren and Sandra were going to head off in different directions, like their meeting was going to be a non-event, like all my worries were for naught. But then, right as Lauren started to step away, comprehension dawned on her face. She paused, pointed at Sandra, and began to talk.

"I was talking to you just the other day, wasn't I? When the conjoined twins had their accident," is what I suspect Lauren said.

Based off the similar dawning of comprehension that spread across Sandra's face, my suspicion was correct. Having identified a shared experience, my one-time fuck and my once-in-a-lifetime love began to talk.

"Shit," I thought. "I hope they don't talk about any other shared experiences."

"Shit? Shit what?" Jones said, confused.

My inner monologue must have gotten away from me. The

expletive that had crossed my mind had, evidently, also crossed my lips. As a result, Jones was now aware of the fact that something was wrong. I decided to be straightforward with him.

"It's bad that they're talking to one another," I said, while offering up a significant look and a head nod in the direction of Sandra and Lauren.

"Oh," Jones said. "I see."

I nodded my head in reply. Jones needed no additional information, a testament to his intuitive nature and his dependable friendship.

"Well, watching them isn't gonna help any. Let's go." He said and headed off in their direction. I followed without hesitation.

As we made our way toward Sandra and Lauren, my anxiety level decreased, a response that both surprised and pleased me. Perhaps it was a positive reaction to taking action. I was terrified by the thought of talking to Lauren and Sandra at the same time, but I was slightly more terrified by the thought of impotently watching as they talked to each other.

Once we were within a reasonable distance I said, "Hey, babe!" There was excitement in my tone. It sounded a little forced, but I don't think Sandra noticed; she didn't have time to. The false ring of my greeting was only in the air for a moment before I dispersed it with a kiss to her cheek and an introduction to Jones.

"And I see that you already met Dr. Campbell," I added, as the handshake between Sandra and Jones came to an end. I intentionally used Lauren's formal title. It seemed an efficient way to prevent Sandra from asking questions regarding the nature of the relationship between Lauren and I. Lauren seemed slightly taken aback by the formal introduction, but she let it pass without question. Sandra noticed nothing.

"Yeah, actually Dr. Campbell and I met once before," Sandra said. "Very briefly, right before the conjoined twins incident that I told you about."

"Really," I replied. "Small world." It seemed an appropriately generic response to Sandra's anecdotal aside.

"Yeah . . ." Sandra said, allowing the conversation to fizzle out lamely.

After an awkward two-second pause, Lauren spoke up, "Well, I'd better go. I have to prepare for this performance," she nodded toward the stage that Jones and I had just set up. "But it was very nice to meet you again, Sandra, and congrats on the new job," she said while delivering an attaboy pat to my arm. "And I'll see you on Monday," she finished, pointing an affable finger at Jones. And that was it. Lauren was gone.

That was it? I thought. *That was painless. Why the hell did I hide in a freak show's fart closet to avoid that?*

My fears put to rest, I suggested that Sandra, Jones, and I take the present and head over to one of the tables in the corner of the lobby. On the way I took a slow and deep breath. As I exhaled I felt the tensions and anxieties that had burdened me for months depart my body.

* * *

Jones left a few minutes after we sat down, he had a night class to attend. He shook my hand on his way out and said, "Don't be a stranger." A simple and classy good-bye, exactly what I had expected.

After Jones left, Sandra told me to open the present. Inside the cumbersome box was a portable drafting table, a digital distance measuring tool, a Lego model of Burj Khalifa, and a page torn out of a high-end lingerie catalog. Sandra informed me that although I would not be getting the lingerie model I would be getting her, in the lingerie, later that night. All together the present managed the nearly impossible feat of being thoughtful, useful, quirky, inspiring, and exciting. Exactly what I would have expected had I been expecting anything.

Sandra and I sat and talked for a while. I'm not sure why we didn't go somewhere else, it's not like I wanted to drag out my last few minutes at the hospital. I suppose that we stayed because there was no reason to move. That urgent, get-the-fuck-out feeling that normally accompanied the end of my workday was not present, and I was no longer anxious about Sandra and Lauren running into one another. Consequently, I didn't feel the need to move our conversation elsewhere, which meant that we talked unimpeded for a half hour.

Our discussion came to an end when Sandra said, "I have to go pee."

As she updated me on the status of her bladder she stood up. Once on her feet, she inquired as to the whereabouts of the nearest restroom, and after I pointed her in the right direction, she said, "When I get back we should go celebrate, grab a drink somewhere."

"Sounds perfect," I said. It did.

I looked around the room while I waited for Sandra. The seats that Jones and I had set up were almost full. I watched as an old man with a wrinkly neck eased his way into one of the few remaining spots. Jesus Christ, his neck was disgusting, the skin below his Adam's apple looked like the vulva of a retired porn star. I couldn't look away. Fortunately, once the old man settled into the chair it became impossible for me to see his floppy-vulva-neck, which allowed me to move my attention elsewhere. Eventually, my eyes made their way to the entrance through which Sandra had made her way earlier that afternoon. When I looked through the glass doors, I caught sight of Lauren. She was far away, but I could tell that it was her, there was no mistaking those tits.

It seemed a little weird to me, Lauren standing there outside. Earlier, when she said good-bye to us, she made it seem as though she was pressed for time, like she needed the next few minutes to prepare for her performance. Evidently, that was bullshit. Thirty minutes later there she was, standing outside, gazing contemplatively into the distance.

That big-breasted liar, I thought as I looked at her staring off toward the late-afternoon sun. Then it occurred to me that I should probably reserve judgment in regard to the telling of falsehoods. Then I decided that Lauren probably had a good reason for excusing herself from our presence.

As I reached this conclusion, Lauren broke from her thoughtful gaze and made her way into the building. She proceeded from the bright sunlit outdoors into the poorly lit foyer and then toward the makeshift performance venue that Jones and I had created in the corner of the lobby. In the time that had passed since Jones and I finished, heavy curtains had been erected between the glass hospital entrance and the performance area. As a result, the chairs and the stage lay in near darkness.

The set-up seemed a little too fancy. What were they going to do, put a spotlight on the performers? Did they hire a fucking light technician? What a waste. The patients would have been happy with a high school a cappella group, they didn't need some extravagant show.

I started thinking about all of the better ways that the hospital could have spent its money but stopped when I saw that Lauren was headed for the rear of the performance area rather than the stage.

Performers typically stand on stage and Lauren was supposed to be performing, so it was odd to see her headed away from the destination that I expected her to be headed toward. For a second, I thought that she was shirking her responsibilities, and that she was trying to get out of the performance, a move that would have been contrary to her character, a move that had me confused. Then, she clicked on the projector and everything became clear.

A beam of light shot out of the lens, across the dark performance area, and onto the wall above the stage. The attention of the audience shifted toward the bright rectangle, and once everyone's eyes were fixed on the far wall, Lauren began. She used her hands and the light from the projector to create shadowed images on the wall. I say shadowed images rather than shadow puppets because the latter is not a just description. They were more than puppets. They were captivating and haunting, and although they portrayed a simple approximation of reality, they were somehow more enthralling than reality. People that were standing behind Lauren and the projector inched forward to remove the creator of the images from their line of sight. They wanted to immerse themselves in the world that she had devised. Although I understood why those people moved forward, I refrained from doing so myself. I preferred to see the shadows and their point of origin.

A few minutes into the performance, Sandra tapped me on the shoulder. "Ready to go?" she said in a half whisper.

"Yeah," I said, part of my attention still on the shadows. "Did you see this, it's pretty impressive."

"Uh-huh," Sandra replied, a tone of indifference in her voice.

I was a little surprised by her lack of interest. My face said as much.

"I mean they're amazing shadow puppets," she said, in response to the look that I had given her. "But I mean come on, they're shadow puppets."

"True," I replied.

We quietly gathered our things and headed toward the exit.

Sandra was right of course. They were just shadow puppets. Still, there was something more to them, not in regard to the shadows themselves but in regard to the effect that the shadows had on others. I don't know what it was, but it was enticing.

As we walked out of the hospital, I thought about taking the time to learn how to make the shadow images. My contemplation of the matter didn't last too long. I quickly concluded that although the shadow images were impressive, it would be a huge waste of time. I mean what's the point? Why the fuck would I spend hours mastering a useless skill? So I could perform for sick people and other audiences in need of charitable entertainment? Pass.

"So, what took you so long?" I asked Sandra, as we made our way toward her car. "You were pooping, weren't you? You said you had to pee when, in reality, you had to BM like a mad woman."

"Obviously," she replied. "It doesn't take me ten minutes to pee. The only reason that I told you that I had to go number one was because I was trying to maintain my allure. I didn't want you to be thinking about me pooping while I'm seducing you in my sexy new lingerie."

"A thoughtful choice," I replied. "A thoughtful choice that I have now spoiled."

"Eh, what can you do," she said, with a grin.

When we got to her car, Sandra took the large box of gifts out of my hands, set it on the top of her trunk, and then took me by the hands. Looking up into my eyes she said, "I'm really proud of you," and then kissed me affectionately on the lips.

It felt nice to hear her say those words. She had said them before, but they had never meant as much to me as they did at that moment. I lifted her off the ground with a hug and kissed her indiscriminately all over her face. It was silly but I think that it demonstrated what her support meant to me. When I set her back on the ground, I noticed that she was blushing. Ninth-grade-I-just-got-asked-to-homecoming-by-my-crush blushing. Unfiltered and irrepressible, it was the type of emotional display that adults learn to hide out of fear that it will scare their partner off. Sandra didn't try and hide it. I lifted her off the ground and kissed her again.

After we got into the car and situated ourselves, Sandra looked over her shoulder in order to reverse. The car had moved less than a yard when she stopped.

"Something wrong?" I asked.

"Yeah, dummy. Don't you have to turn in your ID and keycard?" She playfully flipped the lanyard that carried the cards up into my face.

"Oh, yeah." I replied sprightly. It was an inconvenience, but it didn't bother me. I felt too good to feel bothered. I hopped out of the car and jogged off toward the hospital. I entered through the glass revolving door and then made my way through the crowd that was filing out of the makeshift performance area. I smiled kindly at the woman that took my ID and keycard and then made small talk with her as I filled out the departure paperwork. All together, it took less than five minutes. With the last remnants of my time at the hospital gone, I made my way back across the lobby. As I pushed on the revolving door, I noticed that Sandra had pulled the car up. Once I was outside, I jogged off happily toward her. My hand was on the car handle when I heard someone call out my name. I looked over my shoulder and saw that it was Lauren, her gargantuan breasts bouncing comically as she made her way toward me. I considered ignoring her but thought better of it. That might cause unnecessary problems. Knowing her kindly nature, I decided that she probably just wanted to offer another good-bye. Having been preoccupied by her impending performance, her last farewell had lacked her characteristic enthusiasm. I decided to walk a few steps toward her to expedite the process.

"Hey," she said, slightly out of breath.

I responded in kind.

"So," Lauren continued, a serious but hopeful tone in her voice. "There is something I've been meaning to tell you."

"Oh, yeah?" I said. *No way,* I thought. *She doesn't want to say a better good-bye, she wants to confess her feelings for me.* I had no desire to be with Lauren, but the idea that she wanted me was flattering. As she looked down at the ground and attempted to build up the courage to share her feelings, I searched for the right words to let her down easy. I found the words fairly quickly and began to speak in the hopes that I could help her save face. Let her know that I wasn't interested before she told me that she was. I had no desire to humiliate such a kind person.

"Listen," I said, "you're a wonderful person and you're gorgeous but—"

"I'm pregnant," Lauren interjected.

Part II

Chapter 23

Anal Health

The first time I got hemorrhoids was my freshman year in college. I had been the youngest player to make the travel roster, and as a reward for my achievement, I was given the center seat in the back row of the oldest van in the university's fleet. I use the word *seat* liberally; really it was just the spot where the two actual seats almost came together. It was horribly uncomfortable. The only way that I could make it bearable was to line my ass crack up with the crack between the seats. After nine hours in that position, a little bit of my asshole fell out, thus my first hemorrhoid was born. Of course, I didn't know about it until a couple of hours later, and even then I didn't know what it was.

When I took my pre-game shit, it felt a little weird so I turned around to investigate and saw that the toilet water was stained red. It was not an I-just-ate-a-bag-of-flaming-hot-flavored-chips red, it was blood red. Seriously concerned for my health, I did what came naturally, and kept it to myself. After all, aren't most ailments cured by refusing to acknowledge their existence?

I ended up playing really well that game, perhaps out of fear that it was my last. I struck out seven batters and went 3 for 4 with 4 RBIs. My performance was, however, not the highlight of the evening. That came in the bottom of the sixth when one of my teammates noticed a bloodstain on the ass of my pants and started calling me "period pants." By the top of the seventh, the whole team was calling me "period pants." It was kind of clever, but it wasn't really clever. I'm not sure why it stuck. Probably because of how frequently it was repeated that night. The game wasn't close so the team was freed up. They were allowed to focus more of their energy on giving each other shit, and since I was the only one with a stain on my ass, I was one of the primary targets. They really "piles-d it on." That was clever.

The new moniker didn't bother me. Actually, it made me feel welcome. My anal health, however, did continue to prove worrisome, at least for another hour or so.

On the way out of the locker room, one of the captains slapped me on the back and said, "Good game PP." As I was thanking him, he handed me a tube of cream and said, "You got hemorrhoids freshie. Lube that asshole up. We don't want to lose you to a torn anus. And just to be safe, you better slide face first until that brown starfish of yours tightens back up."

Those were some of the most comforting words I had ever heard.

* * *

The third time I got hemorrhoids was during the spring semester of my junior year. One of my teammates dared me to swallow two packs of gum in two minutes. I won the bet, but I turned out to be the loser. The gum formed a mass in my intestines, the mass led to constipation, the constipation led to difficult poops, and the difficult poops led to hemorrhoids.

* * *

The seventh time I got hemorrhoids was two months after baby Howard was born; their emergence, a result of sitting on the toilet too long. I still have them; it's been nearly a month now and there is no indication that they're going away.

The hemorrhoids hurt, but they're a small price to pay for the solace that I experience while sitting on the shitter. It's the only place where I can escape Lauren and the baby. Cheery, beautiful, kind Lauren and our healthy, happy baby; goddamn they annoy me. Even the baby's name annoys me. Howard, Jesus Christ, that's awful. No baby born after the new millennium should be named Howard. I acquiesced to the name because Lauren liked it so much. Something about her grandfather who did something during World War II. I don't know for sure. I didn't really pay attention to what she said.

Honestly, I have been annoyed, frustrated, and/or disappointed on a consistent basis for the last few months; ever since Lauren told me she was pregnant. That moment shattered me. My ideal life was within reach and then those two words—"I'm pregnant"—took it all away. Well, they didn't take it all away. I still have the job at Soren's firm and I'm still in the running for the library contest, so, career-wise, all is not lost. In fact, in regard to the competition there has been nothing but good news. A month ago, it was announced that they had narrowed down the pool of finalists from five to three—Soren's design, the new neoclassicist design, and mine. It's a little ridiculous that the contest has taken so long. I assume that the listless pace is due in large part to the fact that it's run by local government—a snail among turtles, our city government is slow even by bureaucratic standards. Of the designs that remain, mine is unquestionably the worst, but I'm okay with that. I'm proud of the fact that it has made it as far as it has. I just started to reapply myself. I don't deserve the top spot.

Still, my architectural successes aside, everything in my life has gone to shit. I know that, objectively, it might not seem that way. I have a gorgeous and intelligent girlfriend in Lauren, our baby boy is healthy and sleeps through the night, I have a beautiful home (technically it's Lauren's, but still), I'm financially stable, I have good friends that live a few blocks away, and I no longer have to empty bedpans. By almost anyone's standards, that is a good life. Indeed, had you told me a year ago that my life would look like it does now, I would have been pleased. But that was before I met Sandra. Compared to what I almost had with her, the life that I have now is shit.

Sometimes I wonder what would have happened if I had

ignored Lauren that day, if I had just gotten in the car with Sandra and drove off. Maybe Lauren would have left it alone, maybe she would have lacked the requisite temerity to track me down and tell me about the pregnancy. Maybe she would have raised the baby alone and left me blissfully ignorant. Maybe she would have given up the baby for adoption. He would probably have been better off. He would definitely have been given a better name, something like Jack or Holden or Kwame. The last one might be a bit of a stretch, perhaps if a progressive black family had adopted him. Regardless, any of those names would have been better than Howard, and odds are high that any of those adoptive fathers would have been better than me.

I try to be a good father and, in some respects, I am. I feed Howard and hold him and rock him to sleep, but I don't really love him. I try to feel genuine affection for him, and I pretend to feel genuine affection for him, but I don't actually feel genuine affection for him. I resent him. I resent him because my dreams were in the palm of my hand and then he came along and smashed them with his weird tiny feet and his stupid bowlegs. Plus, I have to change his diapers; just when I thought I had escaped dealing with other people's shit.

Of course, Howard's not alone. I resent Lauren, too. I try not to show it, but I do. I mean Jesus Christ, what hot, sexually active, thirty-year-old doesn't use the pill? And she is a doctor so she can't use that whole I-was-on-antibiotics-and-I-didn't-know-that-they-reduced-the-efficacy-of-my-birth-control shtick. What the fuck is her excuse?

That said, I know that all the blame cannot be placed on Howard and Lauren. I also bear a lot of the responsibility. I could have thrown a condom on or I could have chosen not to have sex with her. I mean I already knew that I loved Sandra, so what was I doing with Lauren? Son of a bitch, thinking about it makes me resent myself.

Despite all of my bitterness, I do my best to treat Lauren and

Howard well. When I attempt to analyze the situation impartially, I realize that they can't be held responsible. Howard was little more than a blastocyst when he unintentionally ruined my life, and Lauren is far too kind a person to have done anything with malicious intent. Actually, Lauren is far too kind a person period. That's one of the main problems I have with her. She is constantly volunteering and fundraising and carrying her food home from the co-op in cloth bags. Goddamn it's irritating. It shouldn't be, but it is. The fact that she's not sanctimonious about it makes it even worse. Most people that perform such good deeds behave as though their actions make them morally superior, and in so doing legitimize my irritation with them, but not Lauren. Lauren doesn't act the least bit priggish, which means that my irritation is completely unwarranted. Realizing this makes me feel bad about being irritated, but it doesn't make the irritation go away, thus I'm left feeling both guilty and irritated.

Unable to express any justified discontent, I typically go along with whatever Lauren is doing. Entertaining cancer kids, raising money for wounded veterans, finding homes for pit bulls that have been rescued from underground dog fighting rings, I do it all and I do it with a smile on my face. On rare occasions I even find it to be worthwhile. One time, I raised money for an Iraq War veteran to get an experimental prosthesis and then got to watch as he walked alongside his toddler for the first time; on another occasion, I found a home for an old, distressed, and battle-scarred pit bull by convincing a fourth grader that the dog's missing eye and crippled front leg made him a cool pirate dog; and another time one of the cancer kid's rich parents decided that I should design his new vacation home. So, it hasn't all been bad. Nevertheless, these redeeming moments, even the self-serving ones, do not provide me with enough satisfaction to overcome my negative feelings.

I like volunteering and acting selflessly but not all the time, and not with Lauren. I want to be able to spend a Saturday getting entertained, not being the entertainment; I want to be able to make fun of unfortunate things and not feel bad about it; I want to be able to enjoy heavily processed food from a company that pays their workers minimum wage, and I want to carry that food home in a plastic bag. That makes me sound like a dick, but it's honest, and ever since I started dating Lauren, honesty has proved to be elusive. That's not to say that I've been lying, rather that I've been pretending to be something that I'm not. I don't think that's the same thing, is it?

Chapter 24

Exteriors, Interiors, and Assholes

"Is it racist that I cheer more for white basketball players?" Brad asked the room at large, a hint of concern in his voice. He passed the vaporizer whip to Robert, exhaled a fog of cannabis, and then continued. "I mean it's not like I think the white guys are superior in any way, it's just that when they're on the court, I find myself really hoping that they do well."

I decided to refrain from answering. There were three of us in the room and one of us was black. It seemed appropriate to let the lone African American field the question. Robert did just that.

"It depends. When you are watching hockey, do you cheer more for the black players?"

Brad sat back and thought for a second before replying, "Yeah, yeah I do. Why?"

"Well then, you aren't racist. You just like cheering for the players that seem more novel."

"That's a good point," Brad replied, with what seemed a comical amount of relief.

I laughed and said, "I miss you guys."

It was true. I did miss them. They had become unexpected casualties of the unexpected pregnancy. I hadn't anticipated how severely limited my time with them would become.

Within a month of finding out about the baby, I had moved out of the townhouse and into Lauren's place. At the time, it didn't seem like a drastic move. I was wrong. It was. Lauren's home is less than two miles from Robert and Brad's, but in reality, it's much farther than that. Between work, volunteering, Lamaze classes, breast-feeding classes, newborn parenting classes, and date nights, there has been almost no time to hang out with the guys. Making things even worse is the fact that save for work, all of the aforementioned activities have been an enormous waste of time, especially the breast-feeding class. My breasts don't produce milk so that course has proven completely useless. Plus, it forced me into a situation where I had to look at a lot of breasts in a non-recreational way. Those boobs were all business. They were there for function, not for fun. What a nightmare. It reminded me of the time when I was five and wandered into the employee's locker room at Disney World. Seeing a worn-out breast flopped out of a nursing bra and into the mouth of a newborn felt startlingly similar to finding out that Mickey Mouse is a sweaty, middle-aged alcoholic in a costume.

Exacerbating the problem even further, Brad and Robert's free time has also become more limited. Brad and Hayden have become more serious, and Robert has started dating Nina. Considering the fact that one is the best friend of the woman whom I fell in love with and then cheated on, and the other is the sister of the woman whom I fell in love with and then cheated on, it should not be surprising to learn that neither of my best friends' girlfriends view me in a positive light. It's a situation that proves problematic for everyone.

I know that when my name comes up in conversation, Brad and Robert do their best to defend me. I tell them not to. I do not deserve to be defended. Hayden and Nina should dislike me. Sandra should loathe me.

That day, when Lauren told me about the pregnancy, I immediately shut down. Mentally and emotionally vacant, I turned away from her, walked over to Sandra's car, got in, and proceeded to tell Sandra that a woman that I had slept with before we were officially together was now pregnant. Amazingly, and despite my lobotomized state, I remembered to throw in that "before we were official" qualifier. It was a last ditch effort from my subconscious, an attempt to salvage the situation through the acknowledgment of a caveat. The subtext read: *This happened before we were together, so please don't let it break us apart.*

Sandra wasn't interested in caveats or subtext. Despondence showed briefly on her face, but it was quickly replaced by determined calm.

"Alright," she said. "That's it then."

Looking straight ahead, she sat silently and waited for me to get out of the car. After a few seconds I did. No other words were spoken. I had no other words to offer, or perhaps I knew that I didn't deserve to offer any other words.

After I exited the car, Sandra left. She didn't peel out and she didn't inch away slowly. She drove off as though she had somewhere to be.

Continuing to operate in a vacant state, I slowly made my way over to Lauren. She suggested we talk things out over coffee, and I agreed. I spent the next couple of hours listening, and, when it was necessary, responding. I tried to put on an understanding and supportive face. Whether or not those sentiments were conveyed in a genuine fashion is unknown to me. Lauren responded to them in a positive way, but I can't imagine that I was overly convincing. It seems as though my mental condition would have precluded a compelling display of emotion. Nevertheless, by the end of the conversation we had decided to give a relationship a try. I didn't really want to, but it seemed like the right decision. At least that way I would get to see her engorged cans. Sometimes you have to accentuate the positive even if you can't eliminate the negative.

* * *

After the contents of the vaporizer turned brown, we walked over to my new place of residence. Neither Robert nor Brad had seen it, and since Lauren and the baby were spending the night at her parents', it seemed an opportune time to change that.

As we made our way toward the house, I realized how excited I was to show off the place. It's one of the few bright spots in my post-Sandra existence. From the outside the house looks nice. It's well crafted, well maintained, and well decorated, and as a result, it stands out from its surroundings. It doesn't do this in a gaudy way; it does it in a subtle way. It's the type of place that improves the neighborhood, not the type that diminishes it by serving as a superior point of contrast.

The inside of the house is different. It seems less concerned with the eyes of passersby. The floor plan is innovative, the finish work is elegant, and the furnishings are luxurious. At first glance, one might describe it as lavish. A few seconds later, however, that person would realize that they had chosen the wrong adjective. It's too comfortable to be lavish, too genuine. The space is impressive, but it is void of pretense.

The first time that I saw the inside of Lauren's house, I was slightly taken aback. It wasn't what I had expected and it showed on my face. As it turns out, I was not the first person to react in such a fashion. In response to my poorly disguised surprise, Lauren said, "Oh, yeah. I know. The place is a little much."

"No, it's not. It's beautifully . . . tastefully, done." The words had stumbled a little as they made their way out of my mouth. They didn't falter because they were lies, they faltered because they were unanticipated.

"Well, thank you," Lauren said, with a hint of bashfulness. "At first I was unsure how I felt about it, and it still makes me a little self-conscious sometimes, but I've come to like it."

"Come to like it?" I inquired. "So you didn't design it yourself?"

"Oh, no. I could never do this. This was done by a couple of interior designers. Actually, you might have met them, they're the parents of one of the sick children at the pediatric hospital where you volunteered with me that one time."

I nodded to indicate that I remembered. I didn't, but I wanted her to continue.

"Well, they said that they wanted to do something nice for me because I always brightened their son's day. I tried to convince them that it was unnecessary but they insisted, so here we are."

After hearing its origin story, the interior of the house made more sense. Lauren would never choose an exquisite space for herself, but she would live in an exquisite space in order to spare someone else's feelings. Jesus Christ, that seems absurd. Who chooses to spend everyday in surroundings that make them feel uncomfortable to protect the sensibilities of a couple of acquaintances?

When the guys walked into the house, they showed the same amount of surprise that I had a few months prior.

Robert said, "This is unexpected."

Brad said, "Where the fuck did this place come from?"

I told them the story, and their confusion quickly dispelled.

"Of course," Brad said. "Only Lauren would feel embarrassed about the ridiculous gift she received for her ridiculous generosity. I think she might be Mother Theresa reincarnated into the body of a pin-up model." He paused for a second and looked at a picture of Lauren holding a sick toddler in some third-world country. "Sometimes her compassion makes me feel kind of like an asshole."

"You are kind of an asshole," Robert said.

"True, but I'm okay with that, so long as I'm not a full-blown asshole."

"You mean like a prolapsed asshole?"

"No, not full blown, like 'blown out.' Full blown, like 'one-hundred percent.'"

"Ah, that makes more sense."

"Well," I said. "Assuming that you two are done talking about homonyms and anuses, why don't we check out the rest of the house."

"Agreed," Robert said.

"With beers in our hands," Brad added.

We did just that. The more of the house the guys saw the more impressed they were. It felt nice to hear their positive reactions.

After we finished the tour, we had a couple more beers and then played video games. The seventy-inch TV made the games better than normal. When we played hockey, Brad scored a hat trick with P.K. Subban. We all thought that was funny.

The guys ended up leaving around midnight. I walked them to the door and watched as they headed down the driveway. All I could see was their backs but I could tell by the bend in their arms, the angle of their necks, and the glow around their profiles, that they were checking their phones. I'm sure that both of them had multiple texts from their girlfriends. They had refrained from replying while in my presence because they knew that it would be difficult for me. They knew that I would have a tough time watching them correspond with the women that they wanted to be with, while I sat in the home of the woman that I'm obligated to be with. Their choice was a considerate one, but it made me feel worse. Despite being impressed with my new residence, they still pitied my new life.

Chapter 25

Fuller, Clemente, and Lauren: Models of Virtue

Lauren and I were on the second floor of our local athletic club. We were running on adjacent treadmills looking out a large window down onto the street below. Although I prefer to run alone, I don't mind running with Lauren. She doesn't talk too much and she doesn't bounce too much. I also don't mind running with Lauren because it means that she's running. Running burns calories, and calorie burning helps people stay fit, and fit people are more fun to have sex with. Lauren is very fit, remarkably fit if you consider the fact that she pushed a human being out of her body less than three months ago. And, in line with the previous statement, she's also very fun to have sex with. Neither the pregnancy nor the delivery did anything to change that. We had sex exactly six weeks after she gave birth and her naughty purse was as tight as ever. She must have been doing Kegels from the moment she popped baby Howard out until the moment I slid back in. Sometimes, I do see the benefits of her thoughtfulness.

Forty minutes into our run another woman stepped onto the vacant treadmill beside me. She was of average size for people that go to athletic clubs, so she was thinner than average. The bulk of her hair was pulled back in a ponytail, her bangs were pulled back in an elastic headband, her sports bra was neon and could be seen through her dry fit tank top, her shorts were short but not ridiculously so, her legs were toned, and her running shoes were used but not old. Both her body habitus and her attire indicated that she knew what she was doing. They were misleading. As the treadmill sped up, it became increasingly apparent that this woman had no idea how to run. She looked like a horse at a dressage competition and sounded like a class of first graders headed to recess. Unsurprisingly, her "running" commanded my attention. Over the course of the next five minutes, I looked over at her at least fifteen times. I looked because I was annoyed and I looked because I was amazed. Both emotions were visceral and involuntary. Her running style was obnoxious enough to elicit that sort of response.

Eventually, the repeated glances caught up with me. Under the impression that I was checking her out, she began to look over at me in an attempt to reciprocate the imagined attraction. In response, I looked straight ahead, out the window, and down onto the street. I maintained that position for ten minutes. The first two were spent wondering if she were still looking at me, the second two were spent appreciating the fact that a random woman thought I was attractive, the next three were devoted to wondering why people care whether or not someone that they aren't attracted to finds them attractive, and the final three were re-devoted to being annoyed with the woman's running style. At no point over the course of those ten minutes did I actually focus on what was taking place on the street below. Consequently, I had no idea what Lauren was talking about when she asked, "Do you think that elderly gentleman needs our help?"

Searching for clarification, I looked over at Lauren and saw that she was pointing to something outside. Following the line that her index finger suggested, my eyes passed over a street vendor, a homeless woman, and some skateboarders, and eventually came to rest on a well-dressed old man who was trying, and failing, to make his way down the sidewalk. The sturdy cane in his right hand and the heavy bag on his shoulder were actively working against one another. Whenever he would inch the cane forward the bag would fall off his shoulder, slide down his arm, and crash into the cane, at which point, he would stop, raise the bag back onto his shoulder, and then start the whole process again. It was hard to watch. Based on his appearance, this old man was, at one time, a very dignified individual, and yet now he moved down the street in a thoroughly undignified fashion.

I said to Lauren, "Yeah, we should help him." My affirmative response was partly inspired by a longing to escape the equestrian event that was taking place on the treadmill next to me, and partly by a desire to end the old man's humiliation.

* * *

"Would you mind if I carried that bag?" Lauren asked, while pointing to the leather satchel on the old man's shoulder.

The question was well phrased. Lauren didn't ask if the old man needed help, that would have been demeaning, it would have made him feel old. Instead, she asked if he would do her a favor, if he would be kind enough to let her carry the bag. In doing so, she both helped the old man and restored some of his dignity. If he was able to do a favor for a beautiful young woman, then he was still worth something. Of course, it didn't really make sense. Why would Lauren want to carry a stranger's bag? Her request was obviously an act of charity, and, yet, it did not feel like one.

One block and twenty minutes later, we arrived at the codger's brownstone. Standing outside his door, Lauren said, "We are parched," and then nudged me a little to indicate that I should echo her sentiment.

"Yes, very thirsty," I said.

"Would it be possible for us to get some water? Maybe some iced tea?"

The old man was delighted. "Of course, of course," he said.

The request of another favor made the old man feel even more useful. It also subtly extended our time with him, ensuring that he had at least one meaningful conversation that day.

We went inside, sat, drank water and iced tea, and talked.

Well, Lauren and the old man talked, I provided an occasional noise of interest or approval. Instead of conversing, I introspected. This self-reflection led to this conclusion: I'm a self-centered asshole.

* * *

After we finished our second glass of iced tea, Lauren wrote down her name and number and encouraged the old man to call if he ever wanted "someone to go out on the boat with." I didn't know what boat she was talking about, but that wasn't surprising. I had paid attention to little of the conversation. The old man assured Lauren that he would get in touch with her; she replied, "Looking forward to it," and we left.

We took a right once we hit the sidewalk, returning in the direction from which we had come. I didn't want to go back to the gym, but I knew we had to. All of our shit was still there. We had left it behind in our rush to assist that doddering geriatric. A decision that, in retrospect, seemed quite stupid. It's not like that dapper old bastard would have scampered away in the minute that it would have taken to swing by our lockers.

We walked in silence at first. I thought about the perspiration that had dried on my back and wondered if it would make me break out. Lauren probably thought about different ways to bring cheer to that ancient dawdler's life. After a minute or so, I resigned myself to the fact that the sweat residue would probably leave me with some bacne. My mind free of clogged pore related concerns, I started thinking about the conclusion that I had reached regarding my status as an asshole. I didn't like thinking about that, so I began a conversation with Lauren.

"Who is your favorite architect?" I asked.

The question was a trap, an effort to make myself feel better about my negative feelings toward her. If Lauren failed to name any architects then some of my antipathy would be legitimized.

Your partner should know at least a little about your primary interest. Sandra knew a little and if Lauren knew nothing then, in that regard, she was objectively worse. I needed her to be objectively worse, and I was confident that my query would provide me with evidence that in at least one way, she is. My confidence was ill founded.

"Good question," she replied. "I suppose, if I had to choose, I would say Buckminster Fuller."

"Interesting choice," I said. *Jesus Christ,* I thought. *Not only did she come up with an architect, she came up with the most ridiculously altruistic and environmentally conscious architect in history.*

"Yeah, his geodesic domes are amazing and he was always thinking about environmental and social concerns; I mean, I think that he's an inspiration."

"Definitely."

"Plus I always liked that metaphor he used about being a trim tab."

"Absolutely, me too," I said. I had no idea what she was talking about. Without segue, I asked, "What about baseball, do you have a favorite baseball player?"

"Roberto Clemente," she quickly replied.

"Great choice," I said. *Fuck,* I thought. *It's like she is a paragon of virtue that has researched all the other paragons of virtue in the hope that they will inspire her to become more virtuous.*

I stopped asking questions and did some more self-reflection while Lauren expounded on Roberto Clemente's philanthropic work. By the time we picked up our belongings and returned home, I had decided that my asshole status was beyond dispute. There was no objective reason for me to dislike the mother of my only child.

Chapter 26

Aye-Aye Don't Cry or Dennis Bergkamp Eat Your Heart Out

Around a year ago I googled "Ugleist ANimals in th World." Google responded by showing me the results for "Ugliest Animals in the World." Near the top of the list was the aye-aye. A sort of lemur/rodent hybrid, the aye-aye looks like it's suffering from a variety of medical conditions including but not limited to alopecia, arachnodactyly, exophthalmos, hypertrichosis, microtia, and retrognathia. Of course, one could easily be confused by the counterintuitive nature of this list. Said individual might express their confusion by saying, "How could a creature possibly look as though it has both werewolf disease and hair loss disease?" Answer: the aye-aye looks like it was born with hypertrichosis but then fell victim to alopecia later in life. Which is to say, it looks like it was plagued with a bizarre disease that gave it thick, head-to-toe body hair and then, in what seemed like a fortunate twist of fate, it developed the exact opposite disease, but rather than curing the existing malady, the new disease merely lessened it, leaving the aye-aye stranded between the two conditions, the lamentable effects of both still conspicuously present.

I had not thought about the aye-aye in ages. It had stopped inserting itself into my stream of consciousness about six months ago and it had vacated my nightmares about a month after that. Unfortunately, the baby on the changing table in the men's room of the children's cancer hospital ended that streak.

The infant was an aye-aye doppelganger. Although I cannot say with absolute certainty that it was suffering from any medical problems, I have to believe that it was. I mean it looked like a fucking aye-aye. Plus, it was in the bathroom of a hospital.

Coincidence? Doubtful.

I yelped when I first saw it. It was a mean reaction but an involuntary one. The baby's father gave me a nasty look as he slid the soiled diaper off his son. I thought about leaving out of embarrassment but decided against it. Turning around would have added insult to injury, it also would have been difficult. I was dressed up as Glauco the clown and the oversized shoes inhibit 180-degree turns. Consequently, I moved forward making my way toward the urinal with high-stepping strides. They were less comical than they used to be; having volunteered with Lauren on a number of occasions, my clown shoe walking had improved.

As I urinated, I thought about the aye-aye's father. He seemed vaguely familiar, but I couldn't place him. Halfway through the pee, I decided that he just had one of those faces. After I finished, I stood at the urinal for an additional thirty seconds. It was my hope that by stalling, I could avoid further interaction with the lemur/human hybrid and the lemur/human hybrid's ubiquitous looking father. My wish was not fulfilled. When I turned around, the first thing that I saw was the baby's big, bulging eyes. The father was headed toward the trashcan on the far wall so there was nothing standing between the aye-aye and I. His gaze was unimpeded, the full force of his disconcerting stare focused on me. Feeling uncomfortable, I broke eye contact and headed toward the sinks. The baby did not approve, it began to cry and shake. With his back to the changing table, the father said, "Hold on, bud," as he tried to dispose of the dirty diaper, while simultaneously taking a paper towel out of the dispenser. The baby didn't respond well to this either. The crying and shaking increased, and in what seemed like an attempt to express the magnitude of his discontent, the baby began to roll. Assuming that he was buckled in, my initial reaction was rather passive.

He's as squirmy as he is ugly, I thought. *Maybe it's the lemur blood.*

Then, as I turned on the sink, I caught a glimpse of the father's face, showing signs of concern, and terror, and "oh shit" all at once. He took off toward the changing table, but it was clear that he wasn't going to make it in time. The baby was already headed toward the floor. Reacting without thought, I reached my foot up and out. The falling baby made contact with the top of my clown shoe halfway down. As soon as its fragile little head touched the end of my flimsy footwear, I began to lower my leg. I brought it down slowly, easing its descent, cradling the unsightly child all the way to the ground, gently bringing it to rest on the tile floor. It was as though the baby had been placed on the ground by the steady hands of a doting mother.

I'm not really a soccer fan, but the image of some guy in an orange jersey bringing down a sixty-yard pass popped into my head. It must have been from a World Cup game, that's the only time I watch soccer. *My trap was better,* I thought. *The guy in the orange jersey didn't save the life of a disease-ridden baby. Plus I did that shit wearing clown shoes.*

* * *

The aye-aye's father ended up thanking me profusely. He even made an announcement at the conclusion of Lauren/Socko's show. The cancer kids and their parents gave me a big round of applause. Some of them offered to get me presents, others offered me favors, all of them offered me approval. It felt nice.

On the way home, Lauren asked me to detail what had happened. I did.

"Oh, my god," she said. "That's amazing. You're a hero."

I replied in a modest fashion.

"No, no," she insisted. "You saved a child's life, you are definitely a hero. And in such a crazy way, too, you would be hard pressed to even stage something like that."

I didn't reply. I had missed some of what Lauren had said,

distracted by the phone vibrating in my pocket. I shifted in my seat, slid the phone out, and gave her a nonverbal indicator that said, "Sorry to interrupt, if you could just hold on one second, I have to take this phone call." She smiled and nodded, a nonverbal indicator that said, "No problem."

The phone call was about the architecture competition— another gala, a final gala, where they would announce their decision. I knew that I wasn't going to win but I was still excited. So was Lauren. She talked to her mother about it when we went to pick up baby Howard, she talked to the grocer about it when we went to pick up butt wipes, she talked to me about it while I changed Howard's diaper, and she continued talking to me about it while we prepared dinner. Her persistent flattery could have been obnoxious but it wasn't. Her genuine nature prevented that from happening.

Chapter 27

Affirmations and Affectations

The week leading up to the final gala was nice. It afforded me some rare alone time. Baby Howard spent the evenings at his grandmother's, while Lauren, due to her new administrative duties and do-gooder boating obligations, spent them at the hospital or on the lake.

I used most of the free time wisely, sketching out design ideas and reading up on new architectural developments. The time that wasn't spent wisely was spent on the Internet, looking up random stuff. At some point, some Web browser led me to some webpage that informed me that Kegel exercises are not exclusively for women. It also said that Kegels help with hemorrhoids. By Friday, mine were nearly gone. It was an actuality that made me very happy. Indeed, when I sat down in the limousine that had been sent to bring Lauren and I to the gala, the first thing that crossed my mind was how much better my asshole felt. The second was how spectacular Lauren's breasts looked in her purple dress. The third was how much I wished Sandra was the one sitting beside me. Although Sandra's breasts are slightly less impressive than Lauren's, I enjoy her presence infinitely more.

I drank two glasses of scotch on the way, an attempt to discourage my mind from comparing this gala to the last one. The one with Sandra, the one where she taught me to be confident but not arrogant, the one where she showed me the benefits of hard work, of being proactive, of trying. The scotch worked. By the end of the car ride I was totally focused on the present, especially Lauren's tits. I got a great view of them as I helped her out of the car. Of course, her breasts were not new to me but the dress she was wearing made it seem as though they were.

As we made our way inside, I received a number of envious looks. I would like to think that they were inspired by my top-three design for the new library, but I knew that they were inspired by the presence of Lauren on my arm. The abundance of covetous eyes served as a testament to the success of her post-delivery workout routine. She didn't seem to notice. She was focused on me and my achievement.

Once we got inside, Lauren headed straight for the room showcasing the final three entries. The displays were larger than they were at the previous gala. "Probably because the number of designs has been winnowed down," I thought. Then I thought, "Shit," and gave myself a mental reprimand for making a comparison to last time.

Standing in front of my design, Lauren started talking about how impressed and proud she was. She hadn't even looked at the work of the other two finalists so her words seemed empty. My mind began to drift, and after a short while, my eyes followed suit. Looking around the room, I caught sight of Soren. Well dressed and well groomed, he looked sophisticated but accessible. *Unnecessary,* I thought. *He could wear stilettos and a thong and he would still win. Fuck, he would still deserve to win. His design is ridiculous.* Moving on, my eyes ran across a couple of people that I might have talked to at the previous soiree. One was talking with big hand gestures, the other was checking something on his phone. Neither of them interested me. Next I saw a rich old woman scolding a waiter. That mildly interested me, in a tacky way. After that I saw four men and a woman arguing in hushed voices in the corner of the room. That seriously interested me, in a significant way. All of the people participating in the disagreement looked familiar, some more than others, but none of them unknown to me. They were all impeccably dressed, they all had an air of importance, and they were all wearing a badge around their necks. It was the contest committee.

It seemed odd and unprofessional, the committee arguing an

hour before they announced the winner. At first I thought that I must be mistaken. That such important and dignified people would never argue in public, not even in hushed voices. But it wasn't a mistake, I was right. The longer I watched, the more certain I became. They were definitely the contest committee and they were definitely arguing. The extremely ordinary looking member was making an impassioned appeal to the others, three of which were shaking their heads in exasperation, while the fourth stood passively to the side digging a finger into his hairy ear. I tried to make out what they were saying but failed. They were a few yards away, talking softly, whereas Lauren was a few feet away, talking loudly. Eavesdropping was an impossibility. Unable to hear, I appeased my curiosity by concluding that their argument must be a business dispute or a political squabble. Aren't those the only topics that raise the ire of the upper crust? That and who gets to "swing the jib" or "turn the aft starboard" or, I don't know, some sailing thing.

In need of another drink, I politely interrupted Lauren by squeezing her arm and asking her if she wanted to head over to the bar with me. She agreed, and we made our way. It took roughly thirty minutes to cover the twenty yards from where we were standing to where I wanted to be—elbow on the bar, ordering a single malt. Our progress was slowed by Lauren's social aptitude. It was amazing. She talked to everyone. Some of them because she knew them from volunteering or work, some of them because she recognized them from the newspaper, and some of them because she liked their shoes. She smiled no matter whom she was talking to and she showed an interest in every-thing everyone had to say. One woman talked about Yorkshire terriers for five goddamn minutes. It made me want to cut my ears off. But not Lauren, she didn't mind at all. In fact, when the woman finally finished Lauren asked her another question, like she had a desperate longing to know more about canine fashion. What the fuck? Canine fashion designers don't want to talk about canine fashion.

After the Yorkie woman, came the mustachioed man that collected antique guns, then the well-dressed Persian that talked about his baccarat winnings, and then the pale twenty-something with strong feelings about the future of fair trade fashion. I wanted to slap all of them on the mouth.

Eventually, I gave up on Lauren and walked to the bar on my own. I took a shot of scotch as soon as I arrived, followed that up with one on the rocks, and then ordered one more. The first two did their job so I drank the third slowly. I leaned my back against the bar, sucked on an ice cube, and watched Lauren converse with everyone. At one point she even talked to the female member of the contest committee. That would have been a perfect opportunity to network, but I refrained. Well, I didn't refrain so much as I veered away at the last second when I heard their topic of conversation. The benefits of getting to know one of the committee members were far outweighed by the cost of having to listen to said committee member complain about the amount of playing time the lacrosse coach was giving her son. Listen lady, his lack of playing time is probably due to his lack of skill.

Last time wasn't this bad, I thought while leaning against the bar sipping the last of my third scotch. The conversations that Sandra and I had with these people were alright. They weren't overly substantive, but they weren't horrible. They definitely weren't this particular brand of no-one-besides-you-gives-a-fuck. Son of a bitch, I said I wouldn't compare…

Lauren found me against the bar, interrupting my self-admonishment. "We should find our table before they start," she said.

I agreed, took an ice cube into my mouth, and followed her to our seats.

* * *

People always complain about the quality of food at large, high-end functions, or at least that's the way it's portrayed in movies and television shows. "Five hundred dollars a plate and all I get is a rubbery chicken breast?" That sort of thing. Based on what I was served at the gala, those people, or at least the on-screen version of those people, are full of shit. The chicken tasted like bacon, the bacon tasted like chocolate, the chocolate tasted like truffles, and it all tasted fantastic. Everything that I ate was better than every variant of that food that I had ever eaten before.

In addition to delighting my palate, the food also served as a welcome distraction. My attention remained focused on my plate rather than on the endless string of dull speakers at the front of the room. Apparently, everyone who ever donated money to the city's libraries needed to be thanked publically and given an opportunity to deliver a falsely modest speech. Only then could the winner of the contest be announced. It took about ninety minutes in all, maybe more. When the time finally came to announce the victorious design, the host literally had to say, "And now the moment you've all been waiting for," to rouse people's attention. It wasn't very original, but it seemed to work. I know that it brought my focus back to the fore. I didn't care what the wealthy philanthropists had to say, but I did care what the impending winner had to say. Soren is one of the greatest minds in the field and when one of the greatest minds in your field speaks, you listen.

Unfortunately, Soren didn't go up to the stage right away. The host had enlivened everyone's hopes with his now-the-moment-you-have-all-been-waiting-for talk and then immediately dashed them by introducing the head of the contest committee rather than the winner of the contest. I should have known that the audience would have to endure one more speaker.

As the committee member with the hairy ears made his way to the podium, I contemplated how he was able to hear the host beckon him. *The abundance of wiry hair occupying his auditory canal must inhibit his hearing,* I mused. Then I thought, *God, he moves slow.*

Using the time afforded to me by the committee chair's plodding pace, I looked over at Soren, taking a moment to appreciate how fortunate I was to be working with a visionary. He was already receiving a congratulatory shoulder squeeze on one side and a handshake on the other. *Keep my nose to the grindstone and continue to learn and that could be me,* I thought. It was an affirmation. Something that I used to do on the pitcher's mound, something that I forgot for a while after I stepped off, something that Sandra re-taught me, something that I re-learned. The affirmation made me feel good, it made me want to get shit done, and it made me antsy that I was sitting there not getting shit done. In order to ease my restlessness, I started working on my current project in my head. I hadn't been at it for very long when Lauren brought my attention back to the present with an excited hand squeeze. Old whisker ears was finally at the podium, situated, and ready to speak. Expecting a long introduction detailing Soren's many accolades, I went back to working in my head. There was, however, no need to return to thoughts of work because there was not a long speech. There was a very short speech and then my name. Me. The winner.

Chapter 28

Insights and Indian Food

"So what did I do?" I asked Lauren. We were in the back of the limousine, headed home. I was still trying to process what had happened. The scotch, the rich food, and the unexpected result were all working in a collaborative effort to obscure the events that had just taken place.

"Not too much really," Lauren replied, an amused smile on her face. "After they announced that you won, you just kind of walked up to the stage looking all surprised and flattered, and then you said something about how honored you were, and then you thanked a bunch of people, including me which was super sweet, and then you came and sat back down at our table. Wait, no, you shook the hands of all the committee members and then you came and sat back down. Then, after dinner, you kindly accepted some congratulations, we made our way back to the car, and here we are."

". . ." I replied, my mind wandering back to thoughts of the committee members.

"I'm really so, so proud of you," Lauren beamed. "You really deserve this."

". . ." I replied again. *No I don't,* I thought. *I do not deserve it. I do not deserve first. I deserve third, Soren deserves first, Soren deserves what I got. I might deserve it in the future but I don't deserve it now.*

Lauren continued talking. Her chipper disposition enabled her to proceed, unfazed by my unresponsiveness. "Why are you so surprised, babe? You did great work."

The inaccuracy of her statement provoked a response. "No," I said curtly. "My design was good. Soren's was great. Soren did great work. I did good work."

"Oh," she replied, a perplexed look running across her face.

After a second's pause, she opened her mouth to continue talking. Another second passed, and she closed it again without a word. Feeling as though she had been unfairly reprimanded, Lauren stared out the window. I felt bad for being short with her, but I couldn't be bothered to make amends, not at that moment. My mind was elsewhere. It was moving off the injustice of Soren's loss and on to recollections of the moments following my acceptance speech. They were moments that were blurred, moments that seemed improbable, moments that were still being processed. One moment, in particular, I could not believe, or, perhaps, did not want to believe.

It was right after the speech, my ad-libbed and horribly bland speech. While the crowd applauded, I walked over to the contest committee and conveyed my thanks. Each of the members stood up in turn and shook my hand. The first one was the tallest of the five. As he shook my hand, he smiled in my general direction but not at me. The second was the chair of the committee, the one with the hairy ears. When we shook, I smiled in his general direction but not at him. I was too distracted to smile at him, the chinchillas in his ears commandeered my attention. The third was the mother of the mediocre lacrosse player. She shook my one hand with two of hers. The fourth was a chubby but well-groomed man with thick, sweaty hands. I wiped my right palm on my pants after the conclusion of our shake. The fifth was the ordinary looking committee member, the one that was arguing with all the others, the one with the face that is one-of-those-faces. He pulled me in as we shook and said, "Thank you so much for saving my son's life. He would have broken his skull on that bathroom floor."

I may have responded, "Aye, aye captain." I cannot say for sure, the moment overwhelmed me.

I was still processing what had transpired that evening as the limousine pulled up to our house. "Son of a bitch," I thought. "That's why I won. My design was not the best; it was just the best of those that were submitted by people that had saved the life of a committee member's child. There were probably not too many entrants in that pool. Me, I'm guessing, and that's it. In a field of one, I finished first. Huzzah! What an achievement. This is how dictators must feel when they win 'elections.'"

Lauren exited the limousine, tipped the driver, and walked off toward the house. She made sure to stay a few steps ahead of me, an indication that she was still upset that I had been short with her. Unfortunate. I really wanted her to hike that purple dress up so that I could put my P in her V. That now seemed unlikely. I accepted the consolation prize of watching her ass as she made her way inside. I continued to watch it as she greeted her mother, kissed Baby Howard, thanked her mother for watching Baby Howard, and then told her mother to drive safe as she walked her to the door. I did break eye contact long enough to offer some gratitude to her mom. I didn't, however, hug her mom like I normally do. I had half of an erection from checking Lauren out, and I didn't want it to brush up against my future mother-in-law's stomach.

Since Lauren was upset with me, sex was unlikely, and the beginnings of an erection were useless. Consequently, I steered my thoughts away from her arousing curves and back to my unfulfilling victory. *I should have known,* I thought. I should have known as soon as I won. Some other force had to be at work. There was no way that I won that contest on merit alone. And how could I not know that the aye-aye's father was on the contest committee? Christ, what an oversight. I mean I had met all the committee members at the first gala, how did I not recognize him? Although, I did meet a ton of people that night, and his physical characteristics are the epitome of ordinary, and it is an unlikely event. Seriously, what are the odds of running into a member of the contest committee in the bathroom of a hospital? Probably very low. Fuck, what are the odds of saving his disease-ridden child by cushioning its fall with a clown shoe? Probably . . .

Lauren interrupted my calculations regarding the statistical likelihood of saving the committee member's offspring with oversized comedic footwear. "Howard pooped," she said. "And I'm getting ready to take a shower. Could you change him?" Her words came in the form of a request, but they were delivered in the tone of a demand, uncharacteristically firm. The way I acted in the limousine had legitimately upset her. I acquiesced to Lauren's request, taking Howard from her hands without a word. My mind remained too preoccupied to apologize for being curt with her.

Having transferred the baby to my care, Lauren walked off toward the bathroom. Her departure seemed cold. I waited a few seconds and then headed to the nursery. As I walked, my mind returned to its primary concern.

Still . . . , I thought. The support of the aye-aye's father wouldn't have been enough to carry me to victory. Other members of the committee must have voted for my design, but who, and why? Perhaps that's what they were arguing about at the gala? No, if that were the case I would have lost. The father of the aye-aye was definitely on the losing end of that dispute. Maybe, I won because . . .

My mind groped for ideas but none came. I kicked over a pile of books sitting on the floor next to the nursery door and then stepped on a couple of them as I made my way to the changing table. The cover of *The Republic* got bent in half and a few pages were ripped out of some Vonnegut paperback. A shame, they were the only two legitimate books among the pile of awful pregnancy and parenting tomes. If I had it to do over again, I would have stepped on *The New Guide to a Gluten-Free, Preservative-Free, Probiotic-Filled Pregnancy.* Dear god, what a title. It manages to make pregnancy even less appealing than it already is. If I ever met the author, I would tie her to a chair and force-feed her pastries from a vending machine.

I laid Howard down on the changing table and took off his

diaper. It looked like he had chicken tikka masala for supper, but I knew that was unlikely. His grandmother hates Indian food. As I wiped the burnt orange shit off his lower back, I contemplated what Sandra would say about my undeserved victory. Probably something like, "You lucky bastard. You better tell Soren that you didn't sleep with any of the committee members because he is definitely thinking that you employed your masculine wiles in order to win. It's the only logical explanation. . . . Still, I'm proud of you. You may not have deserved to win, but you did deserve to be in the running, and you worked hard to get yourself there. The victory was a little bit of luck but getting considered for the victory wasn't." I nodded to indicate to imaginary Sandra that I understood. I also threw away four poop-covered wet wipes and grabbed a new diaper from the shelf under the table. The Sandra in my head continued talking, "And remember this in the future because sometime you will deserve to win and you won't. I mean, getting shit done, working hard, it makes you feel better about yourself, and a lot of the time it pays off, but it doesn't pay off perfectly. Too many people refuse to acknowledge that. Those who think working hard guarantees success are wrong, and those that think it has nothing to do with success are even more wrong. But regardless of whether or not you reap the rewards, effort is a lot better than apathy. I guarantee you that is what Soren thinks. He's probably pissed, but I doubt that he's pouting about the injustice of it all. He isn't pouting because he knows that the system isn't perfect, but he also knows that it is far from bullshit . . . I guess all that I'm saying is . . . Well, look at it this way. Ken Johnson threw a no-hitter and lost. But still, he threw a no-hitter."

I smiled. I liked that imaginary Sandra tied in baseball and that she understood my frustration with the outcome of the contest. Real Sandra would've been the same way, maybe, a little less preachy. I closed my eyes and wished, like a child, that she was in the other room waiting for me. When I opened my eyes, I knew that she was not.

I picked up Howard from the changing table, held him out at arms' length, and looked over his body. He was clean, no sign of his Indian dinner remained. I pulled him into my body and walked over to the wardrobe to grab a onesie. As I dressed him, my thoughts returned to the contest committee. After ten seconds, no new insights had presented themselves so I allowed my mind to wander back to Sandra. She was more fun to think about, more fun but also more painful and more troublesome. Thoughts of her made it hard to look at Howard. If it weren't for him, I would be with her. Howard squirmed as if he sensed my resentment.

"No, no, I know it's not your fault," I said to him. Like usual he didn't listen. Instead, he chose to continue flailing his limbs and arching his back, increasing the difficulty of the task at hand. I managed to succeed in maneuvering his head and one of his arms through the appropriate holes in the onesie. Unfortunately, the second arm didn't come as easily. One of his fingers got caught as I pulled the arm through, bending awkwardly before releasing from the fabric. Concerned, I inspected his tiny little digits. All of them looked fine except for the pinkie finger, which bent in at an awkward angle. It appeared to be broken, but since Howard wasn't crying, I concluded that it wasn't—if you cry when a thermometer is put in your ear, you definitely cry when you break your finger. Confused, I inspected his pinkie again. It definitely had an abnormally large amount of inward bend. I picked up his other hand to provide myself with some contrast. There was none, that pinkie bent in as well. It seemed weird, but weird was good; it meant that I had not broken my son's finger. His last digit had always bent inward. His other pinkie was proof of that.

Relieved, I finished dressing Howard, picked him up, and carried him to his crib. As I lifted his freshly cleaned ass up and over the latticed side, his weird tiny pinkie stabbed me in the eye.

"You have to learn to control those crooked digits," I said, as I lowered him into the bed and repeatedly blinked my eye.

Then, suddenly, I stopped. I wasn't done putting Howard to bed, but I stopped, I had to, something had dawned on me. Once more, I lifted his freshly cleaned ass up and over the latticed side, brought him in close, and inspected his fingers.

"These warped pinkies are weird," I said. "But they're not unique. I've seen them before."

Howard stared at me blankly. He didn't seem to understand the magnitude of my revelation.

Chapter 29

Shadows or What Is Possible

"Lauren!" I yelled.

No response.

I started walking toward our bedroom in a determined fashion, Howard lying tummy down on my forearm his head in my hand. I was carrying him like a football because he likes to be carried like a football. It calms him when he's pissed off. I wanted him to be calm, I was angry enough for the both of us. Angry, but maybe a little excited.

"Lauren!" I yelled again. The second shout was unnecessary as I was less than ten yards from her location. I did it anyway. I did it because I wanted to. Once again she did not respond.

I made my way through our bedroom and into the master bath. Lauren was facing the mirror, wrapped in a towel, combing her wet hair.

"Lauren," I said firmly.

"Yeah?" she replied. She didn't bother to turn around, choosing instead to look at me in the mirror while continuing to comb.

"Look at Howard's fingers," I said stridently, convinced that this would elicit a more significant response. It didn't.

"Yeah, what about them."

"What about them? What about them! What the fuck do you think about them? His pinkies look like goddamn hockey sticks, all turned in at the last knuckle. Those are not my fingers."

"Nope," she said, cleaning her ears with a cotton swab.

"And they're definitely not your fucking model fingers."

"No," she replied, throwing the swab away, irritatingly uninterested.

"Exactly, so what the fuck? They're not my fingers and they're not your fingers and it seems unlikely that they just happened to be that way. I mean babies are not randomly born with crooked fucking pinkies."

"No, they're not."

"Well, if he had to get them from somebody, and he didn't get them from me, and he didn't get them from you, then he had to have gotten them from someone else, and I think I know exactly who that person is. It's that—"

"Yeah," Lauren interrupted. "You do know who it is, it's Abe. That geriatric fuck with the patchy hair."

I didn't reply. I didn't even try to. Lauren had halted my big reveal with a cavalier and expletive-laced admission of the truth. I was confounded. A monumental insight had been made and then immediately discarded as passé, confirmed by the party in question with a casual air and uncharacteristically foul language. I felt like Isaac Newton would have felt if, after he discovered gravity, the first person he told was like, "Oh yeah, you didn't know about that shit."

Lauren retrieved some plastic container from the cabinet and started working its contents through her hair. I slid down the doorframe and onto the floor, the reality of the situation washing over me.

After a minute I spoke. "So, baby Howard isn't mine?"

"Of course not," Lauren replied, still moving the product through her hair.

"He's Abe's. He's the son of a withered old man with gnarled fingers."

"A withered, old, *rich* man with gnarled fingers," Lauren amended.

"So, that's it? That's all there is to it? You fucked some ugly old bastard for his money."

"No, that's not it. That's part of it, but that's not it." She got out the face wash and turned on the water.

Lauren's vague reply along with the continuance of her

nightly beauty routine reawakened my anger. I laid Howard down on the carpet and stood back up.

"Well, then what the fuck is it, Lauren? You lie about being pregnant with my baby. You fuck some old dude for what? Money? And now you're acting all nonchalant about the whole thing. Fuck! Who the fuck are you?" I had used the word fuck as an adjective, a verb, and an interjection. Normally, I would have been disappointed in myself for the pedestrian nature of my language, but I wasn't. Not at that moment. Legitimate anger had overpowered my inclination for erudite articulation.

"Come on now, you know the answer to that question," Lauren replied. She acted as if I were a star pupil who had disappointed her with a poor response. As she spoke, she turned toward me. It was the first time she had done so since I entered the room. Perhaps my persistent use of "fuck" had compelled her attention.

"I thought I did but . . . I don't know." I shook my head.

"You do. You know. We're the same."

"Jesus Christ. What are you a fucking sphinx? Stop talking in goddamn riddles? All I know is that I came here to live with you and take care of a baby that I thought was mine. But, as it turns out, the baby is not mine. The baby is the result of you fucking some rich corpse with mutant pinkies." As I said this, my stomach gave a small leap. If Howard wasn't mine, then neither were any of the responsibilities that came along with him. I could leave, move back in with the boys, plead with Sandra. There might be a chance on that front; she might forgive me after learning about Lauren's psychotic behavior. It was unlikely, but it was possible. A brighter future was possible. But in order to hypothesize about that future, I needed to understand the past. I needed to understand what had happened and what was happening. I forced my attention back onto Lauren.

"Don't play dumb," she said. "You don't need to, not with me. I know that we're the same. I've known for a long time, ever since that day I saw you covered in shit."

"What's that supposed to mean?"

"Please, you know exactly what I mean. That day at the hospital when you came in to help me, but you couldn't because you had shit all over yourself. Yeah, that was your own shit." Lauren was not guessing, she knew. Her certainty preemptively struck down all my potential refutations. Instead of denying the accusation, I sat and waited for her to continue. After she put her face wash away, she did.

"The shit was too artistically applied to be real. Plus, when you came into the room you were lost in thought. If you had actually been covered in someone else's shit, you wouldn't have been lost in thought. You would have been consumed by one thought. Namely, what is the quickest way to get this fucking shit off me?"

I raised my eyebrows, gave a half-frown, and nodded my head once, the yeah-that-makes-a-lot-of-sense gesture. The light-hearted nature of my reaction didn't match the seriousness of the moment. Actually, we were talking about poop so perhaps it did.

"No one else noticed," Lauren continued, "because no one else thought to look for it. No one else considered the fact that someone might want to cover themselves in shit because being covered in shit can have its rewards. It can garner the sympathy and appreciation of others, it can convey a sense of humility and resolve, it can get you out of a situation or it can help you into a new one. There are an infinite number of reasons someone might be motivated to cover themselves in shit. I didn't know what your motivation was, but I could tell that you had one."

"Yeah," I said, as plainly as possible. I thought, *What the hell is this woman talking about. I was covered in shit because I refused to let my lactose intolerance stop me from eating two tubs of cream cheese. Dear god, that makes me sound like an imbecile. What sort of idiot eats two tubs of cream cheese when he knows that his body can't digest lactose? So, yeah, I better not tell her that. No, absolutely not. The best course of action is to allow Lauren to continue believing her own insane theory. Let her think that it was planned, that I did it for some devious reason. . . . Although, I suppose her theory might not be insane, just ridiculous. I mean, after the accident happened, I did try to provoke some emotions. I was already covered in feces, why not capitalize on the opportunity?*

"Actually, if I'm honest," Lauren said, in a tone that was even more casual than the one that she had been using. "At first, I wasn't completely sure about the shit facade; only like ninety percent. Since your motives were unclear, I couldn't be certain. I mean I was fairly sure that we were employing similar tactics, but I wasn't positive."

I replied with a very-interesting-I-think-you-are-onto-something face. Or, at least that's the expression I tried to make. I might not have succeeded because I actually had no idea what she was talking about. I wanted to, but I didn't. Fortunately, Lauren carried on and clarity began to creep in.

"So, since certainty alluded me, I started to pay more attention to you and the more attention I paid the closer certainty came. It was clear that you were masquerading and manipulating just like me. I mean you were obviously not as good at it, but still. The way you read so animatedly to the newborns when others were watching but disdainfully ignored them when you thought you were alone. That was the first point of confirmation. And then I saw you take the soda tabs out of that charity bin and put them back in once I was close enough to notice, acting like you had personally collected them to help the sick kids. That was a good one. Fucking shameless and crafty.

"Anyway, that's when I really became confident that I had you figured out, and basically everything that you've done since then has confirmed my conclusion. It's actually pretty impressive. Seriously, you'll do anything to manipulate a situation in your favor. Subtle, outlandish, doesn't matter. Call me 'Dr. Campbell' in front of your girlfriend so she doesn't suspect anything happened between us. Stay quiet about hitting a terminally ill child in the face with a clown shoe so you don't jeopardize your relationship with any of the powerful parents. Hide in a closet and then knock over Siamese twins to avoid having to simultaneously interact with both your girlfriend and the woman that you fucked. That was my favorite by the way. Watching those fat bastards tip over like that, maybe the highlight of my year. I mean I knew you were hiding in the closet and I had a pretty good idea why, and I was really enjoying fucking with you, walking around the lobby all determined and then asking your girlfriend if she needed help. Hilarious. I can only imagine what your face looked like behind that door. Dear god, I would have paid to see it. But seriously, I never thought that you would push those fat bastards over. That was a ballsy move. Fucking brilliant, but ballsy."

Lauren paused and laughed quietly while staring off into a corner. The memory of the tumbling conjoined twins must have amused her all over again. I tried to keep my face passive, it wasn't as difficult as one might expect. Although I was taken aback by what she was saying, I wasn't shocked. I was too intrigued to be shocked.

Lauren returned from her darkly comedic memory, picking up where she had left off. "But you know, on a larger scale I've always been a little confused by your approach. All of your deceptions and manipulations are too reactionary. And sure, I understand the whole worst-to-first shtick, slum it as a janitor for a few years so that when you make it as an architect everyone will praise you. Hold you up as an icon of what is possible with hard work and determination, a prototype for overcoming adversity. I mean it's good, but it's a little circuitous. Plus, a lot of times your moves lack direction, they're not focused on the long term. If you're going to deceive in order to succeed, then you better look ahead. That's your main problem; you're never looking far enough ahead. Well, except the whole saving of the ugly baby thing. You were looking ahead with that one. Of course, if it were me I would have done it a bit sooner. A week before the winner of the contest was announced, that's cutting it a little close. And your method, rescuing the kid with your foot, that's more than a little unorthodox. But hey, it worked. You're the winner."

"I am the winner," I confirmed. I don't know why I said that. Maybe because my mind was too overwhelmed to formulate an original sentence, or maybe because I didn't hate what Lauren was saying. Her depiction of me wasn't accurate, but it wasn't totally off base either. I wanted to hear more. She obliged without request.

"Tonight though, tonight you've thrown me a little. In the limo, when you acted all upset with the injustice of Soren's loss, that was confusing. That didn't match. It didn't line up with my understanding of you. For a second, it even made me think that I had completely misjudged you. But, now I see. Now I see that I haven't completely misjudged you, I've just kind of misjudged you. Because the truth is you do masquerade and deceive and manipulate, but you don't fully embrace it. You do it instinctively not methodically. You lie to yourself about it. And because of that you fall short of your potential.

"Looking back, I really don't know how I missed it. I suppose I just misread things. But seriously, there were times when it really felt like we were on the same page. I mean how could you not have known what I was up to? How many times have you seen me doting on some rich asshole on his deathbed? Christ, you sat across from me while I worked on that ancient bastard with the sailboat. Not to mention the time that you were right outside the room while I talked to that hairy-eared fuck about changing his will. You know, the same hairy-eared fuck that chaired the contest that you just won."

Surprise and comprehension appeared on my face. I couldn't help it. It didn't go unnoticed.

"Son of a bitch, you really didn't remember him," Lauren said.

"Un-fucking believable, that blows my mind. How did you think you won that contest? The one guy whose son you saved? Please, that wouldn't have been enough. You won because I told old hairy ears that if he didn't vote for you, his wife would find out about how much he likes to lick my asshole, and because I told that other bitch that I knew some college lacrosse coaches that would love to meet her son. Christ, she was easy. I knew the woman for five minutes and I got her to change her vote." Lauren gave a slight grin and shook her head.

I opened my mouth to say something, but nothing came out. I wanted to yell, but I couldn't. I wanted to be enraged and disgusted, but I wasn't. I wanted to hear more. Lauren could tell.

"You won that contest because we decided that you were going to win. We made it reality. That's what you and I do. As it turns out, I'm far more aware of that fact than you are, but still." Lauren paused thoughtfully. A moment passed and then she pushed in a drawer, turned off the bathroom light, walked into the lamp lit bedroom, picked up Baby Howard, and sat on the edge of the bed. I followed her into the light.

"Actually," Lauren said, in a contemplative voice. "I'm kind of amazed at how well you've done thus far, considering the fact that you've been lying to yourself. Christ, imagine what you can do once you fully embrace it. And what we can achieve together, there is—"

"Embrace what?" I interjected. The words came without thought. I needed to know. I had an idea, but I wasn't certain. I needed her to say it plainly.

"The lies, the facades, the manipulations, the shadows."

I gave her a face that showed I wanted more.

"Seriously? You're going to make me spell out the whole fucking thing," she said, looking up from the baby and into my eyes. "Fine, the simple truth is this. Most people are stupid. They don't get it. They see the world in plain terms, clear-cut, black and white, correct and incorrect. They don't see reality. They see shadows on a wall. They're a bunch of fucking idiots. As for the handful that do get it, well a third of them long for clarity so much that they end up actively ignoring the truth; another third waste their time attempting to explain the complexities to the idiots; and the rest just remove themselves completely. What a fucking waste. I say if the vast majority of people think that the shadows on the wall are reality, but you know that they're not, than you might as well fuck with the shadows. It's more fun than completely removing yourself from the shade, and it's more rewarding than trying to educate the imbeciles.

"So, to answer your stupid fucking question, that's what we do. That's what I've embraced, and that's what you need to embrace. Don't be above the shadows, make the shadows work for you. Embrace the lies and the facades. Show people what they want to see because it will help you get where you want to be. Intelligence and hard work will get you a lot, but this, if you add this to the mix, you can have so much more."

"So, that's it?" I asked, not in a critical tone, in a comprehending one. "You distort and deceive. You pretend to be whomever you need to be to get what you want. I mean it's not revolutionary. Everyone has done that at some point. Everyone has pretended to do something or be something so that they could get something."

"Come on now, you know that what I'm talking about is different," Lauren said dismissively, an air of disappointment in her voice. She was right, I did know. It had been childish to pretend otherwise. I asked a more substantial question in an attempt to regain my dignity.

"But if you're constantly pretending, doesn't that just become who you are?"

"Of course not," Lauren replied. Once again her response was stern; however, this time the air of disappointment was gone. My question had a definitive answer, but it was void of the intentional ignorance that beset my previous query. Lauren approved.

"All that appearance is reality business," she continued. "That's bullshit. We're not who we pretend to be. We are who we know we are. That's important so I will say it again. We are who we know we are. By acknowledging that, you afford yourself opportunities. By acknowledging that, you allow your real self to put your pretend self to work. By acknowledging that, you help yourself get what you want.

"You want money from a rich old man? Then your pretend self cares for him or dotes on him or makes him feel virile, whatever the fuck he wants. You want to make connections with influential people? Then your pretend self locates them and acts endearing, and wins over their children, and shows concern for their concerns. You want to climb the executive ladder? Then your real self proves that you are talented and hard working, while your pretend self disguises your insatiable hunger for power. You want to lay to rest suspicions that you're not as warm and caring as people think, suspicions that you might be a little selfish, that your motives might not be what they seem? Then you spawn and let your pretend self act as though that kid is more important than everything else. And if, as an added bonus, you can lock down an old man's fortune by letting him be the father, all the better. And if the old man happens to pass away at just the right time, after you've shown him the prenatal paternity test and he's changed his will, but before he's told anyone about the new development, well then, that's just icing on the cake."

"Fuck," I said on an exhale, a hint of a smile on my face. I didn't want the smile to be there, but it was.

"Think about it," Lauren said, encouraged by my reaction. "Think about what we will achieve together. Look at what we've already achieved, and you haven't even put your back into it. Once you stop lying to yourself and embrace it, once you own it, once you start using all of your tools, once you do that, we will do great things."

Lauren paused for a minute. She really did want me to think

about it. I used the time as suggested. I thought about what she had said, about the night's events, about what we already had, about what we could have, and about what I could have. Once again, I noticed the hint of a smile on my face. Perhaps it was there because I now had a good reason to leave Lauren, because I no longer had any parental responsibilities, because I now had a story so outrageous that it might convince Sandra to give me another chance; or perhaps the smile was there because I liked what I was hearing.

Having provided me with a sufficient amount of time to think, Lauren spoke up once more. This time she delivered her words with a studied composure, a forced calm that only served to amplify the excitement that it was intended to suppress. "And think about Howard," she said. "Think what he'll do. I didn't figure out how to manipulate the shadows until I was older—out of college, well into medical school. And you, Christ, you're just starting to grasp it now. We wasted years, decades, but not Howard. He hasn't wasted any time, and he'll never have to. He'll never have to because we will teach him. From the beginning, we will teach him. We'll raise him on it, the lies, the facades, the manipulations, all of it. His pretend self will get to work on day one, the shadows will be his playthings, and, as a result, his real self will be limitless." Lauren paused and then said it again, softly, to herself, "Limitless."

My smile was gone, replaced by an open-mouthed stare. My eyes shifted from Lauren to Howard and then out the window. I stared off into the dark. I stared in awe. I stared in contemplation. There was a lot to consider.

Part III

Chapter 30

The Minute I Got My Shit Together or Who's in the Bathroom?

I woke up with a headache and blood around the base of my cock. Not a gory-horror-movie amount of blood but rather an I-had-sex-with-a-woman-on-her-period amount of blood. Based on my nudity, the disheveled hotel room, and the sounds coming from the bathroom, the latter description was an accurate portrayal of the previous night's events. I was pleased that the dried, crusty, red appeared exclusively on the base of my shaft. It suggested that a condom had been worn. I was not pleased that the identity of the person in the bathroom eluded me. Lying back on the pillow I covered my eyes with my hands, and strained my hungover brain in an attempt to remember.

I had started drinking early, as soon as the ceremony had concluded. Brad and Hayden were paying for an open bar, it made sense to capitalize on it. I was not alone. At least half of the six hundred guests had the same idea. While sipping my first scotch, I tried to add up how much the wedding was going to cost. The total quickly became outrageous so I abandoned my calculations choosing, instead, to accept the rough estimate that it cost a shit ton.

Fuck it, I thought. *Hayden's parents can afford it.*

I had learned, roughly three years into Brad and Hayden's relationship that Hayden came from old money. It's a testament to her character that it took me so long to find out.

While sipping my second scotch, I wandered over to Robert and Nina. Her legs were crossed toward him, he was speaking softly into her ear, she was laughing. Four years together, yet they still acted as though they were in the honeymoon stage. Their constant affection should have bothered me, but it didn't. It was too genuine to be obnoxious.

I sat and talked with them for a while. As usual, once I arrived, Nina adopted a tone that was accommodating, yet cold. Neither Hayden nor Nina had completely forgiven me for what I had done to Sandra. They had, however, made a conscious effort to tolerate my presence, more for their boyfriends' sakes than anything else. I couldn't complain. If the circumstances were reversed, I would treat them the same way. Perhaps, in time, I can win back their approval, or at least that's what I tell myself.

The conversation between Robert, Nina, and I concluded with me giving Robert shit about his pomegranate martini. As usual he took it in stride. I stood up and continued making the rounds. I talked to a couple of friends from college that I hadn't seen in years and then made my way over to Jones. He was standing beside the stage tuning his guitar, preparing to play. I had heard Jones's band on a few occasions, usually at small local venues. All of the shows had been great. They hadn't been great because the band was particularly wonderful, but rather because the band knew who they were. They had no illusions of fame. They acknowledged and embraced the fact that they were nothing more and nothing less than a reasonably talented group of old guys that enjoyed playing music together. Their self-awareness allowed them to focus on enjoying the moment, on having fun, and, in turn, the audience did the same.

Jones asked me how I was doing. I told him, "well." I explained that Soren had just promoted me, that I was now the highest-ranking employee at the firm. Jones congratulated me with intensity, the first person to do so. Everyone else that I had told had offered shallow praise. To them, the promotion seemed mundane, overdue, a nonevent. To them it was something that I should have achieved years ago, after I won the library contest. At the time everyone had been flummoxed by my refusal to accept any of the offers that were being made in the wake of my victory, and they now seemed even more flummoxed by the idea that they should applaud me for becoming the second most important person at someone else's firm.

Jones's reaction was different because he knew the truth, the whole truth. He was the only one. Brad and Robert and pretty much everyone else knew that Baby Howard was not mine, but that was it, they didn't know anything else. They didn't know the truth about Lauren. Christ, they didn't even know the real truth about Baby Howard. The minute that I left, Lauren took control. She started telling people that Howard was the product of artificial insemination. That prior to our relationship, she was receiving fertility treatments because she desperately wanted a child but that none of them had been successful. That after we got together, she had become pregnant and mistakenly assumed it was mine. That she felt horrible about accidentally misleading me and that she didn't want me to feel obligated to her or the baby. Evidently, every time she told the story she concluded with an optimistic statement. A blushing confession of how blessed she felt, regardless of how things played out. It was another lie, another ploy, another manipulation, and it has proven just as effective as all of her other ones. Maybe, even more effective. Now, people do not just admire Lauren, they also feel sympathy for her.

I suppose that I could have tried to set the story straight, tried to reveal Lauren's true nature, but I didn't. Perhaps I thought that no one would believe me, perhaps I was scared of what Lauren would do to me, perhaps I thought I deserved everything that had happened, or perhaps. . . . Well, perhaps something darker. Perhaps Lauren's philosophy was too alluring to spoil, too useful to rule out. If I exposed it, then I could never use it. I would close that door permanently, and, perhaps, I wanted that door ajar.

Whatever my reasoning, my chosen course of action acquiesced to ignorance, it enabled Lauren, and it left everyone but Jones in the dark. I'm not sure why I told him the entire story, but I'm glad I did. Jones affirmed my decision to leave Lauren, to refuse the job opportunities, to let the shadows be. I needed someone to do that for me.

"Did ya' see that she's here?" Jones asked, pointing over my shoulder.

I didn't need to turn around. I knew that he was talking about Sandra. I had spent most of the ceremony watching her. She was wearing the shit out of a canary yellow bridesmaid dress. A dress that had been chosen in the hope that it would make her look bad; sallow her toasted almond skin, thereby increasing the beauty of the bride by contrast. It did not achieve its intended aim.

During the ceremony, there were a couple of occasions when it looked like Sandra was gazing in my direction, although in a crowd of six hundred it's hard to say who, exactly, she was focused on. Nevertheless, my stomach dropped and my chest rose as I considered the possibility. It was a feeling that I was familiar with, one that I had experienced on a number of occasions. Quite a large number actually. In the time that has passed since I left Lauren, Sandra and I have interacted a lot. The frequency of our interactions can be largely attributed to the fact that her best friend and her sister are with my two best friends; that and the fact that Sandra is far too dignified to childishly avoid an ex. Indeed, her dignity even precludes her from behaving awkwardly around one. Unlike Hayden and Nina, Sandra treats me like a friend. It may even be possible that we are friends, and maybe that makes everything worse.

"Of course I know that she's here, Jones," I replied in a tone that was more defeated than I wanted it to be. "She was on the goddamn stage wearing a yellow dress, it would have been hard to miss her."

"Not her," he said, pointing his head toward Sandra who was standing by the wall off to our right. "Her," he nodded his head upward, indicating the space behind me. I turned and looked. It was Lauren. As always, she looked fantastic.

I had only talked to Lauren once over the last four years. I would have preferred less interaction. The one time we did meet was unavoidable. I was put in charge of designing a new building for the hospital, and since she was the newly appointed CEO, we had to meet to hash out some of the details. Although that interaction was brief and cordial, it was still worthy of note, there was something off about it. I doubt that the other people in the room noticed, but I did. Lauren was not quite on her game. It wasn't fear and it wasn't anger, it was closer to frustration. It was well disguised, but it was there. Still, she held the room in the palm of her hand. She does not need to be firing on all cylinders in order to dominate. Despite internal objections, I had found her compelling and a little arousing.

After a brief pause, I turned back around to Jones and said, "Son of a bitch. What the fuck is she doing here?"

"Well, the bride's daddy is a big shot, which means that there are a lot of big shots here and Lauren, like it or not, is a big shot."

I grabbed a glass of champagne off the tray of a passing waiter and downed it in one. Jones slapped my back, said, "Don't worry about her boy," and then climbed up on to the stage. I grabbed another glass of champagne and drank it with even greater haste than the last. That's when things start to get a little hazy.

I remember that as Jones's band started to play I made my way over to the bar and ordered a scotch and water, an attempt to hydrate myself while dehydrating myself. I sat at the bar, while I finished the drink and then ordered another. Upon receiving the tumbler of pale brown, I spun my stool around to face the room. I watched Lauren for a while, sober enough to follow her movements yet drunk enough to be indifferent toward being caught watching her movements. Her black dress covered her skin but showed off her curves, modest enough to appease the prudes yet provocative enough to be alluring. She made her way around the room conversing with a variety of people, many of whom looked important. Everyone that she talked to enjoyed her company. You could see it on their faces. It was impressive.

At some point, my focus turned from Lauren to Sandra. I don't know what spurred the change, but I do know that when my attention shifted I became more aware of my drunkenness. I also know that the prospect of being caught gawking became embarrassing once more. This revival of self-awareness inspired me to slow my drinking and alter my observing. I sucked on the ice cubes at the bottom of the glass and stole glances at Sandra when the opportunities presented themselves. She spent most of her time talking to friends and the other members of the wedding party. A couple of the other bridesmaids were pretty, but unlike Sandra, the dress succeeded in making them look sallow. Still, they were fuckable.

Sandra laughed freely and expressed herself with a gaiety that showed no concern for the judgmental eyes of the haughtier guests. Her confidence, affability, and beauty were all on display, unconcerned and unfiltered. I remembered how she was once with me, and I felt destroyed all over again. The memory made me want to order another scotch and wallow in self-pity. Instead, I ordered water and resolved to go over and talk to her. The bartender brought the water, I tipped him and started to stand. I was halfway up when I felt a hand on my shoulder. It was Brad. He took a sip of my drink and made a face. He asked why the hell I was drinking water and then ordered us shots. That is when things start to get really hazy.

I couldn't say no to Brad, he was one of my best friends and it was his wedding. We did a few shots and then took a couple with us as we made our way over to the wedding party. I made a mild protest. Something like, "I don't know if they want me over there."

Brad said, "Fuck that shit. It's my fucking wedding if I want you to get rowdy with me then you get rowdy, bitch."

"You're absolutely right," I said. He was.

When we arrived at the wedding party, Brad grabbed the

nearest waiter and told him to bring a round of vodka for the group. The waiter returned a few minutes later with the shots. Everyone took one. I said, "To Brad and Hayden"; there was a sloppy clanking of glass, and then we drank. Once all of the glasses had been returned to the tray, it became apparent that the waiter had miscounted by two. Brad handed one of the extras to me and the other to Sandra. She gave him an indulgent smile.

"Don't give me that," Brad razzed. "You know you want to take a shot with him."

Surprisingly, Sandra didn't object. It wasn't an endorsement of Brad's assertion, but it was a good sign. We touched the little glasses together and threw back the vodka. Brad watched us drink. Having verified that we ingested the liquor, he brought us into a three-way hug and then walked off toward his bride. On the way, he bumped Sandra with his hip, nudging her in my direction. I was appreciative.

"Subtlety is really his strong suit," I said.

"Always has been," she replied.

We proceeded to have a fairly long conversation although I have no memory of what topics were discussed. I do remember that it was frank and tangential in nature. The sort of conversation that can only be had by two people that are drunk and know each other well. Nostalgic storytelling mixed with random debates about topics of mutual interest mixed with moments of sincere confession.

Thirty minutes, or maybe two hours, into our conversation, I had to take a pee break. I had fought the urge as long as I could, afraid that the opportunity that Sandra was giving me would be lost in the time that it took to empty my bladder. Eventually, however, I had to give in. It was that or be the guy that pissed himself at the wedding event of the summer.

I jogged to the bathroom. Upon arrival, I went directly to the urinal, and with my abs and well-toned Kegels shot the piss out as quickly as possible. On the way out, I used the instant hand sanitizer rather than the soap and water, rubbing it in on the jog back. It was one of the quickest trips to the restroom that I've ever had, but it wasn't quick enough. I arrived to find Sandra engaged in another conversation, nodding her head in an understanding fashion. She must have agreed with whatever Lauren was saying.

* * *

I grabbed two glasses of champagne off a passing tray and asked the waiter to bring me a scotch. I drank the first glass down in one and held on to the other for aesthetic reasons. It's weird to see someone at a party without a drink in their hands.

I thought briefly of interfering with Sandra and Lauren's conversation but decided against it. It would have been pointless. Instead, I slid over to a group of people that included some of the bridesmaids and pretended to be part of their discussion. I smiled and occasionally nodded but paid no real attention to their discourse. They were merely a vantage point from which I could watch Sandra and Lauren.

There was nothing exceptional about the conversation that took place. Sandra behaved like her confident and amiable self. Lauren put on her standard charm. They both talked and listened in equal measure.

As the minutes wore on, my initial anxiety ebbed. It gave way to captivation. Both Sandra and Lauren had a raw and undeniable allure. Standing next to one another only served to amplify that reality. Although their appeal was different in kind, it was not different in degree and thus neither was diminished by the other's presence. They were contrasting paragons of greatness standing side by side. I wanted to be drawn to one of them, but I was drawn to both. Bothered by this realization, I downed the remainder of my champagne. Before I had time to set the empty glass down, the waiter arrived with the scotch. I took the cup full of amber liquid, gave the waiter a tip, and dropped the finished glass onto his tray. With the tumbler of scotch in my hand, I turned back toward Sandra and Lauren. As I moved my head, I also, unintentionally, moved my body, bumping into one of the bridesmaids that I didn't know. The alcohol was catching up with me.

The bridesmaid turned around to find the culprit and in the process revealed that she was even drunker than I. After taking a few seconds to get her bearings, she located me and said something. I don't know what she said, but her tone indicated that it was not confrontational. I think that I responded, but I'm not sure. I didn't care. I had no interest in her or what she had to say. She didn't seem to mind, she continued talking anyway.

I did my best to ignore the rambling bridesmaid, shifting my attention back onto Sandra and Lauren. I was surprised to find that they were looking at me. Lauren was talking and gesturing in my direction. Sandra was listening intently, her face was contemplative—eyebrows raised, head nodding slightly, as if Lauren were inspiring her to reconsider a long-held belief. I had no idea whether this was a positive or a negative development.

Lauren was undoubtedly looking out for her own self-interest, but I had no idea what that entailed. Exacting her revenge on me for leaving her? Fucking with Sandra and I for her own amusement? Removing Sandra as a possibility in the hope that it would bring me back? Convincing Sandra to take me back so that I would be appeased and, as a result, less likely to expose her? Charming Sandra because Sandra is an important person and charming important people is what Lauren does? They all seemed like reasonable possibilities and judging the veracity of each was a task beyond my inebriated capabilities.

Overwhelmed, I swallowed the scotch in three giant gulps. When I lowered the glass, I found that both Sandra and Lauren were headed in my direction. As they made their way over, I reached my hand out, toward the yammering bridesmaid and snatched the drink from her hand. I swallowed the last of it right as Sandra and Lauren arrived. That's when the night fades to black.

Chapter 31

Finding Out

No matter how hard I racked my brain I couldn't remember anything beyond that moment. I pressed my head deeper into the pillow and pushed my palms more firmly against my eyes, but it didn't help.

Important events, life-changing events, had transpired, but my memory didn't give a shit. It didn't care that the trajectory of my future had been altered, that the identity of the person in the bathroom would influence who I would become, that it would give me insight into who I was. Sandra, Lauren, some random bridesmaid, it didn't seem to matter to my goddamn memory.

"What the fuck happened?" I asked myself.

". . ." I responded.

The shower continued to run. I looked down at my slightly bloody cock in the hope that it would provide me with an answer. None came.

"Just get the fuck out of bed, walk over to the goddamn bathroom, and find out who the fuck is in there."

The attempt to encourage myself had little effect. My body remained firmly rooted to the bed. Discovering the identity of the person in the bathroom seemed a monumental task. I wanted to know and I needed to know, but the thought of finding out terrified me. I knew who I wanted it to be, but that didn't matter. The event had already taken place. Whoever was in there was in there. I couldn't do anything to change that. All I could do was decide how long I wanted to remain in the dark. I could stay in bed and wait for the unknown person to enter the room, or I could get up and find out.

I took a deep breath, exhaled slowly, sat up, and put my feet on the ground. I walked to the bathroom door and opened it. A canary yellow dress was lying on the ground.

Acknowledgments

Thank you, Beth, for putting up with me, and for calling me on my bullshit, and for reading all my stuff, and for being the love of my life.

Thank you, Daddy Doug and Mama PJ, for pretty much everything. And for not disowning me after reading this book—I'm assuming that you're not going to disown me, if you do then disregard this section.

Thank you, Jessbutt, for being an awesome little sister, and for allowing me to call you Jessbutt even though you're a fully grown human being.

Thank you, Kuskos, for accepting me into your family, and for allowing me to write like an anti-social recluse whenever I'm at your house. Also, thanks for not disowning me after reading this book. I promise, I'm not an asshole.

Thank you, Al Gore and Matt Hodge, for reading this early on and for the encouragement.

Thank you, friends, for being my friends and for occasionally laughing with/at me. This includes but is not limited to the Rochtown crew, the gang from Miami University, the people with whom I endured Fargo winters, all the poli-sci and soccer people in Pocatello, and everyone that likes me in Raleigh.

A Note to the Reader

Thanks for reading my book. If you enjoyed it, then please
go to as many review websites as possible and shower it with
praise. If you disliked it, then shut your goddamn mouth.
More of my writing can be found at borderlineatbest.com and
thedangeratlas.com. My next novel, *Feral Chickens*, should be out
next year.

Roundfire

FICTION

Put simply, we publish great stories. Whether it's literary or popular, a gentle tale or a pulsating thriller, the connecting theme in all Roundfire fiction titles is that once you pick them up you won't want to put them down.
If you have enjoyed this book, why not tell other readers by posting a review on your preferred book site. Recent bestsellers from Roundfire are:

The Bookseller's Sonnets
Andi Rosenthal

The Bookseller's Sonnets intertwines three love stories with a tale of religious identity and mystery spanning five hundred years and three countries.
Paperback: 978-1-84694-342-3 ebook: 978-184694-626-4

Birds of the Nile
An Egyptian Adventure
N.E. David

Ex-diplomat Michael Blake wanted a quiet birding trip up the Nile – he wasn't expecting a revolution.
Paperback: 978-1-78279-158-4 ebook: 978-1-78279-157-7

Blood Profit$
The Lithium Conspiracy
J. Victor Tomaszek, James N. Patrick, Sr

The blood of the many for the profits of the few... *Blood Profit$*
will take you into the cigar-smoke-filled room where American
policy and laws are really made.
Paperback: 978-1-78279-483-7 ebook: 978-1-78279-277-2

The Burden
A Family Saga
N.E. David

Frank will do anything to keep his mother and father apart. But
he's carrying baggage – and it might just weigh him down...
Paperback: 978-1-78279-936-8 ebook: 978-1-78279-937-5

The Cause
Roderick Vincent

The second American Revolution will be a fire lit from an
internal spark.
Paperback: 978-1-78279-763-0 ebook: 978-1-78279-762-3

Don't Drink and Fly
The Story of Bernice O'Hanlon Part One
Cathie Devitt

Bernice is a witch living in Glasgow. She loses her way in her
life and wanders off the beaten track looking for the garden of
enlightenment.
Paperback: 978-1-78279-016-7 ebook: 978-1-78279-015-0

Gag
Melissa Unger

One rainy afternoon in a Brooklyn diner, Peter Howland
punctures an egg with his fork. Repulsed, Peter pushes the plate
away and never eats again.
Paperback: 978-1-78279-564-3 ebook: 978-1-78279-563-6

The Master Yeshua
The Undiscovered Gospel of Joseph
Joyce Luck

Jesus is not who you think he is. The year is 75 CE. Joseph ben
Jude is frail and ailing, but he has a prophecy to fulfill…
Paperback: 978-1-78279-974-0 ebook: 978-1-78279-975-7

On the Far Side, There's a Boy
Paula Coston

Martine Haslett, a thirty-something 1980s woman, plays hard on
the fringes of the London drag club scene until one night which
prompts her to sign up to a charity. She writes to a young Sri
Lankan boy, with consequences far and long.
Paperback: 978-1-78279-574-2 ebook: 978-1-78279-573-5

Tuareg
Alberto Vazquez-Figueroa

With over 5 million copies sold worldwide, *Tuareg* is a classic
adventure story from best-selling author Alberto Vazquez-
Figueroa, about honour, revenge and a clash of cultures.
Paperback: 978-1-84694-192-4

Readers of ebooks can buy or view any of these bestsellers by clicking on the live link in the title. Most titles are published in paperback and as an ebook. Paperbacks are available in traditional bookshops. Both print and ebook formats are available online.

Find more titles and sign up to our readers' newsletter at http://www.johnhuntpublishing.com/fiction

Follow us on Facebook at https://www.facebook.com/JHPfiction and Twitter at https://twitter.com/JHPFiction